NOT WITHOUT YOU

Dianne Venetta

NOT WITHOUT YOU
Book #1

Silver Creek Series:
Romantic Mystery/Adventure
NOT WITHOUT YOU ~ #1
BECAUSE OF YOU ~ #2
ALL ABOUT YOU ~ #3
ONLY WITH YOU ~ #4

Other novels by Dianne Venetta

Ladd Springs Series:
Cozy Mystery/Romance
LADD SPRINGS ~ #1
LADD FORTUNE ~ #2
HOTEL LADD ~ #3
LADD HAVEN ~ #4
LOSING LADD ~ #5
LADD CHRISTMAS ~ #6

The Gables Trilogy:
Romantic Women's Fiction
JENNIFER'S GARDEN
LUST ON THE ROCKS
WHISPER PRIVILEGES

Women's Fiction
CONDEMN ME NOT

Copyright 2014 by Dianne Venetta
All rights reserved
ISBN 9780991118243

Not Without You
Copyright 2014 by Dianne Venetta
ISBN: 978-0-9911182-4-3
Publisher: BloominThyme Press
Editor: Best Foot Forward
Cover Design: Seductive Designs

Acknowledgements

This story takes place almost exclusively in the high country of Colorado, one of my favorite places on earth. I could spend hours hiking the terrain, never tiring of the pristine environment. It's not only beautiful, but clean, thanks to the commitment from locals and naturalists everywhere. Recycling is encouraged, as is the motto, "leave no trace." It's a tenet that has preserved the rugged countryside through education and practice. They're principles I respect, and follow, with each and every visit. If you're not familiar with them, visit any one of the outdoor adventure centers throughout the state, and the staff will enthusiastically bring you up to speed. After all, they live there because they love it! And they don't mind sharing. My gratitude goes out to them, one and all.

Many scenes in this book couldn't have been written without the help of my friend, Ken Smithgall. Founder and CEO of the Trident Consulting Group, Ken's experience as a firefighter proved invaluable in helping me create the dramatic scenes that happen throughout much of the novel. Couldn't have written them without him!

Dedication

This novel is dedicated to all those "granolas" out there like me who love nature and everything about healthy living. I'm never happier than when I am outside, enjoying the simple pleasures of this beautiful planet on which we live.

Chapter One

McIntyre Walsh held the binoculars firmly against his face as he watched the young woman traverse the steep Colorado mountainside. It was a hundred foot drop to the valley floor. A fatal proposition, should she slip. *Don't fall, sweetheart. I'm in no mood for a search and rescue today.*

Walsh grunted. Credit another college girl hiker too independent for her own good. He'd seen them before—single women in their twenties hiking the wilderness alone with nothing more than a backpack and a camera. This one had both, a fancy black camera hanging awkwardly from her neck as she navigated the ridge as though she were walking a sidewalk, her khaki cargo shorts and white T-shirt no protection against the jagged stone and scratchy pine bark. Sweeping over the route ahead of her, he searched for possible signs of her destination. Where could she be headed?

This young woman wasn't on a pleasure hike. Her movements were too determined, intent. She was on the hunt for something. Surveying the landscape, the clumps of scruffy shrubs and sharp-edged rocks, he wondered what it could be. As far as he could tell, there was nothing up there worth seeing. No animal. No special flowers.

When she reached the precipice, she paused. The brunette cupped a hand to the pink bandana she wore over her head, and glanced over the panorama before her. Uncapping her camera lens, she brought it to her face for a few snapshots. Walsh knew that vantage point would give her a spectacular view of a lake-filled valley and distant mountain range. On a sunny day like today, she'd be treated to a mirror reflection on the lake's still surface, the massive twin serrated peaks and evergreen base. It was one of his favorite fishing holes—he'd caught a monster trout up there only last week.

She stumbled as she edged closer to the ledge, sending rocks tumbling from beneath her feet in a free fall to the ground below. His heart thumped. Regaining her balance, she paused and looked down, then looked back toward the edge of the cliff and the view of the valley.

Walsh grunted again. *Give it up, honey. Go back home. It's dangerous out here in the wilderness alone.* A flash of silver caught his attention. Whipping his binoculars toward the object, his intuition hummed as his military training kicked in. *Scan every inch. Look for signs of movement. What doesn't fit?*

It was a technique he had learned in the military. Train your brain to look for the piece that doesn't fit. As a sniper it was crucial. He had to pick out a target, usually well-camouflaged, and the way he did so was to look for clues. Movement, shape or color, something didn't belong and that something was usually his target.

Continuously moving his line of vision over the terrain, Walsh looked for signs of the flash. Something caused that flash, and it wasn't a feat of nature. Did the woman have a hiking partner? If so, why were they separated, outside of visual contact?

It wasn't smart. Examining the terrain behind the girl, Walsh settled on scraggly brush, adjusting his focus as he looked through the branches and leaves, scrutinized rocks—waiting for something to reveal itself. It was an automatic reaction to chance danger. Forget the fact he left his unit more than a year ago, it was part of the deal. Once a Marine, always a Marine.

Methodically combing every crevice of the rugged land-scape for the source, Walsh moved his line of vision back to the female hiker. Other than her, there was nothing moving up on that ridge. But he couldn't suppress a gut feeling. Something wasn't right. A threat loomed. He could feel it in his bones, streaming through his veins, same as he did the day that villager tried to infiltrate his unit. On the outside the guy had appeared like any other local Afghani herder, but when he walked up to one of the vehicles asking for help, Walsh knew something was wrong and fired warning shots at the guy's feet. When he did, the dirtbag exploded, right before their very eyes. Walsh had been credited that day with saving the lives of six men.

He relied on instinct to stay alive. Instinct didn't fail him. Sweeping his binoculars back along the ledge toward the girl, the silvery light flashed again and Walsh was quick to respond. Honing in on the area above her, he laser-focused on a cluster of small spruce. If someone was there, the nearby boulders would provide their best cover to take a shot. Walsh's mind always went to the worst-case scenario. It was possible someone was out for a leisurely hike, same as the girl, but he preferred to assume the worst and be surprised when proved wrong.

He was rarely wrong.

Isolating the target, Walsh deemed there were twenty yards between the girl and the threat. Controlling his breathing through practiced methods, he slowed his heart rate, sharpened his thoughts, and drew his weapon. If an attack occurred, the girl appeared totally clueless and ill-equipped to handle herself. He was too far away to personally intervene, but could easily neutralize a threat from here. Sharpshooting skills came with the training, too.

A spot of black shifted against the gray of rock. A jacketed figure slowly emerged. Walsh fired a shot into the air. The girl froze. The threat ducked out of sight. *That's right*, Walsh mused, his heart pumping up a notch. *You're not alone. You have a witness.*

Me.

To her credit, the girl scrambled down the rock-face, quickly dropping to a lower ledge, the space wide enough to accommodate her and nothing else. With barely a moment's pause, she leapt down to a plateau below, landing in a squat, her camera swinging precariously close to unforgiving rock points. She didn't look up but focused her attention on the way down.

Walsh was impressed. Not only did she move with the agility of a deer, seemed she understood the significance of the situation after all. Maintaining an eye on her, he returned his scope to the hiker above. Would he resume his pursuit? If he did, the girl was an easy target. Granted, she appeared to be a fairly skilled mountain climber, but overloaded with a hefty backpack, she yielded all advantage to the hunter, should he choose to follow.

Anger welled in his gut. Why did young women insist on hiking alone? Didn't they understand there were bad people out there? Did they think they were invincible? Or was it plain stupidity? Walsh grunted. He didn't care. It was a free world. A girl wanted to hike alone and fend for herself, let her. *Just don't do it on my watch.* He had more important things to do, like hunt for his food, enjoy the scenery. Living alone in the wilderness required time and effort, gave him peace of mind. Calm. The way he saw it, his needs ranked higher than protecting the butts of wayward sightseeing hikers.

Nimbly the girl continued her downward trek, adjusting her backpack as she hit gentle terrain, her pace more half-jog than walk. As she made a beeline for the tree line across an open meadow, Walsh watched the ridge a while longer, allowing her to put some space between them.

Minutes passed and no one followed. Whoever it was remained hidden behind the rocks and brush. If the girl continued without detour, she would make it down to the base in about two hours, well before sundown. Inhaling deeply, Walsh felt confident he'd prevented a confrontation, though he couldn't ignore the nagging feeling it wasn't over. He folded his binoculars and slipped them into the pocket of his canvas shoulder bag. Any pursuit now would be easily evaded on her part.

Setting off after her, Walsh cut through a field of pine trees running parallel to the trees where she had sought refuge. Currently a half mile west of his camp, he knew the two forests would converge. On impulse, he decided to follow her, making certain she was out of harm's way. Nothing else to do, he mused sourly.

In the six months that he'd lived on the mountain, he'd yet to run into trouble with wayward hikers or high-country troublemakers. Hidden within the shelter of trees and mountain, his camp was well-concealed but easily moved if circumstance warranted. Circumstance had yet to warrant a move, though it didn't prevent him from planning for one. After dedicating over ten years of his life to serving the American public, Walsh wanted nothing to do with the people he once swore to defend. Civilians weren't trustworthy. They didn't live by the code. They lived by power and greed and self-interest. They were corrupt. It was a lesson he'd learned the hard way, a lesson that cost the lives of his men.

It had been the darkest day of his life. Word had come down from the top. How far up, Walsh was never able to determine, but it was high enough in the ranks—the political ranks—where it was clear they didn't understand the men on the ground they commanded. They sent his team on a suicide mission, then tried to pull them back when they realized the obvious. Two of his men were killed during a mission the political brass denied existed, refusing military cover to get them out. It was too dangerous, they said. It would jeopardize their diplomacy efforts in the region.

It was an order Walsh couldn't obey. Every soldier understood *no one gets left behind*. Dead or alive, Marines retrieved their brothers from the battlefield. One of the men in question had been his best friend.

In a tense standoff with the enemy, and under heavy fire, Walsh had taken it upon himself to stay behind and recover his men. He nearly lost his life in the process but he had succeeded, returning both to their families. The incident left a bitter taste in his mouth, personally and professionally. His superior had explained the tide was changing, moving against them and the war effort, but it was no excuse. In his manual, acquiescing to shoddy leadership equated to acceptance. Tolerance.

McIntyre Walsh could not serve a commander he didn't respect. After eighteen months, he'd reached the end of his term and refused reenlistment, retiring from a job he'd expected to perform for the rest of his life. Now his days were his own, no longer determined by the dictates of political hacks, however empty of purpose they might be.

Overtaking her pace, he caught up with the girl, tracking her figure through the forest of evergreen when he noticed she had stopped. Walsh cursed under his breath. Now what? Brushing wayward strands of dark brown hair that had pulled free from her bandana, she looked back for the first time and surveyed the vicinity. Walsh ducked. No sense in revealing his position. He was only trailing her to make sure she made it to safety—a feat she hadn't yet accomplished. If the individual from the ridge wanted to come after her, she was making it easy.

Un-looping the camera from around her neck, she began scrolling through images.

Walsh bolted upright. Are you kidding me? Now was not the time to scroll through pretty photographs—it was time to get down! When she slipped off her shoulder straps and eased her dark blue backpack to the ground, Walsh's pulse kicked. *This is no time to drop your guard, sweetheart. The bad guy is still out there.*

As she retrieved a cell phone from the top pocket, relief swept through him. Perhaps she was calling for help. That would make sense. Shifting his weight, he waited while she spoke, indulging in the view. The girl was definitely a looker and in exceptional shape. He couldn't make out the details of her features, but could tell her skin was lightly tanned, her brown hair shiny and straight beneath a hot pink bandana. Her thighs didn't bear a speck of fat, the rounded length nothing but solid muscle. Her arms were slender but muscular, her breasts modest in size. He saw no jewelry, only a black watch similar to the one he wore. Dropping his gaze back to her legs, he thought it explained how she navigated down that mountain so quickly. *Probably works out with weights when she's not hiking.*

Did she come up here often? Was she camping over-night? The size of her pack suggested she'd expected to be up here for some time. Desire surged. He wouldn't mind the company of a fine thing like her—if he were inclined for company, which he wasn't. Women complicated life, and these days his life was all about simplicity. But if he were, she'd hit the sweet spot.

Ending the phone call, she packed away her cell, her camera, then squatted down and hoisted the pack onto her back. Rising with a fluid ease he found impressive, she set off in the opposite direction from him—and the route down. His thoughts bucked. *Now where in the hell was she going?*

Chapter Two

Lisa Richardson adjusted the heavy pack so that the waist belt rested comfortably snug at the base of her back. The gunshot had caught her off guard. Hunting season didn't start for another month. Was it a poacher? Had someone run into an animal? Had they shot a bear?

Anger fired through her. If people were afraid of coming face-to-face with the wildlife, they should stay off the mountain. At least stay out of high country. It was filled with beautiful creatures not meant to come in contact with man. It was ridiculous that people felt they were invincible, entitled to hike with the wildlife, entitled to shoot it. Calming the sudden pound of her heart, she inhaled the scent of pine trees, their floppy branches laden with tight clusters of honey-colored pinecones. The thick, sweet scent unfailingly pushed the stress from her mind. After lingering for several seconds, she walked out into open sunshine. Whoever it had been wasn't interested in her.

Looping thumbs beneath the shoulder straps of her backpack, Lisa drank in the vista. Fourteeners, fourteen-thousand-foot high mountains, skyrocketed in the distance, embedded against a brilliant blue sky, walls of edgy gray rock appeared dusted with snow. It was gorgeous country, here where the animals lived and roamed, minding their own business. This was their home. People had no right to come here and scare them, or worse, kill them. But they did. People hiked up to high country and did as they pleased without any regard for the habitat they affected.

Unlike her. She was here with a purpose—a purpose that some careless intruder had just derailed. Turning back, Lisa scanned the mountain ridge she'd ascended only minutes ago and considered making another pass over it to start scouring

the far lake for toads. She'd do it, too, except for the thought
of running into some crazy hunter-type with a gun. Not her
idea of fun. Besides, she wasn't exactly sure where Dale was
at the moment, and she only had another few hours of sunlight. Dale Miller was her partner on this expedition and, as
usual, the guy was nowhere to be found. She'd hoped to make
it to the lake on the other side of the ridge this afternoon, but
at this rate she might have to set up camp here and head over
in the morning, setting them back another day.

Lisa looked around. There were plenty of trees for cover,
wood for kindling. Irritation curdled in her gut. Dale. Where
was he?

The cell phone in her pack rang. Reaching into a side
pocket, she snatched it free and glared at the caller ID.
"Where are you?" she snapped.

"Lisa, I found a primo stream!"

"What? Where are you?"

"About a mile or so east of the mountain we were going
to cross."

She peered up at the ridge from where she had just de-
scended. "You mean the mountain where I'm standing?"

"Yeah. It's loaded with tadpoles. They're everywhere!"

"I thought we had plans to hit the lake."

Dale laughed softly. "We did, but you gotta see this. I
stumbled across it by accident."

His easygoing tone grated on her. "When you were supposed to be following me, you mean."

"Yeah, kinda."

"We can hit it on the way down. Right now, we need to
get up to the lake."

"Lisa, we can't go yet, not until you see this. I'll bet
there are millions of tadpoles swimming in this water, and I'll
bet they're fungus-free. We need to collect some."

He didn't know any such thing but arguing with Dale
was a lost cause. Expelling a ragged sigh, she asked, "Where
are you again?"

"Follow the tree line east. You can't miss it."

"Fine. I'll see you in a few."

Ending the call, she stuffed the phone back in her pack and began walking. Good thing they had a day to spare. Dale Miller was her research partner on this project, but when you hiked with him, you had to plan for detours. The guy had an amazing knack for running off on tangents, most of which proved a waste of time, though some, admittedly, turned up gold. He was a smart guy but easily distracted, always trying to discover the next big find—a lake or stream where he'd uncover a community of toads unscathed by the fungus.

The boreal toad was an endangered species found in a variety of high-altitude wet habitats, including marshes, wet meadows, streams, beaver ponds, and was most active during the summer months.

The toad was under threat of extinction due to a fungus that was spreading through the population like wildfire. Known as the Chytrid fungus, it was wiping out toads at an alarming rate, hurling them toward extinction. There was no treatment for the fungus, though reducing environmental stresses—logging, livestock grazing, habitat degradation, and other disturbances—could help keep outbreaks in check. Her job was to document population and track outbreaks. By doing so, they could encourage healthy populations to expand by performing controlled releases in disease-free zones. June and July were the premier months to study the toad's habitat and collect samples. Come August, the toads would go into hibernation and they'd be hard-pressed to capture samples or study anything.

She and Dale had also been tasked with the job of scouting out areas most suited for the release. If they could reintroduce healthy, fungus-free tadpoles and toads currently being held in the research lab, they could make a real dent in the decimation occurring across the range. It was a job that took time, and Dale's side trips didn't help.

She glanced upward and tension rippled through her upper back. In an hour or so, the sky would turn the corner from brilliant blue to hazy blue-purple, then deepen to a fiery orange over the range before depositing them into pitch black. Heading a mile in the opposite direction would only aggravate their schedule.

Funneling her gaze into the pathway ahead, Lisa tried to look on the bright side. At least she'd managed to capture some choice shots of the lake and range beyond before she'd been forced down from the ridge. They'd make some awesome landscape vista prints for Grant Powell's jewelry store.

A close friend of her father's, Grant owned a jewelry store in town and offered to display her photos for sale. At first she'd been hesitant, doubting anyone looking at jewelry while on vacation in the small resort village would be interested in buying photographic art, but boy had she been wrong. She sold ten prints the very first season! This summer marked her third year in business, and while this season was slow, she'd already sold three prints.

The income provided a nice supplement to her dad's support. She hated that he was paying one hundred percent of her expenses, but he insisted. *Live at home, graduate debt-free. Then you can move out and live off the income from your photography.* Lisa couldn't deny it was an appealing prospect. Grad school wasn't cheap, and her scholarship didn't cover everything, but live off the income from her photography?

She'd never considered her hobby paying enough to live on. She was a scientist, not a photographer. She studied amphibians and worked to save them from extinction. Snapping shots with her camera was something she did for fun. Basking in the view around her, she never tired of her time on the mountain. Most people couldn't manage the trek this far up, and would never be able see this view for themselves. According to Grant, that's where she came in. And her camera. He said she should think of it as doing the world a favor by bringing beauty into their lives. She shook her head. Is that what Grant thought he did with his jewelry? Beautified people's lives?

Imagining her life lived for the sole purpose of making money didn't sit well with Lisa. She wanted to make a difference, make positive contributions to the planet in meaningful ways—not sell things to people so they could feel good about what they wore or what they looked at.

Following the tree line as instructed, Lisa came upon a pond, exactly as Dale had described, except for one crucial part. There was no sign of *him*. Slowing, she scanned the perimeter of the pond, a shallow marshy area surrounded by tall grass and thick sections of pine, the ground dotted by columbine flowers, but no Dale. Odd, she thought. It had only taken her fifteen minutes to hike here. Where could he have gone?

Walking toward the pond, she could see the submerged outlines of muddied stones in the still, brown-tinted water. It definitely looked suitable for the boreal toad. Moving a few steps closer, she scoured the shallows for tadpoles. Excitement ramped up her pulse as she spotted a mass of black dots weaving through the water in unison. "Oh my..."

Dale had done it again—there had to be thousands of them! Professor Stevens was going to *love* this little treasure trove. Moving back from the pond, she slipped free from her backpack, dumped it onto a rock, then rummaged through the interior for a canister of bleach wipes. Quickly swiping them over and around her boots, including the soles, she grabbed her camera and snapped a few photos to document the find, the location. Pulling out one of her plastic containers, she untwisted the top and darted near the edge of the water. The fresh scent of lake water filled her senses as she knelt by the water and scrutinized the depths. Noticing several lines of black dots, her excitement grew. Those were clutches—toad eggs—and lots of them!

Leaning in on hands and knees, Lisa ignored the frigid chill and worked to scoop as many tadpoles into her cup as possible. As she hovered over the water on all fours, black bodies dispersed, darting in waves in escape. "Wow," she murmured aloud. This spot really could prove to be a *primo* find.

"What are you doing?"

Startled, Lisa lost her balance, falling into the six-inch deep pond. Water splashed in her face, soaked her T-shirt. Whirling, she found a strange man standing over her. Her heart leapt into her throat. "What are *you* doing?" she demanded.

"I just asked the same of you." The brown-skinned man peered down into the water, a mounting puzzlement rising in his sea-green gaze. "What are you doing playing in a pond?"

Lisa leapt to her feet, squelching a sudden rise of embarrassment. Her white T-shirt was drenched, revealing the outline of her pink bra beneath. Arms and breast turned into a sheet of gooseflesh. "I'm not *playing* in a pond," she snapped, suppressing a shake in her voice. No sense letting the man know he'd surprised her—though he had—which she didn't appreciate. Not one bit. "I'm doing research," she informed him, wiping hair from her eyes. "What business is it of yours?"

The man stood quiet, drawing her into the depths of his gaze. A flurry of heartbeats battered her chest, floated high in her throat. His eyes were such an amazing green, she found it hard not to stare. Layers of green encased in deep brown skin, more an olive base than a result of the sun. His eyes reminded her of the ocean, a sweeping sea green, his skin the beach. Together, they made for a startling contrast. Startling, yet striking. Add the chiseled quality of his features, the high flat cheekbones, narrow nose with a mild ridge, angular jaw line and, Lisa thought, he looked hard, stern.

Dangerous. Another wave of goosebumps flew across her wet skin. Lines marked his otherwise youthful face as he stood staring, a tan canvas bag slung over his shoulder, blending with the olive-brown color of his fitted T-shirt. Briefly she wondered if there was a weapon inside. He certainly looked capable of carrying one.

"Researching water quality?"

"No," she replied. Unwilling to give the man any more information than necessary, she crossed her arms over her chest, her plastic cup clenched in one hand.

"So what are you doing?"

The gravelly quality to his voice gave the impression he was a smoker, not exactly the sort of individual she expected hiking up to an altitude of almost twelve thousand feet. "I'm collecting wildlife samples," she informed him, purposefully vague. Without fail, the minute she mentioned the fact that she was searching for toads, the jokes followed. "Now what are you doing here?"

Lowering his gaze to the water, he slowly lifted his eyes, skimming the length of her legs before settling on her chest where he lingered momentarily.

Lisa felt a hot flush to her cheeks. The front of her shirt was soaking wet, exposing her to his lecherous gaze. Without Dale, she looked vulnerable, like a defenseless woman alone—which she wasn't. She was wholly capable of taking care of this man and any other that had a mind to do her harm.

Flipping his gaze to meet hers head on, he said flatly, "I came to warn you."

Stiffening, she honed in on him. "Warn me about what?"

"You heard the gunshot?"

"Yes."

"I shot it."

"You?" She jerked back. "But why?"

"I saw you climbing on the ridge. There was a man following you."

Shock swirled in her gut. "What?"

"A man, on the ridge."

"You must be mistaken." She glanced in the direction of the mountain she'd recently scaled. "There was no one up there but me."

The man shook his head. "I saw him with my own eyes."

Lisa stammered, "You must have seen my partner, Dale. He's here with me, doing research." Though if he had called her from this pond, there was no way he could have been on the ridge with her. Had she misunderstood him? Had he followed her up after all?

The man cocked a brow. "Why did you run?"

She screwed her expression. "Run?"

"After I shot my gun, you were in a real hurry to get down the mountain. Why run if it was only your partner up there with you?"

Releasing her arms, she stepped away from the water and walked past him to her pack. "I thought it was some crazy hunter with a gun and I didn't want to get shot by accident."

"Crazy hunter with a gun?" he repeated as she passed, seemingly amused by her word choice. "Do you see a lot of those up here?"

Capping the container, she tucked it into her backpack and said, "Enough to be wary of them."

The man nodded, but it was clear he didn't believe her. Glancing around, he appeared to be searching for something. "So where's your friend?"

"He's here. Somewhere," she said, darting a quick glance around them. At the moment, Dale was nowhere to be seen, making it look like she was fabricating a story. Squinting against the sunlight, she looked into the distance. Where was he?

Nearing her, the man said, "Hiking alone isn't smart."

"I'm not hiking alone," she replied, though she had done so on many occasion without issue.

"You should head down." He surveyed the sky above them and said, "It will be dark in a few hours."

"Thank you for your concern, but like I said, I have a partner meeting me here any minute."

"Uh-huh." Nailing her with a pointed gaze, his response was more of a grunt. "You might want to reconsider. Word has it there's a murderer on the loose."

Lisa's heart pelted her ribs. "Those attacks were on a range south of here."

A glimmer of a smile slipped behind his eyes. "So you're not totally clueless."

"On the contrary, Mr…Mr…."

"The name's Walsh."

"Mr. Walsh," she repeated abruptly. "I'm quite aware of the risks associated with hiking in the upper elevations, including those not *native* to the habitat. Rest assured that I'm very capable of taking care of myself."

Where the man should have softened, he didn't. "Suit yourself, but my advice stands. Head down now, before it gets too dark."

Chapter Three

Walsh retreated to the trees, but only so far as to remain unseen. He didn't believe her story about a partner. It was most likely a lame excuse to make him leave—a wish he'd love to grant but somehow couldn't. Call it the military training ingrained in his psyche, call it his instinctual need to protect a woman, but leaving a young female alone on a mountain where a lunatic was loose wasn't going to happen. Besides, watching her wade in a pond on all fours had its upside. Pulling the binoculars from his sack, he scoped the vicinity before zooming in on her slender backside.

She was definitely in shape. Up close and personal, he couldn't ignore the outline of her breasts beneath the wet T-shirt. Or the spark in her hazel-brown eyes. It was at odds with the light spattering of freckles over her nose and cheeks, her fair shade of skin susceptible to burn. Definitely easy on the eyes, he mused, lingering on her rear.

He felt kinda bad about scaring her, causing her to trip, but it should have proven his point. *It wasn't safe to hike alone.* If he could walk up on her without detection, so could someone else. Especially when she was so intent on scooping her cup through the water.

Watching her crawl through the water, Walsh wondered what the heck she was doing. She claimed she was collecting wildlife samples, but what wildlife lived in a pond? Minnows? Flies?

Movement caught his eye and he yanked his lens to the far side of the pond where a moose plodded onto the scene. It was a bull, one that appeared black from a distance, with spindly white legs, though through his binoculars Walsh was able to discern the grizzled dark brown quality of his body hair. The animal's head boasted a spread of antlers that had to span fifty, sixty inches.

Walsh whistled low and soft. That was some kind of beast. Flashing back to the woman, he noted she of course, was oblivious to her visitor. But then again the animal didn't seem to mind her presence, either. He was probably more interested in cooling off than checking her out. Bulls could get aggressive, but it was pretty warm. Maybe he just needed a bath.

Stepping farther into the water, the animal dipped its head, then lifted, shaking the hang of skin beneath its chin. Panning the tree line, Walsh spotted a man emerging from the trees. His heart thumped. Zeroing in on the single male, Walsh dubbed him mid-twenties, brown hair, medium build, carrying something under his arm. The guy looked like he couldn't hurt a flea, but then again, a weapon and the element of surprise made bold predators out of the weakest of men. Trailing his approach, Walsh noted the woman rose to her feet and waved. *Well, I'll be damned...*

She did have someone with her. A male. Someone she seemed pretty eager to see. The guy grabbed a backpack from behind a boulder that Walsh had missed first time around, stuffed something inside and then headed her way. The two commenced to talking, circling the pond near her pack as they pointed around the water. As they walked in his direction, Walsh's attention was drawn to her face. Adjusting his lens, he zoomed in on her expression. She was relaxed now, animated and happy as she spoke to the kid.

Walsh had to admit, the presence of this guy lit up her features like a cake full of birthday candles. The almond-shaped eyes that had greeted him so coldly were now warm and fluid. Laughing, they disappeared into slits above her cheeks, cheeks round and full like those of a child. Her teeth were a perfect row of white, her brows dark brown and perfectly shaped. She didn't sport a speck of makeup, but didn't need it. She looked good. Carefree and in her element.

Which floored him. He'd just told her there was a murderer on the loose, yet it looked as if she hadn't heard the first word. Walsh continued to watch, mesmerized. Their actions were deliberate, purposeful, as they retrieved pads of paper from their individual packs and began writing. What were they after? Fish, frogs, insects? What could it be?

When the guy pulled on a pair of latex gloves, Walsh had had enough. This kid might be "a friendly," but he was not capable of protecting her, should a stranger arrive on scene.

Struck by a thought, Walsh pulled the cell phone from his bag and dialed. Wade Davis worked with the town police department and was Walsh's direct conduit to all things legal and criminal. The man was topnotch when it came to investigative work, but on occasion his team turned down a one-way street and needed a fresh scent. That's where Walsh came in. Wade would call him to bounce ideas off Walsh's objective perspective in hopes of igniting a reset button for his team. Walsh was happy to help. The brainstorming sessions kept him sharp and the two had become close personal friends.

A booming voice filled his ear. "Hey, Walsh. What's up, buddy?"

"Quick question."

"Shoot."

"Whatever happened with that guy who was killing women on the mountain? Did you guys ever get him?"

"Not yet. In fact, they found another girl last week."

"Where?"

"Near you. Which reminds me, watch your back."

Walsh grunted. "Now you tell me."

Wade laughed. "Hell, I'm not worried about you. I'm thinking you can help the department by bringing the guy in for us! You're up there twenty-four seven. You're bound to run into him."

"Whatever you need," Walsh replied, unable to match his buddy's lighthearted tone. Unfortunately, he had a feeling he might have done just that. Keeping an eye trained on the young female hiker and her friend, he asked, "Same MO?"

"Actually, he used a knife this time."

Walsh's pulse quickened at the mention. The silver flash from earlier sprang to mind. In the past, the perp had used his bare hands to strangle the women. The fact that he was changing tactics might translate to an uptick in attacks.

"This time," Wade continued, "there were two girls hiking. They were separated at the time of the murder, allowing the one to get away."

Curiosity surged. "Do we have a description on the guy?"

"No. She found her friend dead with her throat cut, then nearly killed herself getting down the mountain."

"Damn."

"Why do you ask? You run into trouble up there?"

"Not sure. I spotted a girl hiking alone. A man was following her. I fired a shot and the two dispersed."

"Why do these girls insist on hiking alone?" Wade muttered. "Don't they understand the dangers?"

Walsh understood his frustration. Wade and his men were the people who had to risk their lives to save these kids. From stranded, injured hikers to avalanche victims, it was Wade and his team who had to go in, sometimes at great personal risk to their own lives. "This girl has a partner," Walsh said, "though I don't know how much good he's gonna do her. At the moment, they're playing in a pond."

"A pond?" Wade asked. "The girl doesn't happen to be a thin brunette, does she?"

Walsh's gut tightened. "She does."

"Real pretty, light brown eyes and a lean, solid build?"

"One and the same. Why? You know her?"

"I might. If it's who I'm thinking, her name is Lisa Richardson. Her father is an ortho doc who helps us on occasion with mountain search and rescue."

"Well, someone needs to call her and tell her to get her butt off the mountain. If I hadn't stumbled upon her at the right time, she could have been your next victim."

Wade blew a heavy sigh into the phone. "I'll give Hal a call. Maybe he can talk some sense into her."

"What's she doing up here, anyway?" Walsh asked.

"She's a grad student at the University of Colorado. She studies toads."

"*Toads?*"

"Yeah. I don't know exactly what she does with them, but according to her father, she's a real zealot when it comes to the things. Practically lives on the mountain over the summer so she can track them."

Toads. Watching her and the guy splashing through the shallows with their cups and notepads was beginning to make sense. "Let me know if you hear anything else about your perp."

"You do the same," Wade said and ended the call.

Toads. Walsh shook his head, chuckling to himself. What a waste for a pretty girl like her. Sliding the phone back into his sack, he resumed surveillance. While these two were chasing frogs, they were sitting ducks for a man with malice on his mind. No doubt her pal wouldn't put up a fight should the killer show up with a knife. That's where Walsh came in. He'd love nothing more than to get his hands on the guy who'd been killing female hikers, and he wouldn't need a gun to set things right. He'd do so with his bare hands.

Images from a sandy countryside thousands of miles away filtered into his mind. He and his unit had been ambushed at dusk. Ten against five, ragtag militia had double the men but half the firepower. Walsh had no idea what they were thinking, attacking US soldiers without their normal bomb-laden vests, but attack they had, even managing a sniper assist, for all the good it did them. Walsh's best buddy took the guy out with one shot while he and the others handled the remaining clan of fighters. Walsh remembered the feel of his

hands around a man's sweaty neck, the pulse pounding beneath his fingertips, the sheer hatred staring back at him...

Closing his eyes, Walsh warded off the images of what
came next. He wasn't a killer. He took no pleasure in the act
of taking another man's life. But when it came down to him
or them, there was no choice. He'd protect his own. He and
his unit walked away from the incident with one gunshot
wound to the shoulder and a resolve to succeed mired one
layer deeper.

At the sound of voices, Walsh opened his eyes and
swung his binoculars to the left. A group of four men approached. Four young men, mid-twenties, about the same age
as the girl and her friend, all decked out in jeans and hiking
boots, loaded to the hilt with backpacks.

Not girl. *Lisa*, he corrected. Her name was Lisa.

Toggling his view between Lisa and her partner and the
group of men, the moose no longer anywhere to be seen,
Walsh anticipated the confrontation. Would there be one?
Would they stop, or hike by with a passing hello?

The men stopped, probably drawn by the appearance of
an attractive female in a wet T-shirt. She talked to them while
Walsh noted her partner took a step back—away from the
men. Muttering a profanity under his breath, Walsh wasn't
surprised. The lanky kid couldn't squash a bug, let alone take
on four normal-sized men his age. Snorting in disgust, Walsh
watched one of the men reach out and touch Lisa's arm.
Walsh took a step forward, then checked himself. *Not yet.
Don't reveal position until ready to attack.*

Lisa brushed the arm from her shoulder and, to her credit, remained firmly in place. Give her ten points for courage,
Walsh mused. Another man stepped forward and the two exchanged words. Walsh wished he could read lips but almost
didn't have to. By the leer on the first guy's face it was clear
what he was saying. Inching forward, Walsh prepared to
strike.

A third man intervened, pulling guy number one away
from Lisa. After a few heated words, the foursome continued

on their way. Apparently it was a decision not shared by all. A few glances over his shoulder indicated man number one was clearly having second thoughts.

"Go for it," Walsh mumbled to himself. *Come back and see what happens.*

He returned focus to the "students of toads" who had resumed their study, huddled together at the water's edge. Talk about one-track minds—these two didn't seem to care about anything around them but toads. Walsh laughed softly. Toads. Were they really chasing ugly amphibians at eleven thousand feet? And what made these particular toads so worthy of their attention?

Content to watch them, Walsh shifted between scans of the surrounding terrain, the tree line, the boulders, and the two scientists. Deciding they were too old to be undergrads, he assumed they were grad students. If the kid was willing to trek up here with her and chase toads, he had to be a student. No guy in his right mind would do that for his girlfriend, no matter how cute she was. Suddenly, the guy handed his notepad to her and sprang toward the marshy grass bordering the pond. Walsh zeroed in on him. Crouching, the guy froze, then slowly bent over. After a second, he pounced on something farther in the grass and stilled. Inching up, he walked back to Lisa holding out his hand.

Walsh drew back. *Did he just catch a toad?*

Laying the notepads on top of the guy's backpack, she reached into hers and pulled something free. Sharpening the binocular lens on the article in her hand, Walsh realized she had retrieved a test tube. Handing it to the guy, she reached back into her pack and pulled out a pair of creamy white latex gloves, slipping them on without missing a beat of conversation. Her partner stood waiting as she grabbed a plastic bag loaded with white stuff. She pulled something out. It was a cotton swab. *What the heck?* Was she about to perform some kind of experiment on the toad or something?

Intrigued by the idea he was watching them in the heat of their scientific study, Walsh stared as the guy held the toad while Lisa wiped the swab over and around it and then stuffed the swab into the test tube. Walsh screwed his face involuntarily. Was she collecting toad slime?

That was disgusting.

After securing the tube in her backpack, Lisa reached into the guy's pack and rummaged around until she pulled a ruler free. Placing it against the toad, she appeared to measure its length. Sure enough, she scribbled on her notepad and placed the ruler back in the pack. The guy took several steps away and, lowering, released the toad back into the pond. The animal hopped a few times and was gone. The two exchanged eager smiles and continued to hunt through the grass for more. Walsh shook his head. Talk about good times, boy, these two seemed to be having them!

But still...with a killer on the loose, this was no place for them to be messing around. Walking to the edge of the tree line, Walsh registered the change in hue overhead. Wouldn't be long before night began to fall, and when it did, it would fall hard fast, crushing any chance these two had for a safe departure downhill. And that's exactly what they should be doing—heading downhill instead of playing leapfrog with toads.

With a quick glance side-to-side, Walsh mentally recorded the absence of threat and decided to approach. Crossing the open terrain quickly, he slowed as he neared, bothered that neither of them noticed him. He could have neutralized them both without the first scream of protest. Standing behind them, he shook his head once again. They were sitting ducks. Sitting ducks chasing toads. "Having fun?" he asked quietly.

"Ack!" Lisa cried out mid-motion as she reached for a toad.

The guy next to her jumped out of his skin, kicking water all over his pants as he twisted and fell backward. Walsh suppressed a chuckle. Child's play. The guy would be child's play should Walsh want to entertain him.

Lisa glowered at him. "You again?"

Walsh noted the irritation in her voice, the shock and awe on the guy's face next to her as he spluttered, "You know him?"

"No—yes. I met him earlier," she clarified, casting her gaze down to the pond.

Hurrying to his feet, the guy stepped clear of the water, widening the space between himself and the intruder.

Smart choice, for all the good it would do him. A few more feet wasn't going to prevent Walsh from taking him out, should he so desire. But he didn't. He had no desire to engage any more with these two than the situation warranted. His service to his fellow citizens was a thing of the past. He merely wanted them off the mountain and out of danger. A cell phone rang.

Lisa jogged to her backpack and snatched the cell phone from a side pocket. "Hello? Hey, Dad," she said, slanting her gaze from Walsh to her friend. "Who?" Angling away from him, she continued her conversation in hushed tones.

But not so quiet they couldn't hear. "I can't! I'm running out of time as it is." Walsh noted the pause, and realized Wade had followed through with his warning and called the girl's father, who was undoubtedly trying to talk her off the mountain. "I'll be careful, promise. Yes. I understand." Ending the call, Lisa stared at Walsh. "You did this, didn't you?"

"Did what?"

"Called the police department who called my father."

Walsh shrugged.

"You're trying to scare me and I don't appreciate it."

Dale looked at her, his doe eyes widening. "Scare you about what?"

"Didn't she tell you?" Walsh asked nonchalantly, though the dumbstruck look was all the answer he needed. "There's a murderer on the loose," Walsh told him, then directed to her, "and he's here. On this mountain."

The guy's Adam's apple bobbed up and down as he fastened his gaze to Lisa's. "Why didn't you tell me?"

"I was going to tell you, but we got caught up with the—
"

Walsh honed in on her cutoff. Curious. Why not finish the sentence and admit you're chasing toads?

"Listen," she continued, brushing strands of hair from her eyes, "we've been up and down this mountain all summer. Have you seen anything?"

Dale's right eye twitched. "No."

"Exactly. See. There's nothing to worry about."

"What about those guys who just paid you a visit?" Walsh put in.

Lisa chucked a glance in the direction the hikers went. "What about them?"

"What if they were here to cause trouble?"

"I can take care of myself."

"Really..." Unable to hide his smirk, he added, "And what if they decided they wanted to challenge that assertion?"

"They'd find out real quick it was a mistake."

"Mistake?"

"She has mace," her friend pitched in.

Walsh cocked his head and nearly laughed in his face. Mace was overrated, if you asked him. Gave a lot of people a false sense of security when presented with a serious threat, instead of meeting serious threat with serious response—the way it should be. Addressing Lisa, he said, "Well, that might have helped you with *one* of those guys, but what about the other three?" Walsh flicked a glance toward her male counterpart. "What would you have done then?"

"I would have handled them," she said, her voice taking on a flinty displeasure. "I'm trained in self-defense."

Was she intentionally not including her partner in her insistence of capability? Crossing arms over his chest, Walsh posed, "What if I was the bad guy? What then?"

"How do I know you're not?"

"Because if I was, I would have killed you both by now."

Her boy blinked. She didn't budge.

"Well, you didn't," she smacked back, "which means you're the good guy, right?"

Walsh marveled at her swift change in tone. Did she think this was a game? Next to her, the guy fidgeted, his glance unable to hold strong when eyed directly by Walsh.

Walsh didn't like it. Any man that couldn't look him square in the eye was hiding something.

"Now, if you don't mind," Lisa said, her gaze lingering on his, "we have work to do."

"Exactly what are you doing, anyway?" he asked, knowing full well they were up here chasing toads.

"I told you. We're collecting samples."

"Samples of what?" he pressed, curious as to why she didn't reveal the specifics of what they were doing. Did she think he would try and interfere somehow? Move in on their territory?

The thought was laughable.

"Lisa," her friend said, his voice undeniably shaky. "Maybe we should head down."

"Dale, we're not going anywhere. We still haven't made it to the lake on the other side," she said, pointedly avoiding eye contact with Walsh as she spoke to her partner. "Your find here gives us all the more reason to stay."

Staring at her, the guy ran a hand through his long layers of hair. "You're okay up here knowing there's a killer on the loose?"

"No, but I think we'll be okay. This is a huge mountain. The odds that we'll run into him are highly unlikely. Besides, it's two against one. He won't bother us."

"Last week he took out one of *two* female hikers," Walsh interjected. He held up two fingers, paying close attention to the guy's reaction. "And now he's using a weapon."

"A weapon?" Dale asked. "How do you know?"

"The girl's throat was cut."

Lisa's expression reflected the hit. Minor, but the reaction was there just the same. The stakes had changed. The threat had become a little more real.

After a brief hesitation, she flashed a glance to her partner and tossed a smile in Walsh's direction. "Listen, we appreciate your warning, and we'll head down the minute we finish. We will."

"You will," Walsh confirmed, bothered by the evasive quality in her tone.

"Yes, of course."

"So how long before you plan on heading down?"

Lisa's stance eased, as though her hide had just been removed from a hook. "Soon."

"A few hours soon?"

"Soon," she repeated. "Soon as we finish up with our data collection."

Walsh grunted. He didn't like ambiguity. It left too much to chance. "Watch your back," he said evenly. "I've snuck up on you twice. I'd hate for the next time to have deadly consequences."

Annoyance shot from her gaze. "Yes, well, if it's all right with you, we have to get back to our business."

Walsh slackened his stance and projected an unassuming air. "Fine by me," he returned, followed by a silent *I just prefer not to have any murders on my watch*. After a long look at each of them, he took his leave. "Have a nice evening."

Chapter Four

Sheltered by the cover of evergreen, Walsh couldn't shake the sense of danger. In about an hour or so, visibility would be nil and that guy wouldn't be any more help to Lisa than those toads she was chasing. Not that Walsh was looking to intercede. He wasn't. The last thing he needed was another charge under his protective watch. He'd had about all the protecting he needed for one lifetime, especially when there was no backup. Walsh suspected Wade Davis had only been half-joking when he said the department could use his help in bringing the killer to justice.

Only one problem. While the department would gladly accept his help bringing the suspect in, they'd deny any and all ties to him in the event something went wrong. It's the way government worked. Handing out the dirty assignments was easy. But when the jobs became messy, the bureaucrats went to the sink and washed their hands, leaving men like *him* to rot.

Staring at the pair, Walsh wished he could be as callous, washing his hands of these two without a second thought. Sure would make his life a whole lot easier. But that wasn't his style. His stomach growled, a reminder he'd been on his way to fish when he stumbled upon the girl.

Lisa, he corrected. She was no longer an anonymous girl hiker. Her name was Lisa. And she had a hiking partner, Dale, the unmanly and completely ill-equipped hiking partner. Walsh shook the disgust from his thoughts. Maybe he should set out and hunt the killer down for himself. At least it would be problem solved and he could get on with his life. This wasn't his battle. These were two grown adults making poor decisions. Casting a glance back toward the "students of toads," Walsh did not turn toward his camp.

Damn his inability to let it go. Marines had a code of honor one didn't leave at the door when they checked out of the military. It stayed with a man. It's who he was. When someone needed help, a Marine stepped in.

Walsh calculated the odds of Lisa and her boy setting up camp here or moving elsewhere. They seemed pretty intent on what they were doing at the moment which meant they'd probably be there for a while. At least until they couldn't see the toads anymore. Then they'd be looking to set up tents.

Assessing the forest around him, Walsh reckoned this was as good a place as any to pitch a tent. There was plenty of level ground, dead wood for kindling, shelter from weather should they need it. He sniffed the air. Dry and woody, no rain was forecast tonight. In fact, after an extremely wet winter, it had proven to be a fairly dry summer. But he knew that when the clouds did open, it could be fast and furious. It was one of the reasons his tent was wedged beneath a rock overhang within the mountainside. Burrow in, become part of the landscape. That's how he survived.

He had a good view of her through the space between the trees, with floating layers of pine branches and thick, knotted trunks the only thing between the oblivious toad hunters and him. How had he missed them? Didn't she say they'd been hiking this mountain all summer? Had she meant the mountains nearby? The north face instead of the south? Odd they hadn't crossed paths before now. He'd chosen this particular area due to its proximity to town. Should the need arise to access the facilities, he wanted to be close, but not too close. Located opposite the resort area, this section reduced his run-ins with summer tourists. Not that he was without visitors. The entire range held appeal for hiking enthusiasts, offering the perfect cut-through for those looking to conquer the "fourteeners" located beyond this mountain. But only the grittiest came through this terrain. Lisa looked anything but.

His stomach grumbled again, making an audible protest that anyone standing within ten feet of him would've heard. Walsh needed something to eat and he needed it now, but he wasn't about to go fishing. That would take him too far out of range from these two. He'd have to head back to camp for food. Coincidentally, tracking the girl back to this pond put him almost on top of his place. It was located less than two hundred yards from here, allowing him to easily grab a bite and get back with plenty of time to resume watch before nightfall. At the moment, the "students of toads" were trekking the muddy perimeter of the pond.

Turning, Walsh snickered. *Students of toads.* He was beginning to enjoy his nickname for the duo. Cruising over a forest floor of pine needles and wood debris, scrub bushes and the occasional flower, he knew that on the off chance he did miss them they'd be easy to find. Together they couldn't move very fast, not loaded down with those heavy packs. But it was beside the point. Something told him they wouldn't venture far from that pond. His "students of toads" would want to stay close to the action.

Half an hour later, Walsh traveled through pillows of thickening shadows, sunset pulling its shade on the mountain for the evening. In another hour, it would be pitch black. Nothing but darkness and animal calls, all par for the course—a course for which he was prepared. Not sure how long he'd be out tonight, he packed a flashlight and headlamp and an extra energy bar. The beef jerky and smoked fish he'd consumed back at camp wouldn't hold him for long, and if living on the mountain taught a man anything, it was to plan for the best but prepare for the worst. From storms to starvation, living in the wild was a crapshoot. Fish were plentiful, but they weren't always cooperative with a hook and hunting season didn't kick in for another month. Over the summer he'd survived largely on fish and the occasional rabbit, plus a hefty collection of MREs. Meals-ready-to-eat were the failsafe foodstuff of the military and would sustain a man until better grub could be obtained.

Catching sight of movement, Walsh froze. It was about thirty yards to his right. Adrenaline fired through his body, priming his reflexes for action. Lowering to his haunches, he scrutinized the depths of green and brown and gray. Was it an animal? A person? The pond was approximately a hundred feet from here, give or take. If Lisa and her friend had set up camp nearby, they might have an unexpected visitor. Stealing forward, Walsh combed the landscape for signs of motion. Could be a deer, could be a moose... There—

Between the trees, he spotted an object on the move. It appeared too thin to be a bear. Could be a mountain cat, though it looked too big for a cat. Pulling the gun from his waistband, Walsh tracked the course of his target. At least it was traveling away from Lisa and her friend, a small but welcome relief.

Closing the distance between them, Walsh continued to trail the object, unable to make out its identity. There were too many trees, too many obstacles between them. Up ahead, a massive tree lay in his path, branches jutting up and completely blocking his view. He needed to get closer. Inhaling deeply, Walsh reminded himself to take it slow and cautious. It could be the most dangerous animal of all—a man with murder on his mind.

Keeping his footsteps light, Walsh tracked the target to an open clearing. Logging the pace at which they were traveling, he eliminated moose and deer. They tended to move slowly, foraging for food as they walked. A man on a mission would not. He'd walk at a pretty good clip. Walsh edged around a tree for a better look. Walsh's breathing stopped.

It was a man.

Walsh ran the new information through his brain. Was it the murderer? A stray hiker? He wore a jacket similar to the one he'd spotted earlier on the ridge. Heart pounding anew, Walsh maintained position, his weapon leveled on the man. Watching his mark emerge from the shelter of forest, Walsh lowered his gun in disbelief. Out in the open, the man's identity became clear.

It was Lisa's partner! Walsh wanted to rush forward and demand to know what the guy was doing leaving the girl alone, when it occurred to him the kid might be out for a bathroom break. The thought evaporated. Walsh's gaze narrowed. Not with a backpack on his back, he wasn't. Walsh whipped a glance toward the pond, then back to the guy. Was Lisa still on the mountain? Was this guy ditching her? Fighting a rush of anger, Walsh shadowed him as he continued on his way, practically jogging over the rocky expanse of ground. The kid lost his footing, then disappeared into a cluster of trees. Walsh followed, struck by the rapid departure. It was that of a man on the run. A frightened coward willing to leave a defenseless woman behind.

Walsh stopped suddenly. He'd seen enough. If Lisa was making camp on her own, she wasn't safe. Like a bolt of lightning, he resumed his original course, running through the trees back toward the marshy pond where he'd left her this afternoon. Hopefully, she was okay. Images of her throat bleeding from a knife flew at him like spears as he jumped over rocks and logs, dodged trees and branches. The man on the ridge could have followed them. He could have been there and gone in the time Walsh had left them. Is that why the kid left? He'd freaked?

Urgency drove him forward—faster, furious—he'd kill that kid if he left Lisa to fend for herself. Then he'd rip himself a new one for leaving her in the first place.

Chapter Five

Lisa zipped up the front of her royal blue fleece and lifted the hair from between her shirt and jacket. With the sun sinking into the range, the temperature would drop like an ice brick and she needed to get a fire going before she froze her butt off. The first shavings of temperature were already evident. Changing into jeans had been her first line of defense, but until she was wrapped up in a down sleeping bag, she'd need the warmth of a fire to keep her comfortable.

Pulling the collar snug around her neck, she set out to hunt for wood and shrieked—

A hand flew to her breast as she cried out, "You scared the crap out of me!"

"Sorry."

"You could have given me a heart attack!" she exclaimed, realizing at once he meant no harm, but the damage had been done. Her heart was pounding like a jackhammer. Staring at the hardened man from this afternoon, she noticed his chest heaving, too. Had he run here? Was there trouble? She glanced around him and said, "You could have at least warned me, ya know."

"Sorry," he said again.

Sorry. *Sorry*? "What are you doing here, anyway?" she asked, incredulous over seeing him again, slightly unnerved by his penetrating gaze. "Is something wrong?" In the dimming light, his green eyes appeared all the more startling within his dark-skinned face. Was he following her? A stalker?

"Where's your friend?" he asked.

Shoving hands into her jacket pockets, she funneled her gaze into him. "My friend?"

"Your science partner."

"Dale?" she asked, surprised by the reference. "He went down," she muttered without thinking.

"Why?"

Drawing back, Lisa didn't want to say why. She didn't want to admit that all *this* man's talk of murder and danger made Dale run scared. Though hiding the fact would be irrelevant. It wouldn't change anything. Dale was gone. "All your talk about a killer on the loose rattled him."

Walsh grunted. "Smart boy." Glancing at her tent, he asked, "Why didn't you follow?"

"Because I have too much work to do."

"Can't get a lot done when you're dead."

"Are you some kind of paranoid?"

"Careful," he said coolly, his gaze chilling several degrees. "I'm careful."

Lisa felt his gaze look clear through her. She was careful, too. It wasn't *her* fault Dale ditched her before the job was done. And it needed done. Summer was breeding season for the toads and that's when she needed to be here. Professor Stevens had scheduled a major release for next week and it was her job to scout out the best site. Her job and Dale's, though it seemed her fair-weather partner had forgotten that time was of the essence. It wasn't like they could do this in a few months. It had to be done now. And honestly, the likelihood of some madman attacking her was low. She was more likely to run into a bear than a nut job.

The man stood staring at her with a queer look in his eye, but she ignored it. She didn't care what he thought of her. She didn't care that he thought she should've headed down with Dale. She was in a critical stage in her research and twelve hours more hours on the mountain wouldn't kill her. She swallowed back the thought. She'd make sure to keep an extra eye out for strangers. "I'm off to find wood." Moving past the sullen stranger, Lisa stopped suddenly, startled by the iron grip on her arm. "What are you doing?" she snapped.

"Are you some kind of fanatic, or plain stupid? You can't stay up here alone. Didn't your father get that message across to you?"

Glowering, she tamped down a swell of resentment. Lisa was determined, focused, passionate about her work—not a fanatic. She was saving a population of animals from extinction, something this Mountain Man obviously couldn't grasp. "I'm neither. I'm a woman with a job—a job that you're impeding at the moment."

"A job chasing toads?"

Astonished by the mention, she refused to break stride and clipped, "A job saving a particular species of amphibians from extinction."

For a moment, he stared at her with an unreadable look in his eyes, eyes that pulled at her. In the faint light of dusk, his short-cropped black hair and brows emphasized an image of peril, yet his eyes remained soft, supple. They were the strangest green she'd ever seen, a green that was fluid and deep within his dark skin yet could turn hard in an instant. She gulped.

Heated, as they were now.

"Let me help you," he offered quietly.

About to object, the secure hold on her arm and the finality in his voice warned that any protest would fall on deaf ears. With a shake of her head, Lisa replied, "Fine. Just don't get in my way."

He released her arm and she breathed easier, save for the renewed thrash of her pulse. *Mountain Man was here to stay. Get used to it*, she told herself. It'd be easier than fighting him.

Moving about the trees, she kept watch on him through the corner of her eye as she went about her business. Squatting and rising, she gathered small and medium-sized branches, including a handful of pine needles and fine twig kindling. He, on the other hand, was going for the big pieces, several of them six inches in width.

At least his brawn would come in handy. Dale always let her go after the big pieces, feigning he didn't see them. Dale. Good riddance was all she could think. The only reason he'd come up here with her was because Professor Stevens insisted. Dale was smart enough, but he was so weak and timid, there'd been a few times she worried he was going to die of heat exhaustion, forcing her to drag his spindly body down the mountain.

Sneaking a peek at the man working in silence by her side, she mused, no weak or spindly going on with him! The man was cut like a jagged rock, including the line of his jaw and neck. Yet despite his solid size, he moved with the dexterity of a mountain cat, as though he could bolt at any second and take down his prey. Lisa suppressed a smile. Her dad said he was ex-military, Special Forces of some sort. Looking at him, it was easy to believe.

The man stood, waiting while she stuffed as many more branches into her arms as she could.

"Here"—he grabbed half a dozen big sticks from her grasp—"let me help you with those."

The sticks were gone before she could object. Adjusting her lightened load, Lisa led the way back to her tent and tossed the armful of wood to the ground. "I'm building my fire here," she said, pointing to a cleared area about twenty feet from her tent, which she'd pitched clear of the trees, thus avoiding the possibility of falling branches.

The man made no motion of protest, instead, taking up residence as idle onlooker while she formed the finer kindling material into a nest-like bundle, then used her pocket knife to fleck some magnesium into it. To create a spark, she scraped the blade of her knife over the metal striker strip on her magnesium block and one, two—third time was a charm! The dried material caught fire in a burst of flame. Immediately she blew on it, flames crawling up and consuming the twigs she added to the mix, gradually introducing larger kindling until a good-sized flame had taken hold. Adding a few more pieces of wood at a teepee-angle, she knelt down, lowering her face to ground level and blew, engulfing the entire structure in flames.

Lisa didn't bother at conversation with the man. She didn't want to encourage him to stay any longer than he already had. She needed to organize her notes and make a plan for tomorrow. With or without Dale, she intended to hit that lake over the ridge before heading down in the afternoon. It was crucial they took every opportunity while they had the chance. Rising, she brushed the dirt from her palms and her pulse skipped. The guy was poking the flap of her tent open with a stick.

"Nice job," he commented.

Wondering why he was being so nosy, she cleared her throat and said, "Thanks. As you can see, everything is fine. No need for you to waste any more time here."

He looked at her but said nothing.

"Seriously, I'm fine. I'm going to eat, make some notes and go to sleep."

He nodded and sat down on the round of a fallen log.

"You don't need to stay," she said firmly, urging him to take the hint.

"I do."

Lisa stared at him. Did it not occur to him that she was a single female who didn't want him here? That it was rude for him to be so presumptive?

"Don't worry," he said. "I won't bother you."

Uh, too late. But hit by a wave of exhaustion, Lisa decided to let it go. According to her father, the man wasn't a threat. He was a close personal friend of Chief Davis and was going through a rough time. Recently released from the military, he was having a hard time finding his place in society. Lisa had heard stories like his, vets who couldn't assimilate into civilian life after spending time in a war zone. Post-traumatic stress disorder, nightmares, trust issues...

Lisa felt for the vets. It had to be tough. Once a person saw the ugly side of life, of the human spirit, it couldn't be erased. They were images people had to live with for the rest of their lives. It was a concept she understood well. Maybe not on the same level, to the same degree, but the scars were the same. There were some things a human heart shouldn't have to endure.

Glancing at him sitting quietly on the log, his implacable strength, his steely determination, she thought, then again, a man like him could prove handy should anything unexpected happen. Lisa didn't kid herself. Camping in the wild came with a risk. Animals, strangers looking for trouble, she understood the danger, but felt well-equipped to deal with it. She was trained in self-defense. She carried mace. She could out-hike most people—including men—if she had to make a quick getaway. She'd be fine.

Rooting through her pack, Lisa went about the business of preparing her dinner. Adele's gourmet granola was on the menu tonight; rolled oats, raisins, almonds, and a touch of agave nectar. Adele Simms was a close friend of her father's and an amazing chef who owned a restaurant in town. She used only the freshest, locally grown, organic ingredients to prepare her dishes, a practice Lisa appreciated. Respect the environment, eat healthy, live healthy.

Plucking the plastic baggie free, Lisa grabbed a bottle of water and joined Mr. Walsh near the fire, now double in size. Smiling at her handiwork, she set her food down, removed her shoes and placed them inches from the flames. Hiking in soggy boots wasn't good for the feet, which is why she always packed a spare pair. The extra boots also made it easier to keep clean, a necessity in managing the spread of fungal disease across the toad's habitat. Before entering a new area, she made a habit of bleaching her boot soles and equipment to reduce the risk of unwittingly carrying the fungus from site to site.

Sitting cross-legged on the ground, she tucked her socked feet beneath her and dipped into her bag for a handful of granola. Waves of welcome heat hit her as she plopped the first handful into her mouth.

"That's all you're eating?" he asked, not bothering to conceal his disapproval.

"It's a complete meal, including protein, carbs and fat. What more do I need?"

"How about maintaining a sufficient caloric intake? Hiking takes a lot out of a body, especially at high altitude."

Lisa didn't appreciate him looking at her like she was an idiot. As a vegan, she was accustomed to people making uninformed remarks about her nutritional needs. *You need protein. You need meat.* What a bunch of baloney. Lisa would put her health and fitness condition up against anyone's and she'd bet she'd come out on top. Wasn't like she was some neophyte when it came to hiking and camping. On the contrary, she was well-trained and very knowledgeable when it came to what her body needed and when.

Crunching down a handful of granola, she stared at the flames, purposely ignoring his continued stare. If the man thought he was going to intimidate her, he was wrong. Mentally scrolling back through her day, she estimated three suitable sites for releasing the tadpoles, provided the results came back negative for the Chytridiomycosis. Reintroducing healthy tadpoles back into the habitat would go a long way toward rebuilding the population. Their catch from this trip would make for a sizeable release, too.

Catching a nut hard between her teeth, Lisa worked the bit free with her tongue, then followed with a swig of water. Professor Stevens would be pleased. Earlier in the summer, they'd documented a few toad populations that had managed to persevere, despite the prolific spread of fungus, though the reason was still unclear. Testing revealed they might have some genetic resistance, but it was too soon to know for sure. There was more work to be done in the area, work that was challenging because in the absence of toads, the fungus could persist and wasn't easy to detect without their stout little bodies to swab. One more reason why every toad they could test was imperative to the cause.

The fire spit and cracked, a huge spark nearly hitting her toe. Smoke filled the air around her, shifting direction with each mild change in breeze. She loved the smell. It felt raw and natural, a powerful force contained within her fire ring. Though Lisa was ignoring the man, she could feel him staring at her, assessing, pondering, which didn't particularly bother her. It was human nature to wonder, to be curious about others. Most people analyzed and judged without realizing they were doing so. They made snap appraisals based on first impressions and locked people into boxes. Reaching for another handful of granola, Lisa bet he'd pegged her for a clueless college girl more concerned with staying fit than making a real and lasting impact on the planet.

Flipping her face toward him, she asked, "So what's your story?"

"My story?"

"Yes. My father says you moved onto the mountain after returning home from the military. Do you intend to stay up here for good, or is this a temporary gig?"

Lifting his brow, lines rippled across his forehead as though he was mildly amused. "Haven't decided, yet."

"How do you survive?"

"I brought up a stock of food with me, but I also fish. I'll hunt when the season opens. What more do I need?"

"Do you live in a tent, or did you build a shelter?"

"Tent."

"You don't get lonely?"

"Not a bit."

Lisa returned her gaze to the fire, debating how much to ask. She didn't want to hit any sensitive areas, but she did find his choice curious. While she enjoyed hiking and camping in the mountains, enjoyed her time alone, she didn't want to completely wall herself off from people and community. She couldn't imagine a life without her father and Adele, or her best friend, Kinsley Fairchild and Professor Stevens... How could he?

"How about you?" he asked, interrupting her thoughts. "What's your story?"

"Me?"

"Yeah. Why are you up here when you know there's danger? Are your toads that important?"

"Yes," she clipped. "The boreal toad is on the verge of extinction, and our research is the only thing standing between the animals and certain death. If I don't find as many fungus-free zones as possible, I'm condemning them to a death sentence. Summer is the only time I can document populations. It's their mating season."

Walsh smirked. "Sounds like fun."

"It's when they're most active, *smart* guy. We released a huge number of tadpoles on the opposite range ten days ago. After we release here, we'll go back and check the progress of the others."

"Grizzly bear is threatened, too. Gonna track him down as well?"

"There are no grizzlies in Colorado. Or not enough to worry about at the moment, and technically speaking, the government is about to remove the grizzly bear from the endangered species list due to their increase in numbers."

"Really?"

He seemed genuinely surprised, but why shouldn't he be? What did he know about wildlife protection? As an expert involved in the practice, even she found the entire process a bureaucratic maze of hoops and jumps. Then there were the conservationists and special interests who acted as though they had the best interests of the animal at heart, but Lisa thought otherwise. Many were more concerned with power and control than preservation.

"The federal government is planning to revoke the grizzlies' threatened species status in the Yellowstone area," she continued, "because the wildlife managers feel they've become too numerous around the park."

"Too many human encounters," he stated flatly, his face assuming a strange yellow hue in the firelight.

"There are a number of reasons, but yes, I blame people mostly. They expect to roam around and view the wildlife in its natural habitat and then get mad when the wildlife doesn't like being watched. It's ridiculous." Wood cracked loudly, drawing her attention briefly to the fire. Warm and growing hotter, it erased all memory of chill, coating her skin with heat. Turning back to Mr. Walsh, she continued, "You place an animal on the endangered list to increase its population and then complain when the numbers grow. It's beyond comprehension. Then there are the hunters who want to declare open season on the animal just so they can stuff the carcass like a trophy. Next thing you know, the animal will be facing extinction again. It's stupid and preventable."

"Huh." He gave a slight nod of his head. "You don't like people."

Lisa gaped at him. This, coming from the man who ran off to live in the woods alone? It was almost laughable—if it wasn't basically the truth. She didn't like people. Not trampling through nature, she didn't. Not changing rules and regulations on a whim. Not spouting off about how they cared about the wildlife only to prove otherwise with their actions. Allowing the heat of anger to pass, she observed mildly, "You're one to talk about not liking people."

"I dislike them for different reasons."

"Care to elaborate?"

"Not really."

Returning her gaze to the fire, Lisa considered his reasoning. He probably didn't want to dredge up painful memories from his past, which was fine with her. She didn't need to press, though all this talk about endangered species was making her blood boil, and if she didn't change the subject soon, she might have a "come apart." Lisa didn't care whether it was the grizzly bear or the boreal toad, saving an animal's life was saving an animal's life. All were equally important to the ecosystem. All were worthy of her time and effort.

Unable to save them all, she had to choose one. She chose the toads.

Setting forearms to his thighs, he leaned into them. "I still think you should have headed down with your friend and come back up with reinforcements. It's not smart to risk your personal safety, even for a good cause."

"I don't come up here blind. I'm trained in survival skills."

"Crazy people don't care if you know how to live off the mountain. They care about taking your life."

"I'm also trained in personal defense." She glared at him over the sway of flame, undeterred by the concern in his gaze, deepened by the glow of fire. "I meant it when I said I could take care of myself."

"I've surprised you three times."

Lisa ground her jaw and looked away. Picking up a stick, she poked the white-hot embers, sending flames higher, popping loudly as they shot up into the black of night. Most people didn't sneak up on people in high country and, if someone ever did, she'd make it pretty darn hard for them to take her down. Even the superior Mr. Walsh. So what if he surprised her? She hadn't been on guard. She had been focused on her work. But if he had meant trouble, she could have given him a stiff fight. With his military training and obvious good shape, it was possible he could take her down, but it wouldn't be easy. Who knew? She might even win against him. A few well-placed jabs would be all she'd need to disable Mr. Muscular.

Stewing over the imaginary confrontation, she felt a squeak of caution slip through her barrier. Maybe he was right. Maybe she should be prepared and clip her canister of mace to her pocket when she hiked to the lake tomorrow. Never know what she might run into.

A sound cracked in the distance. Lisa stilled. Mr. Walsh drew a finger to his mouth signaling *quiet*. Lisa dialed into the surroundings as he scanned the darkness around them. After a few tense moments, there was another crack, this one farther away. Lisa latched onto him and his gaze drilled right through her. It could be an animal. Could be a person. Growing uncomfortable beneath his hot stare, Lisa knew it could be anything.

When nothing more was heard, she dubbed the noise inconsequential. If it had been an animal with trouble on its mind, it would have made its presence known by now. Most likely it was a squirrel or rabbit jumping through the brittle forest debris. Mountain cats were too stealthy to let their presence be known. Clearing her throat, she said, "I have some work to do before I set out in the morning."

He nodded but made no move to leave.

"Mr. Walsh, don't you have something—er, to *do*?" she asked, but realized at once that a man who pitched a tent up on a mountain for months at a time probably didn't have a thing to do.

"The name's Walsh, not Mr. Walsh. And for the time being, I'm good." He pushed out a smile and wrapped an affable green-eyed gaze around her. "Thanks for asking."

Lisa hesitated, turning the name over in her mind. He didn't strike her as a "Walsh." He seemed more like a Steve or Dan, something hard and stern. Walsh seemed too easygoing and friendly. "Well, Walsh," she said, thrusting the name from her lips, "you don't intend to sit here all night, do you?"

"Sounds like a good idea to me." Glancing toward her small tent, he said, "Have a good night, Lisa."

A squiggle of alarm scurried through her breast. "But where will you sleep?"

"Not your concern." He gave her a sideways look and focused on the fire. "Goodnight."

Chapter Six

Alone by the fire, Walsh plunged his thoughts into the licks of flame, the muted spits and crackle, the heavy drifts of smoke. The temperature had dropped to a brisk forty degrees, the chilled silence folding the night around him. Lisa's headlamp had long since gone off, her tent dark and impenetrable. Whatever work she had to do was done, time for a good night's sleep before she set out on her adventure tomorrow. He, on the other hand, was doing the same as he always did. Sitting alone with the silence.

If only his mind could be silenced. His curiosity. Walsh couldn't stop thinking about the young woman who lay sleeping mere feet away. She was a purist. Determined. Passionate. Single-minded in her opinion when it came to the wildlife of the mountains. They were traits he admired. Softening his gaze on the fire, the orange-yellow flames dominating the darkness, Walsh faintly registered the call of a coyote in the distance. Lisa asked if he was paranoid, as if he were some kind of psycho living in the wilderness. His insides twisted. She assumed he had a problem because he'd decided to live on the mountain in solitude. Assumed he had a problem with people. Funny, but the real answer might surprise her. He'd wanted to say, *I'm fine with people. I simply don't trust them.*

Not anymore.

He wanted to say he preferred living in wide open spaces versus the confines of society, the foolish actions and decisions of others. He wanted to say it was safer, smarter. People acted illogically, impulsively. Like she said, they placed animals on endangered species lists and then removed them because they became too plentiful. They signed on to a relationship only to quit midway through. They ordered men into combat only to yank them back like dogs on a leash.

Lisa was right about one thing. People were the problem. In general, if there was a problem with something, there was usually some fool idiot person behind it. But she was wrong about him. McIntyre Walsh was no paranoid, despite her attempt to pin the label on him. He was no psycho recluse. Truth was, life had a way of changing people, some for the better, some for the worse. Not that Walsh considered his time spent in the military a waste. On the contrary. His years in the unit were some of the best damn years of his life. Living with men who thought the way he did, believed the way he did, solidified a man's direction. Walsh had always known where he wanted to go, what he wanted to do, who he wanted to be. The military was his life. Those men were his life. It wasn't until the upper brass stepped in and undermined his trust and confidence with the swipe of a pen, the click of a mouse, that his mission changed.

People acted in their own self-interest without regard to what was right and just. His wife had been case in point. While on extended tour of duty, Tracy decided pining away for a soldier wasn't for her. Did she wait and tell him in person? Did she have the decency to think of how he would take the news in a phone call?

No. And as if to prove how little she cared about him, she gave his dog away when the animal became inconvenient. She wanted her freedom, wanted to travel, and Max was in the way. Two months after dumping Walsh, she dumped Max off at her cousin's house. She could have given the dog to his family, but they didn't want him. A pet was too much trouble.

Because his parents were dealing with their own batch of trouble. After thirty years of marriage, they were walking away. Giving up and starting over. What the hell for? They managed for this long. What were a few more years between friends?

That was the problem. His parents never were friends. They were sweethearts and then they were parents. Same as he and Tracy, though thank God they never made it to parenthood. That would have sucked. Losing his best friend and a kid?

Walsh shook the sudden chill from his body. Whatever. It didn't matter anymore. He was finished with them all. His blood brothers from the unit were different. They would remain his brothers—always—but the connection they shared had become distant. No more missions, no more camaraderie among men. His brothers continued with a sense of unity and purpose while he was out on his own. No unity, no purpose, his sense of cohesion was gone. Walsh feared it might be gone forever.

Space, he'd told himself. He needed space to get his mind straight. Except for the fact his six months on the mountain had done nothing to pinpoint a new direction, a new course of action. A skillset like his was hard to transfer to civilian life. Terrorist threat assessment, sniper proficiency, survival competency... Outside the theater of war, his skills weren't needed. Wade Davis had offered him a position on the police force, said they could use a man with his intellect and ability, but Walsh had declined. While he didn't mind helping out on a case-by-case basis, he wasn't sure law enforcement was something he wanted to make a career of.

Too many bureaucratic buffoons.

Recalling Lisa and her talk of toads, envy rolled through him. While he missed the significance of saving this one species of toad, there was no way he could miss the passion in her voice, the enthusiasm she exuded as she chased them in the pond. It was visceral. Tangible. That girl was where she wanted to be, doing what she wanted to do. Where he might score her low in sensibility, she scored nothing but tens in fervor and dedication. Two qualities he admired in a person, man and woman alike.

Paranoid. He grunted. That was the *last* word anyone would use to describe McIntyre Walsh. Anyone who knew him, that is. Flicking a glance toward the tent, he soured. She hadn't the first clue to his identity, the man he was on the inside. She asked about his "story," but she wasn't interested in anything but filler, nothing more than empty conversation to fill the void between people. She didn't really care where he'd been, where he was going. She couldn't understand a man like him. Few could.

And she'd never need to try. He was here because he had a job to do. There was a killer on the loose looking for innocent victims and Walsh wasn't about to stand by and let him take another young life, no matter how cavalier she seemed about the same. She was young and foolish. She didn't know any better. He did.

Another sound popped in the distance. Walsh stilled. Was that a coyote? A mountain cat on the hunt? Silence penetrated the black of night around him, but no warning signs flashed. Walsh slowed his breathing, sharpened his ears to the open land, the dense forest around him. Perhaps it was nothing more than a passing animal, a transitory sound in the night. After several long seconds, he returned focus to the fire and reaffirmed his decision. He wasn't going anywhere. He'd post watch outside her tent until morning and then let her flit off in search of her toads while he shadowed her from a safe distance. When she'd had her fill, he'd watch to be sure she headed down to safety. It's what he did. It's who he was. *That* was his story.

As the sun rose the next morning, Walsh stretched the stiffness from his shoulder, an old injury resulting from a surprise ambush five years ago. The bullet had gone clean through, but the damage to his muscle had been permanent. Without consistent flexibility exercises, the shoulder would freeze up, severely limiting his range of motion. He'd slept little through the night, but he learned long ago how to survive on minimum amounts of rest.

Dressed in navy cargo shorts and pale yellow T-shirt, the collar of which was visible beneath her zipped jacket, Lisa popped out of her tent carrying a lemon, a green plastic cup, a napkin and a small knife. "Good morning," she greeted, lowering herself to sit in near the same place she'd vacated last night. As though it were the most normal course of action in the world, she cut the bright yellow fruit in half, squeezed its juice into her cup and setting rinds and knife aside, stirred a finger through the water-juice combination. Sucking the juice from her fingertip, she downed half the cup.

"Not a fan of orange juice?" he asked, detecting the faint scent of sunscreen amid the rancid ashes of fire.

"Lemon juice is by far a better choice."

"How so?"

"It's cleansing, for one."

"Cleansing?"

"Lemons are anionic, which means they have more electrons of energy compared to cations in their atomic structure. In fact, they're one of the few foods that have more anions than cations. It's a wonderful stimulant to the liver, dissolving uric acid and other poisons in the body which aids elimination. The atomic structure of lemon juice is similar to that of saliva, hydrochloric acid, and your stomach's other digestive juices."

Walsh laughed at the scientific terminology streaming from her delicate lips. "Who knew?"

"Anyone with a mind to," she retorted matter-of-factly and pulled a bag of dried fruit and nuts from her jacket pocket. Sliding a blue tab across the top to open it, she pulled out an apricot and plopped it into her mouth. "If you drink it regularly," she added, "your body can eliminate waste more efficiently."

Eyeing the baggie of fruit in her hand, he said, "Doesn't look like you eat a lot of junk to warrant a need for lemon juice."

She grinned, her eyes disappearing into slits above her full cheeks. "I don't. I enjoy the taste, and besides, they say it's good for your skin."

Mildly amused, Walsh couldn't disagree with her on that point. Lisa's skin was flawless. In the soft morning light, it appeared freshly washed, though how she would have managed that he had no clue. Watching her consume half a bag of fruit, he massaged the back of his neck and asked, "What's on tap for today?"

"I'm heading over the ridge. There's a lake on the other side I want to test before heading down this afternoon."

Glad to hear she would be on her way down, he asked, "Test for what?"

"Chytrid fungus."

"What's that?"

"It's the fungus I told you about that's threatening to wipe out the population of boreal toads. The name is Chytridiomycosis, to be exact. It's a skin disease. It's caused by the swimming spores of an aquatic fungus called chytrid and is wreaking havoc on the toad population. They're a pro-tected species in the state of Colorado but not by the federal government—a fact we're working to change."

Digesting the information, Walsh knew at once it wouldn't soak in further than his ears. Fungus and govern-ment were of no concern to him, though she'd made the state of affairs sound of grave importance. "What does testing do to stop it?"

She looked at him as if he were an idiot. "I track popula-tion, determine the affected toads and document how exten-sive the proliferation of the fungus has been. The research staff at the university has put together a program to help stem the tide of infection. Basically, we locate fungus-free zones and reintroduce healthy toads and tadpoles back into their native habitat and hope they stay fungus-free, but it can be a crapshoot."

Walsh raised his brows. "How bad is it?"

"Pretty bad. The fungus is pretty easy to spread. It's one of the reasons I hike the more remote areas of the mountain. The farther we are from civilization the better, except that humans aren't the only ones who can spread the fungus. An-imals can spread the spores across the entire mountain." She frowned. "It's not like we can clean elk feet."

Though something told him she would if she could.

"We're set to release a batch of tadpoles next week, and it's my job to be sure we're not setting them loose in a contaminated environment."

"I see."

She returned a look that suggested otherwise then chucked back a handful of raisins. Chewing them, she drank the remainder of her water and stood. "I'll be gone in about fifteen minutes, so you can get back to your normal routine."

Walsh rose as she deposited the lemon rinds into her empty baggie, then returned the baggie, cup and knife to her backpack. Ducking into her tent, she emerged with her notepad and headlamp, repacking those as well. Without pause, she proceeded to break down her tent. "Hey, let me help you with that."

Brushing him off, she replied, "I got it." Grabbing the slim cross bow over the top, she popped it free and the red and white nylon material collapsed on itself. She popped the stakes from the ground, deftly folded the pieces together, then rolled it up and stowed the kit in her pack.

Walsh was impressed. His tent was heavy-duty military-grade compared to her lightweight contraption and took ten minutes to break down and pack away.

Brushing fingers through her hair, Lisa retied the hot pink bandana around her head, then pulled sections of shiny dark hair forward over her shoulders. Despite the fact she'd had no shower, she appeared amazingly clean and refreshed, her hazel-brown eyes bright and alert.

"Thanks for taking care of the fire."

He nodded. It had become habit over the months. When the fire went out, he waited until the ashes cooled and then dispersed them completely. If someone hadn't seen the fire the night before, they'd never know there'd been one. Ensured the security of his privacy.

"So...it was nice meeting you, Walsh." Lisa extended a hand.

"Likewise," he said, enjoying the feel of her soft skin in his palm.

"Hope you enjoy your stay up here. There are certainly worse places you could use for an escape."

"I'm not escaping anything," he replied abruptly.

"You know what I mean." Lisa offered a half-smile, but the backpedal in her eyes told a different story.

"I choose to be here because it beats the alternative."

"Yes, I'm sorry. I didn't mean to insinuate you were running away from anything."

Yet that's exactly what you implied, he mused privately but said nothing.

Squatting, Lisa backed up against her blue pack, slipped the straps over her shoulders and stood, making the fifty pound-plus lift seem effortless. "Have a good day!" she chirped and hiked off without another word.

Walsh watched her go, a mix of respect and displeasure swirling in his gut. She certainly wasn't afraid to handle the business of hiking on her own, nor the effort that went with it. In the time he'd known her, there was no doubt in Walsh's mind Lisa was fully capable of leading an expedition of her own to the top of any fourteener. Yet there remained an air of naiveté about her that he didn't like. Sure, she was strong and fit when it came to the physical side of camping, but she seemed oblivious to the dangers. Why would her father allow her to hike up here alone? Or maybe he thought she was with her male counterpart.

That's it. He'd call Wade and inform him that the young woman's partner had abandoned her. Maybe then her father could talk some sense into her. Walsh dialed the number.

Wade's voice boomed through the receiver, "Two calls within twenty-four hours? What's up, buddy?"

"I wanted you to know that the girl's hiking partner went down last night."

"What do you mean?"

"I told them about that recent murder and the guy heeded my advice to head down."

"But Lisa didn't?"

"You got it. She's heading farther up the mountain."

"Sounds like Lisa."

"And you're okay with it?"

"What do you want me to do about it? She's an adult woman. I can't order her down, if that's what you were hoping."

"I was hoping you'd put in a call to her father. Maybe he can talk some sense into her." Wade laughed, the sound grating on Walsh. "Wade, this is serious. The girl could be in real trouble."

"Oh, I don't know. Sounds like you've got her back." Wade paused and chuckled. "She's a looker, isn't she?"

Walsh riled at the implication. "I'm worried about her *safety.*"

"Well, there's no better man for the job than you, my friend. I'll call her father if it'll make you feel better, but don't hold your breath on that account. If you told her there's a bad guy on the loose and she's still up there, I doubt there's a lot her old man is going to say to change her mind."

Walsh grunted as he followed Lisa through the forest.

"How about you keep an eye on her until she heads down?" Wade laughed softly. "And try to enjoy the view while you're up there. I hear it's gorgeous."

Ending the call, Walsh didn't care for Wade's smug commentary. He wasn't interested in gawking at some college girl—though he couldn't argue the point about her looks—he was concerned for her well-being. If it was his daughter, he'd order her down immediately. Headstrong or not, she needed to understand what was at stake.

Unfortunately, it was a sentiment he seemed to hold alone.

Whatever. Walsh would trail her up and over the ridge, careful to remain far enough behind that he'd remain undetected, tracking her until she headed down as scheduled. Lisa disappeared around a thick patch of evergreen.

Game on. Adjusting his bag to sit on his back hips, Walsh hurried to pick up her trail. Tracking her the mile or so back to the ridge, once again he was surprised by her agility and physical capability. Sporting a loaded backpack, she still managed to scale the cliff with relative ease, ascending to the rocky ledge where he'd first seen her in less than fifteen minutes, but this time she didn't stop and take pictures. She cruised around the corner and out of sight.

Walsh jogged over the base and leapt onto the nearest boulder. If she could do it in fifteen, he could do it in five. Grabbing hold of another rock, he hoisted himself up, moving stone-to-stone with hands and feet in coordinated movement. As he reached for a pointed rock above, his hand slipped, the rough edge scraping his palm. Cursing, he grabbed hold at a different angle and half-pulled, half-jumped to the next rock. The last thing he needed was to lose sight of her. He knew where she was headed, but anything could happen between here and there, especially considering this was where he'd spotted the stranger yesterday.

Continuing upward until he reached the ledge, Walsh looked downward but didn't see her. The trail wasn't a linear shot down. Instead, it was marred with small trees and big rocks. Calming his heart's rapid pump of exertion, he took in the distant view, scanning the horizon for signs of threat. Below him was a decent-sized lake, its surface flat, not a ripple to speak of. Beyond, slants of trees angled down in a V against the jagged backdrop of snow-capped mountains. Massive boulders dotted the base, a few implanted in the grassy land surrounding the lake.

Looked like another beautiful day in high country—one Walsh intended to keep that way. Lisa would hike down, collect her toad samples and be on her way, hopefully within a few hours' time, and he would get back to normal. He might even take Wade up on his request to hunt down a killer. Give him something to do, anyway.

Walking briskly down the incline, Walsh scanned the curved mountain face. She was most likely around the corner and hidden from view, though the fact that he didn't have her in his sights bothered him. Hiking down, he continuously raked his gaze over the landscape, careful to keep himself concealed as he traveled. But after several minutes and no sign of her, Walsh's antennae began to hum. He should have caught up with her by now. The sharp drop-off to his right would force this trail as her only route. It wound around and eventually led into the valley below.

Moving toward the edge, Walsh stole a peek below, half-expecting to see her making a sheer descent to cut time. He laughed softly. She could probably handle it, too. But Lisa hadn't gone straight down. Picking up his pace, he race-walked the two-foot wide path marred by uneven stones. He'd feel better keeping her within sight, close enough should any action on his part be required, yet far enough away not to intrude or reveal his position to any potential on-lookers. If there was a killer with his eye on Lisa, Walsh wanted the man to think she was alone. He would own the element of surprise and use it to full advantage.

Working his way down the rocky terrain, the path strewn with boulders, many rounded, others sharp-edged, the result of years of erosion and earth-splitting rifts, Walsh maintained as fast a pace as he could manage. High country wasn't for the meek. It called to the brave, challenged the strong. Walsh had heard of climbers bent on conquering the peaks only to fall to their death or succumb to hypothermia, dehydration, and plain old exhaustion. Hiking at altitudes of twelve thousand feet and above took a toll on a body. A sobering reality he'd become all too familiar with as he assisted Wade and others on search and rescue missions.

Earlier this summer, a father and daughter team had set out to climb a fourteener, promising their family they'd be home in four days, but the pair was never heard from again. Ground teams, dogs, and helicopters were sent out after them and within a few days, the bodies were discovered on a grassy stretch of terrain about thirteen thousand feet. Wade's team used a helicopter to evacuate the bodies, the family confirming their identities that afternoon. It was a shame. The girl had been only twenty-one years old.

Shaking the memory from his mind, Walsh ejected the negative thoughts. Lisa would be okay under his watch. He'd make sure of it.

Chapter Seven

As Lisa returned to the ridge from the day before, she pondered Mr. Walsh's claim about a man following her. Walsh, she thought. His name was Walsh, not Mr. Walsh, though a part of her still had a hard time putting that name with his face. The intense eyes and gravelly voice belonged to a man with authority, a man that demanded action, results. A gritty man. A warrior. Walsh seemed too passive and agreeable a name for a man like him.

A man like him. She didn't even know him! Who was she to make judgments regarding his personality and name suitability? She shook her head. It was a silly thought to have in the first place. Mentally settling in for the arduous hike, she estimated the time to the lake to be about an hour, leaving her all day to collect her samples. From there, the hike down would be about three hours.

Focusing on the ground ahead of her, Lisa amped up her pace, mindful to walk on rocks instead of dirt and grass wherever she could, disrupting the natural order of things as little as possible. With no established trails, it was her responsibility to minimize her footprint. Leave no trace. It was an ethical motto to live by for outdoor enthusiasts. Don't disturb, don't disrupt, don't dispose—don't be disrespectful. Humans were visitors up here. Guests.

Overhead the sun baked the bandana scarf on her head, heating the hair beneath, making it very warm. Breathing steady and even, she kept her water bottle handy and drank regularly. Sweating wasn't a concern, not with the lack of humidity, but dehydration could sneak up on a gal, especially on a beautiful day like today. A westerly wind kept her body comfortable. The trip would be a breeze.

Upon reaching her destination, Lisa dropped her pack a respectable distance from the lake and performed a quick wipe down of her boots. Spying a scraggly twig on the ground, she grabbed it. That would come in handy, she thought. Flipping open the top flap of her pack, she gathered her box of gloves, followed by a container of empty test tubes and cotton swabs, careful not to disturb the samples already taken. Setting the trio of supplies on her pack, she pulled two gloves on, wriggling her fingers inside until the latex snapped into place around her wrist. Interlacing her fingers, she secured the fit, grabbed a tube and swab and headed into the marshy border of the lake.

Thin strands of grass feathered across the water's surface, the sun casting the landscape in a buttery glow. This was her favorite time of day, when the world was quiet, save for the sounds of nature. Inhaling the crisp cool air, her body well-acclimated to the lung-straining altitude, she grabbed her twig and perused the shallows and grass, watching for signs of toads. Beneath her, the ground grew soft and muddy, sucking her boots into mud-sicles, squelching as she plodded through sucking, oily-sheened bogs. Skirting the deeper water, she waved her twig above the grass like a blind woman in an attempt to flush the toads out into the open. Boreal toads were famous for hopping between marshes, lakes and streams, giving her the perfect opportunity to catch them. She heard the squeak and whirled, knowing the grass-flute sound would reveal the toad's position. Ah, *yes...*

Bending, Lisa plucked the toad from its perch between blades and aptly flipped it belly side up. Rubbing a cotton swab over its stomach and webbed feet, she admired the dark blotches on its belly. This fella was a pretty good size. Looked healthy, too. Releasing him, she glanced around the marshy area and sighed. Hopefully this section remained untouched by the fungus. Once a population was infected, only about ten percent survived. It was a devastating statistic, but armed with the facts, she and the others involved with the project intended to make a difference.

Circumnavigating the pond, she collected samples, made notes on the number of tadpoles, clutches and adult toads present, pleased by the abundance of juveniles. It wasn't even noon, yet she'd managed quite a treasure trove of samples. It had been a good session. Taking a break, she eased down on her pack and chugged half a bottle of water, followed by a handful of unsalted pistachios. Struck by the need to use the facilities, she glanced around and decided a patch of trees to the north would suit her needs. Not that anyone would see her out in the open, but one never knew.

After relieving herself, Lisa walked to her pack, infused with energy as she drank in the view. The sheer magnitude of the Rocky Mountains filled her with awe. More than beautiful, they represented the power of nature, its complete and total dominance of all things human. Here in the wild, the world was in balance. Harmony. Animals shared a symbiotic relationship with the earth around them, whereas humans did not. Humans consumed resources, exploited natural wonders, depleting the planet to the point of no return. It wasn't fair. It wasn't right.

It shouldn't be allowed to happen.

Working in solitude cleared her mind, made her feel at one with nature. Taking note of a smaller pond to the north of the lake, marsh grass joining the two into one larger aquatic zone, she trekked over and with zen-like focus, proceeded to collect a dozen more samples, the last three proving difficult to get. These little guys must be spreading the word about her presence. *Hop for your lives! Giant Sasquatch woman on the prowl!*

Lisa laughed at her description. If only the little amphibians knew she was working for their best interests! She shook her head. Didn't matter. She knew, and that was enough. Thoughts of Walsh bubbled to the surface. He certainly didn't understand what she was doing. Probably thought she was a loony for traipsing through ponds after a bunch of toads. At least that's the way she'd felt when she revealed her plans for today. He didn't see the significance in capturing toads and testing for fungus. All he cared about was getting her off the mountain.

Last week he took out one of two female hikers. The girl's throat was cut.

A shudder raced through her and Lisa quickly shook it off. Her habit was to hike with a partner, knowing there was safety in numbers, even if that meant two. The only reason she was alone at the moment was because Dale bailed on her. Because there was a killer on the loose. With a knife. With an involuntary scan of the landscape around her, Lisa registered nothing out of the ordinary. The tree line was a good distance away, the steeper mountain terrain a mile farther back. She was in the midst of an open expanse of grassy land, making it easy to spot an incoming intruder. She was fine.

Thinking back to Walsh's ease of sneaking up on her, Lisa attributed it to his Special Forces background. He was trained to advance on an enemy without detection. Not that she was an enemy, but she doubted some lunatic murderer in the mountains would prove as stealthy as Walsh.

Lisa swallowed, her throat suddenly dry. The mere thought of someone on the hunt for women to kill was terrible. She had full confidence in her ability when it came to self-defense—she'd been trained by a local martial arts expert at the insistence of her father, due to a rash of rapes on the campus the spring before her freshman semester, but still... It was creepy.

And while she believed in her ability to survive, she had never been tested. Glancing about, Lisa was overcome by an uneasy feeling. Not in real life, anyway, though she was sure she could defend herself and get away. Softening her gaze on the tree line in the distance, she thought back to her days of training. The sessions had been pretty fun, her practice and skill earning her near black belt rank. It wasn't as though her instructor had gone easy on her. He hadn't. And if she could handle him, she could handle a stranger on a mountain. After all, that's the reason she'd trained.

Calmer now, Lisa reassured herself she'd be okay. Pulling a bottle of water from the side pocket of her backpack, she downed half of it in one long swallow. Her cell phone rang.

Wiping spillage from the corner of her lips, she grabbed her phone. "Hello?"

"Hey, Lisa."

"Dale. What's up?"

"Where are you? Are you coming down?"

"Later, yes." She glanced around the shallows of the lakeshore. "I'm at the lake collecting samples." Where he should be. "I've swabbed over a dozen so far and will head down later." When he said nothing, she asked, "Why? What's up? Rethinking your decision to head down last night?"

"No. Professor Stevens was asking."

Lisa realized he'd taken offense and instantly felt a prick of guilt. This was his discovery as much as hers, and it wasn't really his fault he went down early. It was Walsh's. If he hadn't scared him, Dale would still be up here helping her. Thinking back, she should have called him to make sure he'd made it down all right. "Tell him I'll bring them by this afternoon."

"Sure."

She would be bringing them by and not Dale, something that would have bothered her immensely if their positions were reversed.

"I'll let him know," Dale said and ended the call.

Pulling the phone from her ear, she mulled over the significance. It was odd that he'd called. Every grad student felt the pressure, the competition to be the first, best, but Dale had never struck her as particularly competitive. He was diligent but not fighting to be number one, not like some of the other students. Why call and check on her?

Taking another sip of water, she checked the time. One-thirty. She'd done well for the day but considered hanging around for another hour or so, maybe scout out this section of land a bit before heading down. She had another pack of test tubes. It would be a waste to let them go unused, not when she was here and had the time. As it stood, she had more than enough daylight to get down and get her samples to the lab. The more she could find, the better the statistical data.

Startled by the sound of her cell phone, Lisa's pulse skipped. *Was that Dale again?*

She snatched the phone. "Hello?"

"Lisa, it's Dad. Why didn't you tell me that Dale left you up there alone?"

"What?"

"You know you shouldn't be hiking alone. It isn't safe."

"Dad—" Lisa shook the confusion from her brain. "Did Dale call you?"

"No. Wade did. He told me that Dale left last night. We've talked about this before. You promised you wouldn't hike alone."

"Hold on a minute—how did Wade know?" But as she asked the question, a crystal clear image of Walsh's face popped into her mind's eye. Was he broadcasting her every move?

"His military friend, the one I told you about."

Yes, she figured as much. Lisa cupped a palm to her forehead and dropped her head back. Did the guy think he was doing her a favor by calling her father? He'd only worry to think about her up here alone. While her dad trusted her, he expected her to hike with a companion. Drawing her head forward, Lisa said, "Dad, I'm fine. It was an unexpected turn of events. Dale headed down last night and I'm right behind him."

"According to Wade's friend, you're going up the mountain, not down."

Lisa fumed inwardly. Had he given them a blow-by-blow on her entire whereabouts? Struck by the thought, she glanced back up the mountain ridge she'd passed over to get here. *Was he following her?* Searching the trees and rocks for sign of him, she responded evenly into the phone, "I'm checking one last lake and heading down. In fact, I'm pretty much finished."

"Good. What time can I expect you?"

"Give me a few hours. I have a couple more tubes to fill and then I'm good to go."

"Be careful, Lisa."

Mildly disturbed by the edge in his voice, she replied, "I always am, Dad. You know that."

"I know. It's the only reason the helicopter isn't on its way as we speak."

"*Dad*." Lisa tried to laugh it off but couldn't.

Because her father meant it. An orthopedic surgeon in town, he was also a member of the search and rescue team. He had connections. Add the fact that he was close personal friends with Chief Davis and she had no doubt a helicopter would be overhead within the hour, if her father wanted one. Part of that thought was comforting. The other, somewhat jarring. "Tell Adele I'll be home for dinner."

"Will do," he said, his usual warmth returning. "Love you."

"Love you, too."

Ending the call, she blew out a ragged breath. Overhead the sun was bright. Hot. Not usually prone to sweat at this altitude, she felt a growing sheen of perspiration across her head and above her lips. Loosening her bandana, Lisa pulled it free and wiped her face. Her throat felt scratchy. Water. She needed water—and another round of sunscreen. Blame it on her blond father and his naturally freckled skin. The man couldn't go anywhere without first drenching himself in zinc oxide. As a kid she used to tease him about the white film on his nose. Now she understood the benefits. Fortunately for her, technology had advanced the formula, reducing the size of the zinc oxide particles through a micronized process practically eliminating all trace of chalky white residue so her skin didn't look painted white.

Of course with her family DNA, she would have used the old formula if that's all she had. Cancer killed. A wave of melancholy overcame her. Some forms were more preventable than others, some more survivable, but in the end, cancer killed.

That was the takeaway message her mother had left.

Lisa shook the sudden gloom from her mood. Life was short, so make it sweet; that was her motto. Love what you do, live what you love. You never know how many days you had left on the planet, so make the best of the time you had and leave the earth better than you found it. Breathing in lungs full of air, she exhaled and re-centered on her work. This was her life's purpose. Saving the boreal toad from extinction gave her great satisfaction, a sense she was accomplishing something bigger than herself. People these days cared more about stuff—things—than they did nature. Everything was about the newest device, the latest and greatest app. It was as if life didn't exist outside their handheld screen.

Insane. Nobody talked anymore, they texted. Nobody cared about the waste they were creating. They only cared about getting something new. Not her. This was her source of fulfillment. Armed with gloves and swabs, Lisa continued her hunt for the pudgy little guys. As expected, most of the toads she'd tested were male. This was breeding season. The females would deposit their eggs and disperse from the site, but males would continue to congregate around the area for weeks.

With no stress from the chytrid fungus, these toads could live long and healthy lives, some estimates tacking their age to over ten years. Add the fact that each female could produce as many as twelve thousand eggs per clutch, or strand of eggs, and it began to add up. Lisa laughed, doing the math in her head. That's a lot of toads! It was good news she'd found so many in this lake.

Heartened by thoughts of her amphibians, she swiped at a leaping toad and missed. "Oh, that was a *close* one." No problem, she'd grab the next one. But after an hour and only four more toads, Lisa got the message. The toads were avoiding her. Chuckling, she pulled the gloves from her hands and carried them back to her pack. Some days you win, some days you lose, she thought, though counted today as a win. This lake was fairly remote, increasing the odds of finding a fungus-free population. The less human traffic to carry and spread the fungus spores the better.

Securing the samples in her pack, Lisa changed her boots, storing the muddy ones in one of four large plastic bags she carried. Besides, one never knew what conditions awaited, which is why she made it a habit to pack extra footwear. Her dad used to kid her about being a professional Girl Scout, predicting that one day she was going to be president of the organization. "No way," had been her standard reply. Presidents were stuck in offices, a veritable jail sentence for her.

Drinking in the vista—slants of gray rock capped by snow, a V of evergreen flanking their base and opening to a lush carpet of green—Lisa couldn't imagine her life anywhere but here. This wide-open country was where she dwelled. Professor Stevens teased her about hating to get stuck in the lab—could she imagine getting stuck in an office?

She cringed. The mere thought was repulsive.

Re-wrapping her bandana, Lisa squatted, slipped on the shoulder straps for her pack and stood. Hunger pangs rumbled through her belly. Maybe she should eat something now and then head down. She still had several more hours of sunlight for a hike that would only take about three hours. Suddenly famished, Lisa removed the pack and located a baggie of kale chips, followed by a snack bar. Another one of Adele's gourmet treats, this gem of a bar was cranberry-almond and oh-so-delicious. Packed with protein and carbs, it would give her the energy needed to hike down and make good time.

As usual, Lisa had spent more time mountaintop than she'd planned on, but she'd make it back on schedule. Biting into the snack bar, she relished the soft-textured crunch, savored the sweet scent, the nutty flavors mixed with the tang of dried cranberries. When hiking high altitudes, her body didn't crave fat. Instead, she found it somewhat distasteful. While she loved a spoonful of flax seed on her salads or a plate of sliced avocado, she didn't prefer them while hiking. After a bit of research, she'd discovered that carbohydrates required less oxygen for metabolism—a real consideration for the overtaxed oxygen economy of her body at this altitude.

Taking her time, Lisa ate and drank. Finishing up her kale chips, she packed away her trash, hoisted the pack onto her back and secured the belt at her waist. Looking around, she double-checked to be sure she hadn't accidentally left any trace of her belongings behind, took a deep breath, and shifted into hiking mode.

Walsh's heart skipped. *Finally* she was on her way back. Lucky for her. If she'd stayed much longer, he would have marched down to the lake and hauled her butt back up this ridge and down the mountain. He didn't like the fact that she was taking her sweet time down there. It left him unsettled. Adjusting the focus of his lens, he scanned the perimeter of open terrain, unable to shake the feeling they were being watched. Like an invisible itch, it felt like they weren't alone, like someone else was in their midst. Pulling the binoculars from his eyes, he glanced overhead, squinting against the sunlight. As far as he could see, they were alone. Alone.

From his perch on a panel of rock, Walsh rubbed his eyes, the high ridge of his nose. If Lisa had a pair of binoculars and had chosen to scan the vicinity, she would have easily seen him. But totally consumed with the mountain lake she'd been wading in, she had no interest. Definitely single-minded when it came to those toads of hers, and completely oblivious to the perils that might lay in wait for her.

With nothing to block his view, Walsh had watched as she crept through the water, catching and swabbing her toads. He wasn't sure if Lisa thought she was sneaking up on the toads, but by the way she crept about, stalking the creatures, waving a stick through the tall reeds of grass and pouncing, that's exactly what she appeared to be doing—trying to sneak up on them. Pretty hilarious way to spend your time, if you asked him.

A pretty long time, too. He figured she'd be down there for an hour tops, but as hour number three rolled around it was all he could do not to head down and demand what was taking so long. How many toads did she need to catch to convince herself they were fine and well and doing just dandy without her? And didn't she say this was mating season? How about not barging in on the animals while they were doing what came naturally?

Walsh had been on a fair number of surveillance missions, but this one beat them all—on several levels. While her actions made him laugh, her figure did anything but. More than once his gaze had been drawn to the lean muscle of her thighs, the curve of her rear, the trim waistline of her shirt, her slender but well-muscled arms... Half of him hoped she'd trip and soak that light yellow shirt of hers, outlining her curves as had happened yesterday. Recalling the episode, he chuckled. She liked pink, for her outerwear and her underwear.

Bringing the binoculars to his eyes one last time, Walsh calculated she'd be at the base of the ridge in ten minutes. From there she'd scale this section in fifteen, twenty, taking another twenty to thirty to round the top and make it back to their camping site from last evening.

Her camping site, he corrected. He was a silent bystander in this research jaunt of hers, self-appointing himself to make sure she made it down the mountain and home to safety where she belonged. Then he could pick up where he left off—in peace and solitude.

Taking several steps up the trail, Walsh decided to wait at the top, the area directly above the route she'd have to take to cross over and head down the other side. The vantage point would give him the best view of her coming and going. The best view. He laughed softly as Wade's words floated to the forefront of his mind. *Enjoy the view while you're up there. I hear it's gorgeous.*

Right on, buddy. You nailed it right on.

After a brief reconnaissance of the trail going up, Walsh located the perfect spot to wait. Situated between a boulder and a wall of rock, he had a clear view of the terrain below. Checking his watch, he estimated her time of arrival to be about five, ten minutes. From what he'd witnessed so far, she could have made it by now, if she wanted, but she had no reason to hurry, so Walsh gave her the benefit of the doubt. There was no other way to go. With mountain on one side and cliff on the other, Lisa would have to travel the course he laid out in his mind. It was the course she'd taken down to the lake. It was the course she would take up.

Situating his body in place, it was time to wait. Patience was necessary in his line of work. His old line of work. Today was a fluke, an off-duty job that landed in his lap by chance. Sitting and waiting for the bad guy was something he used to do, but not anymore, though the heightened state of his senses and the taut readiness of his muscles said otherwise. The physical sensation of sitting wedged between trees and rock took him back to another mountainous terrain, a continent of chaos and upheaval halfway around the world from the serenity of Colorado.

Pulling his thoughts from the past, Walsh urged himself to focus. Focus on the here and now. *You're not waiting for a terrorist to show up. You're waiting for a college girl, a grad student out for a research project.* Constricting his thoughts to the narrow path below, he curbed his impatience with practiced, rhythmic inhalations. She would be here soon.

Minutes passed and Walsh lifted up, craning his head to see farther down the passageway. Nothing. As the minutes ticked by, the quiet began to gnaw at him. Lisa should have been here by now. Instinct pressed him to abandon position and go after her, but if she was taking her time, any move from position would expose him.

It was a chance he wasn't willing to take. Letting on to the fact he'd been shadowing her would serve no purpose. She'd be here. Probably stopped to take a break. Electricity crackled through his limbs. Lisa didn't need to take breaks. She was fitter than fit. It was possible she was taking pictures.

Springing from his hiding place, Walsh swiftly climbed down the rock face and dropped to the level space of ground. Something was wrong. He could feel it. Edging around the jutting stone, he peered down the trail. Nothing. Walking several steps, he ducked beneath a horizontal spear of mountain when he glimpsed movement. *Lisa.* His heart kicked. What the—?

She was moving at a good clip—but in the opposite direction!

Walsh took off running. She looked like she was running *from* something.

Was there someone on the trail behind her? Dodging spiked obstacles and pine trees, his boots pounded over uneven ground as he zeroed in on the trail downhill. Leading with a hand to avoid branches smacking his skull, he shouted, "Lisa!"

A sharp curve choked his view. The backside of a man's figure came into full view. Dressed in jeans and navy hoodie, dirty-blond hair, about five-ten in height, hundred and ninety pounds—Walsh committed the description to memory as he bounded forward.

Heart pounding, he lost his footing and nearly went over the cliff. "Lisa!" he shouted at the top of his lungs, grabbing the rough bark of a branch for stability.

She slipped, fell, and tumbled over the cliff.

Walsh's heart stopped. "Lisa!"

The stranger sprinted down the mountain.

Walsh reached the site in seconds. Skidding to a stop, he nearly toppled over the brink as he tried to digest the scene below. Pulse thundering between his ears, he saw a sloped ground, large rounds of rock pushing up through overgrown grass and flowers. There was a drop-off rimmed by a line of pine tree tops. Chest heaving, he saw no Lisa. Nothing. Raking a hand over his head, he scoured the terrain. But she went down here. He *saw* it happen. She couldn't have disappeared into thin air!

He whipped a glance down the empty trail. The stranger was gone. Momentarily stunned, Walsh was at a loss. "Lisa!" he called out. Cupping hands to his mouth, he yelled louder, "Lisa!"

Chapter Eight

Lisa rolled off the cliff—*crack, crack, crack*—her body thundering through tree limbs like twigs. Landing with a hard thud, she gasped. Everything came to a standstill. She stared up, a tangle of heavy dark branches blocked her view of the sky. She couldn't breathe.

She couldn't breathe!

Her lungs felt flattened, hurt with every attempt at breath. Above her, the sunlight came in slits and swaths. She couldn't move. The forest closed in around her as she tried to inhale. *Breathe.* She couldn't breathe.

Lisa's mind began to clear. The wind had been knocked from her lungs. They were constricted, but she'd be okay. *Wait through it.* Slow, easy. It would be okay.

"Lisa!"

Panic caught her heart. Walsh!

She cried out but couldn't manage a whisper. *Walsh. I'm here.* Struggling against the fresh tightening in her chest, Lisa heard him call out her name again. She called back, but no words came from her lips. *Walsh, I'm here. I'm alive!*

He had no way of knowing. Lisa briefly closed her eyes. The devastation sank in. He had no way of knowing, but she did. She was alive.

It was all that mattered at the moment. *Calm. Stay calm. Breathe.*

She assessed her condition. Everything hurt, but nothing felt sharp or debilitating. Slowly regaining her breath, she wriggled her fingers, moved her feet side-to-side. The trees had taken the brunt of her fall. That, and the "tuck and roll" tactic she employed prior to hitting them after rolling off the lower cliff. *Protect the valuables.* It was a strategy she learned in one of her hiking clubs. In case of accidental fall, tucking and rolling would limit the physical damage to her body.

Fall. Hers was no accidental fall. She'd slipped when a man started chasing her. *The killer*. Lisa closed her eyes, warding off the reality as it seeped in. It had to be. No one else would have gone after her like that. Tears burst beneath her lids. She had to move, she had to get out of here. That man would come after her again. But Walsh—he would come too, wouldn't he?

Of course he would. He'd been there, hadn't he?

She heard his voice. Deep and rough, it had to be him. It had to be a sign—a sign that everything would be all right. Splayed over the lump of her backpack, Lisa brought hands to her shoulder straps and winced. Her right wrist was hurt. Broken, sprained, she couldn't be sure, but it was hurt. She lifted her head. It felt okay. Probably saved from hard impact by her backpack.

Using her left hand, she slid the shoulder strap from her right shoulder and eased her arm free, gently pushing the opposite strap aside. Tightening her core, she lifted up and appraised the damage. As expected, her legs were scratched and turning red, same as her arms, but there was nothing gaping or bent at odd angles, nothing gushing blood, which was a relief. Superficial wounds she could ignore. Broken bones and open wounds she could not.

Drawing her knees up, she felt the swelling before she saw it. Her left ankle was injured. How badly remained to be seen. She reached down to examine it, but stopped at the faint snap sound. *Was someone coming?*

Heartbeats battered her ribs. Fear lodged in her throat. Was the killer coming for her?

Sweeping a glance around her immediate vicinity, Lisa saw no place to hide. A field of evergreen surrounded her, but their branches hung feet above the ground providing no cover at all. Behind her the earth rose sharply, a mountainous wall of obstacle. Other than rocks and forest floor debris, there was nothing.

She was totally exposed. Vulnerable.

Fighting a growing urgency, Lisa forced the negativity back. *Think*. Maybe it was Walsh. Maybe it was *him* coming for her instead of the bad guy. But she couldn't take the chance. She had to get out of here. In self-defense, they advised distance—put as much distance as possible between victim and attacker. She couldn't outrun this danger, but she could hide from it and then call for help. First, she needed to tape her ankle. Twisting around toward her pack, she flinched. *Add a few bruised ribs to the list*, she groaned, gritting her teeth as she opened a side pocket on her pack. Her first aid kit would provide the basics to wrap her ankle, though not enough to wrap her wrist.

Under the circumstances, mobility was the higher priority. She never thought she'd need the medical supplies but was glad she came prepared. *Like a Girl Scout.* Memories of her father's voice echoed through the forest of trees. Her father. Thoughts of his phone call pulled at her as she unwound the soft band of tape. Glancing in the distance, straining to detect new and closer sounds, Lisa decided he was next. Once she got herself moving, she'd call and ask her father to send help.

Removing her boot, she quickly taped her ankle, mentally ticking through her first aid basics—rest, ice, elevation, compression—she was working in reverse order, but without time for rest, no ice to be found, and elevating her foot not an option, she had to do what she could. Pausing, she tuned in to the air around her. Musk rose from the shaded ground, wet earth underscoring the scent of pine and wood. Mostly blocked from sun, this area was quiet.

Dead quiet. Lisa loosened the laces on her boot and slipped it on over her foot, assuring herself the noises she'd heard were nothing. Even if a killer was on the loose and looking for her, it would take him time to get here, giving her time to get away.

She would have liked to wrap her wrist, but had only brought one bandage roll. She was prepared for an unexpected emergency—not a full blown calamity. On impulse,

Lisa took the bandana from her head, unfolded it, refolded it lengthwise and using her mouth to assist, wound it around her wrist, pulling it snug. Tucking the ends beneath the layers of material, she secured it in place. It wasn't much, but some support was better than no support.

Gathering the essentials—phone, water, solar cell charger—she debated whether to add a magnesium stick, knife, and head lamp. She didn't intend to stay on the mountain. She intended to make a beeline for the bottom. But as any good Scout knew, plan for the worst and hope for the best, so she packed her pockets with as much as she could carry then tied her fleece jacket around her waist. She'd have to leave her backpack, the thought of which killed her. All her samples were inside, all her notes. Her camera, too.

Had anything broken in the fall? Were her tubes shattered? Her camera?

With no time to check, she could only hope. Rising to her knees, Lisa pushed her pack across the ground. It snagged on a rock, but with a brisk shove, she managed to get it loose and beneath the overhang of a rock. It would be safe until she could return.

Gaining her bearings, Lisa crawled around a massive pine tree and stood. Her ankle throbbed. Clenching her teeth against the pain, she wiped the dirt and pine needles from her palms and double-checked the compass app on her phone. The best way home would be to the right. Sucking in another deep breath, Lisa set off.

Walsh cursed under his breath. In his split second of indecision he had not only lost the assailant, but Lisa, too. How? Forging back up the mountain, he stared down at the vacant slope of land. Where could she be? He saw her fall here, in this spot. His gaze was drawn to the tree line over the ledge of cliff. Had she made it that far? Had she fallen over?

A sudden current of awareness tingled through his senses as though he realized he was being watched. Walsh trusted his instinct, amping the sensitivity of his internal antennae to

full blast. He took an automatic step back, partially concealing his body against the mountainside. Nothing yelled "put a
bullet through my head" like standing out in the wide open.

Or a knife in my back. Calming the sudden jump in
pulse, Walsh dialed into the quiet, dry alpine air. After living
up here for six months, he knew the sounds of mountain living. He knew the rhythm, the tempo. Once the sun dropped,
the sound of wildlife would begin. Visibility would be reduced to nothing. Temperatures would plunge.

With a fleeting glance over the edge, Walsh knew he had
to find her and fast. Surveying the area, facts crystallized in
his brain. If Lisa had indeed gone over, she would be injured,
even—

Walsh scratched the possibility from his mind. She was
fine and he was going to find her. Bolting, he ran down the
trail. He wasn't about to cry "uncle" when it came to a missing coed. Not on his watch.

Lisa shut the pain from her brain. She'd found a man-
gled branch, a fallen pine limb that was sturdy enough to act
as a walking stick, and used it to help ease the burden from
her ankle. Unfortunately, her boot was aggravating the situation. Her foot felt like an inflamed water balloon she'd tried
to cram into her shoe.

But it couldn't be helped. She wasn't leaving her boot
behind. The mounting throb in her ankle warned she should
stop and rest, but she had to keep moving. There was a stream
about a half mile or so down, closer if she detoured due east.
It was a detour she wouldn't be making. Due east would take
her through open meadow for an extended duration, and she
wasn't chancing it. Slow and straight and hidden from view
would win this race, not to mention a little help from her father's friends. In a few minutes, she would stop and try to call
him again. As it stood, her goal was putting distance between
her and whoever had been chasing her.

Fifteen minutes later, the contour of the mountain veered
left. Trying to retrace her steps from the upper ridge, she dis-

covered this level wasn't a match to that above. The mountain sloped down at an angle, giving the lower terrain a much wider girth. But she had to be close. The trees were beginning to thin, allowing light to stream onto the ground, a sure indication she was nearing open land. If she could make it to the edge of the trees, she could use her phone with greater likelihood of success. Cell service tended to work better in open areas.

Rounding the spread of a mammoth pine, she suddenly stopped. Air escaped her lungs. *No!* Sixty feet ahead of her a tumble of huge boulders completely blocked her passage. She could see light above them and instinctively knew she wanted to be on the other side. Under different circumstances she would have climbed over those rocks, taking advantage of the numerous protrusions and footholds, but without two good feet and hands, there was no way.

Expelling a tired sigh, Lisa shrank beneath a swift wave of defeat. On a good day she could take that challenge. Today wasn't a good day. At this rate, she'd end up stuck on the wrong side of the ridge *and* in the dark. If only she knew where Walsh was. Sudden, urgent, she felt the distinct need for his presence. Walsh was ex-Marine. He was in extreme physical condition. He could help her get down, over or around whatever she needed. But he wasn't here.

Because she had insisted he leave her be.

Leaning on her stick, Lisa succumbed to the regret coursing through her. She should have invited him along on her trip to the lake. Wasn't like he was doing anything else. If she'd been thinking, it would have been the perfect solution. It was always better to hike with a companion. Her father's rule, common sense's rule. But she hadn't been thinking. Not about some murderer. She refused Walsh's insistence that she head down because she had work to get done.

Advice given because a killer was on the loose. A shiver scurried up her spine. Tapping her back pocket, Lisa credited herself for grabbing the mace. It would slow down any potential attacker, giving her a fighting chance at defense. Unfortunately, it would be a defense without the help of her dominant hand and one good foot.

Shake it off. Lisa shook her shoulders, her head. She blew out her breath, inhaled a fresh drift of sweet spruce. *Shake it off. Let it go.*

Centering on the scent of forest grounded her. Calmed her. *No self-pity parties allowed.* Though what an easy party it would be to throw, she mused dolefully. *C'mon over, sit down. Stay awhile and sing another round of "Stinks to be You."*

Pulling the cell phone from her pocket, Lisa tried her father's number again, but frowned at the screen. *No service.*

A branch snapped.

Lisa froze. Suspending her breath, she listened. Seconds passed. Heartbeats thrashed in her chest. When she heard nothing, she turned, scanning a one-eighty to her rear. Lisa peered through densely entwined pine branches and trunks, scraggly underbrush and massive boulders, unable to gain a distant view. A myriad hiding places surrounded her. Gaze darting about the landscape, she realized anyone could be tucked behind a tree trunk or boulder and she'd never see them.

She had to keep going. She had to get closer to open space and call for help, maybe flag down passing hikers. Or Walsh. His image filled her for the umpteenth time since her fall—the hard line of his gaze, the square of his shoulders, the tapered lines of his muscular body. No one had to tell her he was ex-military or Special Forces. It oozed from the man's every pore.

Reaching level ground, Walsh cut back and ran toward the area where Lisa would have gone down. Ahead, a packed line of trees complicated matters, but he vowed to methodically search every square inch, leave no stone unturned. He'd find her. One way or another, McIntyre Walsh would find his mark. Standing at the edge of trees, he pulled his cell phone and dialed Wade. The man answered on the first ring.

"Hey, buddy, we've got to stop chatting like this."

Walsh ignored the grin in Wade's voice and clipped, "We've got trouble. Lisa just had a run-in with your mountain murderer."

"What?"

"I scared him off before he could get to her, but she went over a cliff."

"*What?*"

"I think she's okay," Walsh said, automatically working to reassure the panic in Wade's tone. "There's a forest of trees. It might have broken her fall."

"Might have? What are you saying, Walsh? Do you know where she is?"

"Not exactly. I'm on my way to her now, but I wanted you to send help. Get a team up here, stat."

"Got it."

Pressing the screen on his phone, Walsh cupped a hand over it to block the sunlight and called up his exact coordinates, then relayed them to Wade.

"Roger."

"I'll call you when I get to her," Walsh said.

"Thanks."

Ending the call, he ground his jaw. He couldn't make the same promise when he found her attacker. With a quick glance to the sky, Walsh ran into the forest of evergreen. He had little over three hours before dusk. If he didn't find her before then, things could get dicey. Real dicey.

As Lisa walked, dodging the pricks of pine needles and scraggly limbs, she thought through the worse-case scenario. If she didn't find the open clearing she was looking for, she had water, a bag of granola. It was enough to sustain her through the evening and into morning, if she had to park her butt here. Her jacket would keep her warm, her boots would keep her feet comfortable. Shaking off a quick chill, she assured herself it would have to be enough. When she could, she would go to the stream, soak her ankle, elevate it, and prepare for the hike down tomorrow. As it stood, night would lock her on the mountaintop. She had texted her father but with no response.

Translated: she was on her own.

Reaching the edge of trees, a break of grass between her and the next clump of forest, Lisa tried her father again. Forty-five minutes had passed since her last attempt. Forty-five long, excruciating minutes, but she couldn't give up.

The call was going through and her pulse quickened. "Yes!"

Her father answered, "Hello?"

"Dad! It's me, Lisa! I've had an accident—I need you to send help—"

"Hello?"

"Dad—can you hear me?" she cried, gutted by the garbled quality of his voice. Did hers sound the same?

"He...Lis...Di..."

She slumped. The connection was crap.

Groaning, she glanced in either direction and spoke over him in the off chance he could hear her. "I'm up on the mountain, west of Montrose Ridge, headed down." He'd hiked this area with her before. He'd know exactly where she meant. "I sprained my ankle. I can't walk well." Not without taking forever, not without doing more damage. "Send help."

Ending the call, Lisa sat down on a flat section of rock jutting from the base of the mountainous ridge. From this angle, her back was protected, affording her a clear view of anyone approaching. Slipping a hand into her side thigh pocket, she circled her fingers around the cylinder of mace. She was ready, should the need arise. Surveying the open space between here and the next section of trees, she saw no one.

At this point, her plan was to wait it out until darkness fell and make her escape into the forest across the way and down to the stream. She knew exactly how to get there. Once in the woods, she could use her head lamp for illumination. Nerves tingled in her breast. Maybe not. Using her light would make her a beacon for anyone looking for her. Not using it would force her to travel blind.

If only she knew where Walsh had set up his camp. She could go to him, ask him to hide her out until morning. Lisa balked. Hide her out—like *she* was the criminal. Peering back through the layers of evergreen—tightly packed pine needles and scruffy bark, many trees dead and gray, victim to the infestation of a tiny beetle—a tiny part of her did feel in the wrong. She had taken stupid chances. She was in this predicament because she hadn't heeded Walsh's warnings.

Closing her eyes, Lisa breathed in the heady scent of forest. Intense, decadent, the cooler air of the shadows opened her senses, infused her with the sweet smell of pine. She was alone, but alone with nature. This was her territory.

Like your mother, you always preferred to be outdoors. Memories peeled back the moment, dropping her back in time. *You're strong, tough. You get that from your mother.*

Lisa didn't remember her mother that well. She had splintered memories of the woman who had graced her life so long ago, happy memories, fond memories. But she didn't remember her being strong and tough. Lisa only remembered her smile, the gentle touch of her hand, the light stroke of her mother's fingers as she combed them through her hair. Lisa remembered the connection more than the details. It was her father who filled in the rest of the story.

You have her eyes. You have her love for nature. No creature was too small for her to care about their well-being.

Drawn to the throb in her ankle, Lisa opened her eyes and took a look. Lifting her leg, she propped it up on the boulder where she sat. The cold edge of stone cut into her Achilles, but at least her foot was elevated. Touching fingers to the area, she lightly pressed the swollen tissue. Tender, smarting, but not broken.

The hike had been tough, but it was doable. She retained function in her foot. If she had to put weight on it, she could—had done so to get here—but it hurt. It hurt, but it would heal. She blew out her breath. Now, she waited. For once, the darkness would be her ally.

Storming through the wooded section, Walsh couldn't understand it. There was no sight of her—anywhere. But there was no way she could have fallen much farther than here. Shadows were deepening around him but he could still see, could still discern approximate time and distance. He'd been walking for almost an hour, yet he saw nothing. The fact that he couldn't find her had to be a good thing. Glancing upward, a slice of fear cut through him. Unless she was stuck in the trees, splayed across branches, unconscious, unable to move. Had he missed her altogether because he'd been searching the ground and not the trees?

No. His method of search automatically scanned up and down, accounting for any and all possibilities. The training he received for reconnaissance missions had been ingrained in his psyche. It had become second nature to him. Search all angles, all aspects, leave nothing to chance. He knew how to search an area. He'd seen nothing. There was no sign of her. Rooted in place, Walsh felt the seconds ticking like a time bomb. The man he'd seen had disappeared. Walsh assumed he was hidden somewhere on the ridge above, but didn't know it for a fact. He could have gone, abandoned this target, but until Walsh knew with dead certainty the man was no longer a threat, he had to assume he was. If Lisa was okay, if she had somehow miraculously survived and made her way out, she was still in danger.

Glancing ahead, he made his decision. If Lisa was okay, she'd head for familiar terrain. She'd go down near where she came up. At this point, she had a good hour on him. If she had fallen and survived, she'd had to have sustained injuries. But if there was one thing he'd learned about this woman thus far, she was made from tough fiber. She wouldn't quit.

Trying to chase her through this cluster of trees was a waste of time. She'd have made it through and onto the next batch before darkness fell. Hiking up and over the ridge would be quicker for him and give him a chance to catch up to her.

Walsh took off running, back the way he came.

Chapter Nine

Finally, the sun was sinking into the horizon behind her, flaming the distant mountain peaks, drenching the lower elevations in shadows. Tucked out of sight, Lisa could already feel the drop in temperature. Complete darkness would coat the mountain within the next hour. It was time. Replacing the cap on her empty water bottle, Lisa slid it into her side pocket. She'd refill it once she made it to the stream. Right now, it was time to go. Slipping her jacket on, she prepared for the next leg of her journey.

Lisa jumped as a sudden, high-pitched noise pierced the silence. Flinging a hand to her chest, she could feel her heart pounding beneath. She caught her breath, reminding herself it was totally fine, totally natural. The sound had come from an elk. Like the scratch on a violin by a hack musician, the call was distinct. Grating to her nerves, but completely natural. Over the last twenty minutes a crescendo of screechy calls had burst from the hollows of quiet, reminding her she wasn't alone. Wildlife occupied this space with her and dusk intensified their movements. Luckily hunting season for the animals didn't start for another month, or she'd be dodging arrows as well as the blade of a killer.

The blade of a killer. Lisa hadn't seen any sign of him, which was comforting. Then again, she hadn't seen sign of anyone. That part wasn't so comforting. No hikers, no Walsh—she'd been completely alone. Impulsively searching the trees, she had to believe Walsh was making his way back. For whatever reason, he'd been on that ridge and saw her fall. He had called out to her. He wouldn't let her lay there and die. He'd come for her. Walsh was a Marine. He feared nothing. He'd search the area, double back to his tent for supplies, do whatever it took to save her.

That's what she told herself, anyway. It was a logic she found reassuring. He'd gone to the trouble of calling Wade Davis, which meant he was the kind of man concerned with a woman's safety. He'd look for her. The thought of running into Walsh was comforting.

Calming.

Casting another caution-heavy gaze over the open meadow, Lisa listened as a bounty of squirrel chirps peppered the air. Noisy, busily on the hunt for food, they sounded more like birds.

Food. Lisa would need to conserve her stash of granola and split it between tonight's dinner and tomorrow's breakfast. Hiking downhill was decidedly easier for her, but she'd still need the energy stores.

Rolling through scenarios in her mind, she pondered when exactly to make her move. If she waited until pitch dark, she'd be concealed from overhead view—the last place she knew the stranger to be. She could make it to the woods, but would then need her head lamp light to see. If she went now, she could cut her travel time across open land, but would risk being seen from overhead. Two bad choices. Assuming her father had been able to comprehend her message, help would still be a good hour or so away. But had he heard her?

She couldn't be certain, and she wasn't about to wait for something that wasn't a sure thing. No. She had to cross and she had to cross now. Deciding in an instant, Lisa took a deep breath, pulled the mace from her pocket, calmed the sudden patter in her breast, and inched forward. She'd head straight in, then due east, through the trees and down to the stream. Once there, she'd soak her ankle, re-wrap it, and get some sleep, then head down at first sunlight. It was a plan, and having a plan made her feel better. With a goal, it became one step at a time.

Put one foot in front of the other...and soon, you'll be walking out the do-oooor!

The verse from one of her favorite Christmas cartoons popped into her brain out of nowhere. A blast from her childhood, it was automatic, reflexive. And made her smile. Glancing both ways before entering the open space, she thought she could use a peppy dose of "happy" right about now.

Hobbling forward—one foot and stick at a time—Lisa moved as quickly as she could, scanning the trees ahead of her, sweeping her surroundings with an alert gaze, checking back over her shoulder. No one. She saw no one.

Halfway across, she was struck by a bad feeling. A feeling of doom.

Whipping a glance behind her, Lisa half-expected to see someone following her, but she didn't. There was no one there. She glanced up to the ridge. No one. Spewing the breath she hadn't realized she'd been holding, she tried to jog.

Bad idea, she grimaced, nearly tripping. Walk. Hurry.

Almost there.

Upon reaching the line of trees, she took several steps in and bent over. Why was her heart pounding so hard? She should be relieved! She made it!

But she couldn't shake the feeling. Something was wrong. It felt as if someone was watching her. Swallowing over the knot in her throat, Lisa continued her trek. If someone had been watching her, they'd be hard-pressed to find her now. The cover of forest was her friend.

Walsh closed the distance to the top of the ridge, the muscles in his legs burning, but he couldn't stop. Wouldn't. Not until he was there. The rocky trail was taxing as he ran. It was all he could do not to twist an ankle, but on the positive, he'd seen no one on his way up. The man had fled the scene. Now that the stranger realized Lisa wasn't alone, Walsh hoped it stayed that way.

The guy was a coward. He attacked single women. Took them by surprise and took their life. He was sick. Not as sick as some perps Walsh had seen, but he was sick just the same. At the top, he paused, combed the area below. Light had been reduced to embers, the deep haze of night licking at his heels. Dropping hands to his knees, chest heaving, Walsh caught his breath. At least there was no sign of trouble. But now he was at a standstill. What next? Take another go-round through the woods along the ridge? Backtrack up and over?

Lisa wasn't up here. He'd seen her go over the edge. She wasn't on the mid-level terrain, either. He'd searched it. She was one of two places: hidden in the trees below him or hidden in the trees ahead of him. Intuition propelled him forward. Lisa wasn't stupid. She would call for help. She would head down.

It was his job to help her get there. First, he'd need supplies. Back at his camp he'd gather the basics for a night search. Night vision goggles, jacket. Extra bullets.

He wouldn't be caught unprepared a second time.

Edging down the steep incline, Lisa used everything and anything to keep pressure off her ankle, hands to rocks, limbs. She could hear the stream, feel the rise in humidity from the rushing water as she neared. She was close. The scent of decaying leaves and dirt filled her nostrils. She was close to victory and it felt good. Mulling over the ordeal of the past few hours, Lisa deemed she'd won. The first round, anyway. She'd made it to a safe haven and would easily be able to conceal herself until morning. She'd ice her foot in the cold water, re-hydrate her body, and set out first thing. She'd overcome great hardship, and the accomplishment gave her a deep sense of pride. It wasn't over yet, but she was halfway there.

Settling onto a rounded boulder at the stream's bank, Lisa carefully removed her boot and unwrapped her ankle. Using the red LED mode on her headlamp to illuminate her surroundings, she noted this section of stream was quite narrow and littered with rocks, which would mean she'd have to scoot down between the rocks to fill her bottle and ice her foot. But what choice did she have?

Dry and scratchy, her throat warned she was long over-due. Hand, boot, bare foot, she eased her way down to water level one step at a time, careful to keep weight off her right hand. Although not as bad as her ankle, her wrist remained painfully tender to the touch, making it difficult to negotiate between the rocks. When her foot hit the icy water, she braced against the shock reverberating through her system. Despite the fact it felt as if the chill was streaming clear up through her veins and into her chest, pumping ice-cold blood through her arteries and back out into her body, she kept her foot submerged.

This is good for my foot, she chanted silently, turning off her headlight. *This is good for my foot*. Focus on the sound, she told herself, immersing herself in the babble of water flow. Steady, persistent, mountain streams were like salve to the soul. They rushed over the mind, swept thoughts clear as they cleansed heart and soul. *Give in to the sound, release your brain's focus*. Streams were a gift of nature, one more facet of the mountains she loved. Sitting near one equated to a lovely end to a beautiful day. Until she dropped off the edge of a cliff, of course.

Afraid of what invisible bacteria might be lurking in the water, Lisa filled her bottle and drank, shoving her wet hand into the warm fleece of her jacket pocket. Dunked in the wa-ter for barely a minute her fingers felt painfully frozen. The intense cold infiltrated her bones, threatened her overall sense of warmth and well-being. Scooping water from a stream wasn't her first choice, but hydration was hydration and this was no time to be fussy. Her body would have to deal with whatever nasty bugs invaded her interior space so long as she survived.

Once finished drinking, she needed to elevate her leg. If she could stand it, she'd plunge her foot once or twice more before securing a spot for shut-eye. The more she could do to reduce the swelling, the better. Switching her light back on,

Lisa directed it downward, red light glimmering on the sinewy surface of water. Using the dimmed red light instead of bright white would reduce her risk of being seen, yet still provide visibility as she searched the ground for a place to sleep.

Glancing around, her gaze landed on a huge flat rock farther upstream. A good-sized overhang sticking away from the water, Lisa dubbed it perfect. It was on the same side of the stream as she and would provide all the cover she needed, plus a place to sit, elevate her foot and eat her granola in the meantime.

After a few minutes, she capped a full bottle of water, climbed out, grabbed her boot, her stuff, and headed over. Stretching out on the stone, her body felt as though a huge weight had been released. Joints popped and muscles lengthened as she eased back. It felt good to allow the tension to float free from her aching, stiff body. Memories of her fall itemized every injury—as if she'd forgotten. She hadn't.

Everything hurt. Everything hurt and the rest felt luxurious.

Flicking off her light, she indulged in the sensation for several long moments. Opening her pack of granola, she set it on her belly, crossed bad leg over good, and began to chow. Overhead, the gaps between branches revealed a night punctured by stars—stars of every shape, size, and constellation. They were literally everywhere!

August was a great time to watch for shooting stars and meteor showers. The Perseid meteor shower occurred mid-month. The granddaddy of meteor showers, it produced more fireballs—the really bright meteors that streaked across the sky—than any other shower. If she was out in the open, she'd be able to see them with ease, but here under the trees, she could only imagine what they looked like. Her science professor from freshman year said the brilliance was due in part to the shower's progenitor, the Comet Swift-Tuttle. Every year the Earth passed through a trail of dust left behind in the comet's wake, where in turn, the dust burned up in the Earth's atmosphere creating the brilliant shower.

Of course, it could also be due to the comet's size. The Comet Swift-Tuttle had a gigantic nucleus, about sixteen miles wide, allowing it to produce a huge number of meteoroids, many capable of producing fireballs. She smiled as she crunched. Nothing like camping to make a girl feel in tune with Mother Earth!

Swallowing, she reached for another handful of granola and froze. Over the sound of water, she thought she heard something. She stilled her breathing and strained to listen. The constant rush of water competed for her attention, drowning out her ability to hear anything beyond. Releasing the zip-tie on her breathing, she second-guessed herself. Had she heard something?

She'd have sworn she had, but maybe she hadn't.

Maybe she was hearing imaginary Boogey Man sounds. Slowly transferring granola to her mouth, she chewed soundlessly, scanning the darkness. As if she was going to see anything. Though the night was pitch black, the moon was on the rise, depositing light between the trees and rocks, it wasn't enough to see by, though it would outline her figure should someone be searching for her.

Someone with evil in their heart.

Lisa quickly rolled off the boulder and onto soft ground with a thump, wincing against the pain. *Ouch.* Biting back a cry, she wasn't about to give up her advantage by sitting out in plain view for someone who might be searching for her! Stuffing the plastic bag into her coat pocket, she pulled out the mace. Better to give it a few minutes in the off chance the sound hadn't been her imagination.

Crouched and ready to pounce, she keyed into the sounds around her. Gurgling water overwhelmed her senses. Steady and constant, suddenly her wonderful calming stream had become a hindrance. If only she wasn't right next to the water, she could hear better and know for certain whether it was a noise from nature or not!

Feeling a punch of rock and dirt beneath her foot, she remembered her boot and bandage were still sitting up on the rock. *Dammit*, that would give her away. She should grab them—

Wait, she counseled her impatience. Wait.

Seconds turned into minutes. There had been no other disturbances, nothing out of the ordinary, nothing she could pinpoint. Lifting up, she peered over the stone and caught glimpse of movement. Ducking, she felt her heart thwack her ribs.

Ohmigod—was there someone in the woods?

Pressure filled her chest, pumped through her veins. Tightening her grip on the narrow can of mace, the cold metal reassuring in the palm of her hand, she reminded herself it *could* be an animal—though if it were, it'd sniff her out in a second. If it was a person, she was completely covered. Safe. Except for her bandage up top, there was no way he could see her. Pressing into the rock, Lisa struggled to calm the batter of pulse. Maybe it was anxiety. Maybe it was nothing.

Seconds pulled at her nerves as she mentally ran through her options. She couldn't outrun anyone, but after she sprayed the mace, she could turn on her light and blind them. She could charge them, chop her hand into their throat and cause deep tissue damage. Curling her fingers into a half-fist, Lisa created a hard edge on her hand for use as a weapon. It was one of the more lethal moves she'd learned, one she'd practiced many times. She'd rehearsed it in her brain. She'd leap up, punch straight forward using the momentum of her body, and deliver a punishing strike.

Heartbeats drummed. Nerves stretched and burst. The night air seeped through her clothes, seared the bare skin of her legs. She could do this. Then she heard it. It sounded like someone walking. Close. Clenching her mace, she shifted her weight to her right foot and prepared to jump.

"Wh—"

Lisa leapt up and sprayed in the direction of the voice.

A man yelled. Lisa cried out as shock poured through her limbs. *Walsh*?

Chapter Ten

Lisa flicked on her light with a shaky hand and stared. The gravelly voice was unmistakable. Rubbing his eyes, the side of his face, Walsh glared at her, his green eyes stark in the brown of his skin. "What the hell did you do that for? And turn off the light, will you?" he snapped. "I'm not gonna be able to see a thing!"

"I thought you were the bad guy..." she murmured, extinguishing the light at once. Gazing through a temporary black hole in her vision from the abrupt change, a tidal wave of relief swamped her fear. It wasn't the bad guy—it was Walsh. Her heart sung. *Walsh*!

Swiping a hand across his left brow, he scowled. "Lucky for you, it missed."

"What?" She'd done the right thing by spraying him. He was a stranger in the dark. Why was he mad?

"I called your name—didn't you hear me?"

Struck dumb, she muttered, "I thought you said 'Where are you?'"

"I *said*, 'Lisa, are you there?'"

"Oh." Arms dangling at her sides, at this point she didn't care. All she cared was that it was Walsh. Pleasure bloomed in her chest. "How did you find me? How did you know I was here?"

"I spotted your light."

"My light?" Her spirits drooped. And she had thought to be so careful. "But where were you that you could see it? I had it turned down to red."

"I was heading back from my camp and I saw it moving," he told her, turning his own light on to a muted beam angled toward the ground.

"Your *camp*," she seized on the mention. "Is it close?"

"About a quarter mile from here." Then, as if seeing her for the first time, his expression changed. In soft wash of moonlight, concern gripped his gaze. "Are you all right? I saw you fall..."

The naked tenderness in his voice cut deep. *He'd seen her fall*. She'd been right. He would have thought the worst. Then it dawned on her. How did he happen to be there when she fell? Had he been watching her?

Taking a step backward, she winced under her breath, her knee buckling. Heartbeats pulsed anew as she replied, "Yes. I saw a man and he began to come toward me. I started to run, he started to run, and I slipped."

"I saw you. I tried to go after you, but couldn't find you." Walsh ran his gaze from head to toe, examining her as though she were a freak of nature and stated, "It's incredible you weren't hurt."

"I'm hurt," she objected. "The trees broke my fall, but I sprained an ankle, my wrist." She held out her limp hand for him to see, as though to prove it. Still bound by her pink bandana, it looked pathetic. "I'm covered in scratches, bruises."

Walsh came to her, guiding her back to sit on the expanse of rock. "How bad? Let me see," he insisted, not bothering to wait for a reply.

"Nothing's broken, but my ankle's pretty swollen," she told him, mildly jarred by the fact that he was already inspecting her foot for himself. Squatting before her, he turned on his headlamp and gently cupped a hand beneath her heel. Running a light hand over and around her ankle, he scrutinized her injury.

Despite the cold air, her skin felt warmed within his hands. "I soaked it for a few minutes and was in the process of elevating it when you showed up."

Walsh looked up at her. Beneath the dim glow of his lamp, his green eyes were crystal clear. Penetrating. Wearing a charcoal gray jacket and pants, his attire was dark, melting into the night. His eyes were the only part of him she could see.

"There's no way you're going to make it down," he declared. "I'm surprised you made it this far."

"Yes, well..." She swallowed, surprised by the tight nut in her throat. "I did what I had to do."

"You might have caused more damage by walking on it than if you had stayed where you were." Setting her foot down, he asked, "Why didn't you stay put? I would have found you."

"Stay put?" Surprise and indignation flared hot in her breast. "How about there was a bad guy after me, and I didn't want to make it any easier for him to get me than necessary? How was I supposed to know you were coming after me?"

"Didn't you hear me calling you?"

Once again, Walsh was blaming *her* sense of hearing. "Yes, I *heard* you, but there wasn't anything I could do about it." Growing irritated, Lisa added, "When you get the wind knocked out of you, it's kinda hard to speak, let alone yell."

Walsh stood. Stuffing her boot and bandage into his shoulder bag, he said, "I'm taking you to my camp. You can stay the night and I'll get you home in the morning."

Peering up at the man with the spotlight in the middle of his forehead, a flutter of relief swarmed her breast, erasing all anger and frustration. It was exactly what she was hoping he'd say. But still, the man could give her some credit.

Reaching a hand to help her up, he seemed impatient.

Placing her hand in his palm, she replied, "Okay. But you'll have to be patient with me. I can't walk very fast."

"You're not walking," he said, and scooped her up into his arms.

Lisa shrieked, clasping her arms around him. "What are you doing?"

He turned to face her head on, his headlamp nearly blinding her. "I'm carrying you, what does it look like?"

Suspended within his hold, her arms looped around his neck and shoulders, their faces inches apart, Lisa felt awkward, uncomfortable, like she was naked or something.

She didn't care for it one bit. "I *can* walk, you know."

"No. You *can't*."

Despite her protest, Walsh firmed his grip and carried her uphill and away from the stream, weaving his way through trees and around boulders as though he knew the way by heart. Lisa could feel his every step, could hear the grunt of his exertion, the escalation in his breath. She wasn't heavy, but he was moving at a pretty good clip. She dipped her head with his as he ducked branches, marched in and around the trees, the man moving as if on auto-pilot, like he could find his way with his eyes closed.

He must have an established trail. He must have trampled a single path that he used over and over again. At least she hoped so. Leaving a minimal impact on the land was crucial up here. Everywhere, she thought, but especially up here in the seldom-hiked parts of the mountain.

As he walked in silence, Lisa's attention was inescapably drawn to his profile. His brows were black against the brown of his skin, his gaze intent upon the way ahead. His cheekbone was set high on his face, giving way to a slight contour of his cheek, landing in a firm line along his jaw. His neck was solid muscle as was his body. She couldn't miss the muscular build of his arms and chest, firmly pressed against her as they were.

Even through the soft down of his jacket, she could feel every muscle work as he walked. Every muscle moved and jumped and contracted. This close, she could even smell him. No cologne, his scent was all man and fresher than she'd expect. Clean, rugged, Walsh smelled of a man who worked for a living, played hard, lived hard.

Hard. Walsh was definitely a hard man.

Lisa didn't want him to think she was staring, but it was hard not to. Actually, she couldn't keep her eyes off him. His pale green eyes and stern expression were mesmerizing. Their cheeks touched on several occasions, flushing strange sensations through her.

Odd to be this close to him, yet nice. Welcome.

After several minutes, they neared a wall of earth and he slowed. The mountain went up, a blockade without passage. She saw no campsite. No tent. In the subtle cast of light, she could see the outline of trees and logs, the boulders and dead branches, the slide of rocks, but no personal belongings.

"Are we almost there?" she asked.

"We're here," he announced, circling around a duo of trees.

That's when she spotted his tent. Hard to make out against the landscape, it was army-green and practically wedged up against the mountain. But that was it, save for a small fire ring. Alongside it was a metal bar he could place over a fire and hang items for cooking. Nearby, a good-sized log cut to about four feet in length had been situated to the side, as though placed there for the purpose of sitting. What she expected to see, exactly, Lisa wasn't entirely sure. This was his entire existence. This was where he spent every day, every night.

Walsh stopped and eased her to the ground. "You can have my tent for the night. It's probably not the most comfortable you'll inhabit, set up on a couple of rocks, but it will keep you warm. I've layered it with sleeping bags."

"No, Walsh, you don't need to do that," she replied, pulling her jacket down into place around her hips. "I can sleep outside. I've done it hundreds of times."

"You'll sleep in the tent. I'll sleep outside." He reached into his tent and produced a lantern. Walking to the nearest tree, he hung it from a barren branch and turned it on. The area flooded with light.

Once again, she felt awkward. He was bestowing a "special person" status on her that she didn't deserve. Glancing around the spray of light, she noticed housing for a portable camping stove, a rolled up tarp. Nothing but the bare basics. She peered at him. How did he sustain himself? Fish? Wildlife?

Walsh crawled into his tent and reemerged with a rolled sleeping bag. "Are you cold?"

She shook her head. Considering the fact she'd been warmed by the close contact with his body, she felt pretty good. "No. Not really."

Making a point to stare at her legs, he said, "Your legs have to be cold."

They weren't really. They were beginning to feel air, now that they were no longer tucked within his arms, but they weren't bad. A shiver raced through her. Actually, she hadn't thought about the temperature until he mentioned it.

Lisa felt a rise of heat to her cheeks. She'd been too focused on him. "I'm fine," she replied.

Walsh unzipped his sleeping bag and wrapped the satiny orange interior around her shoulders. A small smile touched his lips. "Your goosebumps say otherwise. How about I build a fire?"

"No, the lantern's fine." Besides, she didn't want to send any signals that might help the stranger locate them.

"Sure?"

"I'm sure." As though he understood her rationality, he didn't push.

"Let's get you seated," he said, guiding her to the log. As she lowered, he situated her comfortably in place, drawing a flap of sleeping bag over her bare skin. Then he pulled a phone from his bag and said, "I need to call off the dogs."

"Excuse me?"

Resting the phone against his ear, he said, "I called Wade and asked him to send up a search and rescue team."

Surprise mingled with joy. "You what?"

"I didn't know where you were, but I knew what happened. They're scouring the area east of here." Into the phone, he said, "Wade, I found Lisa." He nodded, gave her the thumbs up.

The gesture sent an unexpected thrill through her.

"Yes." He winked at Lisa. "Tell her father she's safe and sound. A little bruised but nothing that won't heal." Walsh nodded with a slight grin. "Aw, c'mon, buddy. You know better than to worry when a young woman is under my watch."

He laughed and Lisa found the sound infectious. Joy wound through her as she watched him. Walsh was easy and natural, a man content. Comfortable. Strange that he'd feel so gratified by informing Chief Davis that he'd secured her safety. It wasn't like he knew her. They'd only just met.

When he ended the call, she asked, "You called my father, too?"

"Wade did." With a sheepish grin, Walsh admitted, "I didn't have time."

Because he was going after her. Bubbles of pleasure skirted through her. "What happened to the man? Do you know where he went?"

Walsh's gaze darkened. "No."

"Oh." Lisa pulled the sleeping bag snug around her shoulders. All wasn't perfect in the world.

"Let's get that ankle wrapped," he said. Lisa leaned forward to do as she was told, but Walsh waved her back. "My job." Pulling her boot and bandage from his shoulder bag, he knelt before her. Setting her leg over his raised knee, he wrapped her ankle with the skill of a medic. Not too tight, not too loose, the soft material hugged the curves of her foot in precision layers. Cupping his fingers over her toes, he warmed them. "You're cold."

With a sharp intake of breath, she mused, *Must be no blood flow. It's all in my neck and cheeks.*

After returning her leg to the sleeping bag, Walsh went back in his tent, emerging with a heavy backpack. "You can use this to elevate your leg."

"Thank you," she replied, and watched as he gingerly lifted her leg up and place her calf over top of his pack, mindful of keeping it warm and covered.

"You really should have that leg above heart level."

"I will. Later."

"Are you sure? I can set you up in the tent where you can lie down."

Lisa suppressed a grin. "I'm sure." It was amusing to see a big, strong man act as nursemaid. Sweet to know he had a sensitive side. Too bad he lived squired away up here in solitude. The world could use more people like him.

Eyeing the pink bandana wrapped around her wrist, he said, "I have something better for that hand." Ducking back into his tent, he retrieved a roll of white tape and changed out her bandage. "Are you hungry?" he asked.

"I have some granola. I was eating it when you showed up."

"You need serious food."

Pulling a red plastic bag from his coat, the second he opened it, she knew what it was. "I don't eat beef jerky."

"It's one of the best sources of protein you can find. With all your knowledge, you have to know you need protein to stay strong."

The pungent scent of salty, smoked meat assaulted her nose. "I'm plenty strong, and there are other sources of protein. Non-animal sources of protein."

For a moment, he stared at her with the oddest expression but dropped the subject. "Suit yourself."

"Thank you."

Walsh found a spot on the ground nearby, tore off an end of knotty jerky and chewed, the action rippling across his entire face. His movements were determined, purposeful, a man on a mission in everything he did.

As she sat swathed in the warm blanket with her ankle throbbing, her wrist and bruised muscles stiffening with an allover malaise, an intense curiosity took hold of her. Who was this man? What was his story? Beyond the military, beyond his escape to high country, Lisa felt compelled to learn the truth. Should she ask? Was it her place?

Taking the granola bag from her jacket pocket, she tried to keep the cover around her shoulders as she opened the baggie. Her left hand was doing a miserable job as double-duty baggie-holder and blanket-clip, while her right hand tried to pluck the granola free.

Rising, Walsh came over to her. "Let me help you with that."

Feeling somewhat foolish, Lisa was forced to accept the fact that she couldn't multi-task under these conditions and allowed him to take her bag of food. "Thanks."

Sitting next to her on the log—a log with barely enough room for two—he began to hand-feed her granola. Clumsily accepting the first chunk of toasted oats, she said, "This is silly."

"It's not silly."

Ignoring the meaty stench of beef jerky on his fingers, she grinned despite the fact. "Yes, it is. You don't have to feed me. I'm not starving."

"Indulge me," he said, a flicker of sensuality lighting up his eyes, suddenly sultry and suede smooth.

Warmth exploded deep in her belly as he placed another bite into her mouth, his fingertips grazing her lips. Lisa held his gaze until the pressure of direct eye contact overwhelmed her and she glanced away.

Swallowing, she murmured, "Thanks for taking care of me."

"My pleasure."

Lisa tried to ignore the softening in his voice, the intimate tone he was assuming. It was slightly unnerving to be this close to him, to a man she'd thought about all day, a stranger who felt familiar. "I've never had anything like this happen to me before."

"Wish I could say the same," he said.

The sadness in his voice pulled at her. "You probably rescued a lot of damsels in distress while in the military, huh?"

"Not many damsels in distress," he replied, following with a wink that felt forced, "but I have saved the butts of a lot of soldiers and a few civilians in my time."

His time. Walsh was referring to his time in the military. Had it been hard? Had he enjoyed the service? Could anyone really *enjoy* their time in a war zone? "It must have been hard, what you did for a living..."

"Hard, gratifying, rewarding." He gave a brisk shrug. "Being a Marine is a lifestyle, not a living."

"A lifestyle? Even now that you're not in the Marines anymore?"

"Even now."

Lisa wasn't sure how to respond. She didn't know anything about the military, other than they defended the United States of America against threats, foreign and domestic. Her father never served. She had no brothers. She didn't know anyone with personal experience in the service, other than Wade Davis and some of the guys that worked with him at the police department. Had Walsh fought overseas? Had it been scary?

The minute she thought it, Lisa chastised herself. No man would admit to being scared, especially a man like Walsh. "Do you like people?"

He screwed his expression as though he took offense. "What kind of question is that?"

"Well, you live up here, alone... I thought maybe it was a bad experience with people that sent you up here."

A rigidity formed around Walsh like a force field. His mouth tightened, his gaze assumed an edge. Tension seized the air between them and she wanted it gone. "I'm sorry. I shouldn't have probed."

"You're fine." He looked away. "War is ugly business. The men I worked with were topnotch, the best of the best, but the work wasn't. It was dark and ruthless, turns a man's soul black where few recover. It's a waste of humanity."

Lisa blinked. Did she just hear what she thought she heard?

When she didn't reply, Walsh took the opportunity to plop another piece of granola into her mouth. The hard crunch against her soft tongue evoked strange emotion. Walsh was an odd mix. Tough and gritty on the outside, yet soft center. Very soft, judging by the delicate way he'd handled her foot. His skin had been callused from a life outdoors but tender in its hold. Lisa finished chewing with a rough gulp.

"Thirsty?"

"No. Yes," she said, desperate to clear the granular residue from the back of her mouth. Adele's granola was great but really needed to be consumed with water. Walsh went to grab a bottle of water, and Lisa felt a distinct void by her side at his absence. As he disappeared once again into his tent, a chill clutched hold of her side until he returned.

"Here you go." He handed the bottle over and eased down beside her. "Sorry there's no lemon to go with it."

Lisa smiled. "It's okay. I've had my daily quota." She drank hungrily and without shame, not realizing how thirsty she was until the water flowed freely down her throat. Downing the contents in practically one swallow, she laughed. "Guess I was thirsty!"

He cocked a brow. "Guess so."

Setting the bottle aside, she snuggled into the sleeping bag, picking up hints of Walsh's scent. It wasn't gross and sweaty, a man unwashed after days in the wilderness, but natural with a trace of male fragrance. Did he sleep with this bag? Did he use it as a pillow?

Lingering in question, she thought it strange to be thrown together with a man she hardly knew, and wonder things about his personal space. Lisa wasn't much for dating. She didn't have the time, not with her research consuming her every thought. It would be different if there was a guy on the research team she liked. But other than Professor Stevens, none were even attractive, let alone enticing. The team was filled with guys like Dale, whose entire life's focus centered on the boreal toad, and all had the social skills to prove it. Lisa paused on that notion for a moment. Her focus was wrapped up in the toad, too, but she enjoyed other things. She liked hiking, socializing with her father and Adele, taking part as they hosted dinner parties. Stealing a sideways glance at Walsh, she was struck by a thought. Did he think *she* had the social skills of a lab rat? A woman with a one-track mind consumed with toads?

No, she decided abruptly, shaking the absurdity from her mind. She was nothing like Dale, nor did she come across like him. She had the upbringing of two wonderfully socially-adept parents who could waltz their way around any high society gala event, and that made her different. Dale's parents were nerds, like him. Her parents had taught her to be well-rounded, sophisticated. Lisa shivered.

"Cold?" he asked.

"A little," she said. The temperature had dropped by about twenty degrees since the sun had gone down and she didn't have her jeans, one foot was bare. Wrapped, but bare.

Walsh slid an arm around her body and pulled her close. She balked at the gesture and he squeezed gently. "Don't worry." Then he rubbed his hand briskly up and down her arm. "Just doing my part to make sure you return home in good condition."

Tucked within the crux of his body, Lisa couldn't ignore a swell of disappointment amidst the jolt of desire. He wasn't trying to take advantage, though a tiny part of her almost wished he were. She'd never been with a man like him, a man who radiated strength and dominance. A man who exuded quiet power. Walsh pulled her close and she leaned in, relishing the contact as she rested her head against him. So what if he was only being a gentleman. He was warm. Solid. She bet he'd make a great hiking partner. Maybe she should invite him to join her on her next trip up. She could teach him a thing or two about toads, and he might discover he actually liked it. She chuckled.

"Something funny?"

"I was thinking you might like to come along on my next research trip and learn about toads."

"Already planning your next hike, despite your near-death experience?"

"Of course." Gazing into the yellowish lamplight cast about his campsite, she joked, "You don't think I'd let a little old deranged madman interfere with my science, do you?"

Walsh laughed softly into the top of her head. "Ya know, I don't know you that well, but what I do know makes me doubt anything less. Not many civilians I know could have done what you did today."

Nerves ripped and tore through her midsection as she wondered, *Did that mean he'd join her next time*?

Chapter Eleven

Lisa woke early, battling a slew of metal rods shooting through her body. Walsh wasn't kidding when he said he set up his tent on rocks—her back and shoulders felt every single one of them. Groaning, she rubbed the sleep from her eyes and followed the center line that ran the length of his tent roof, dark green material sloping down from either side. Minimal light permeated the interior, a slice of morning eeking through the flapped entry at her feet. She couldn't see outside, but the scent of smoke was a sure sign Walsh was up and at it. Probably made it a habit to rise with the sun. She did, when she was on the mountain.

Likely, he'd want to get her down the mountain without detour.

A trip she wanted to discuss with him. Lisa wanted to retrieve her backpack. With him by her side, there shouldn't be any trouble. No man was going to attack Walsh and if he did, Walsh would no doubt prevail. And she needed her backpack—her data. It was too important to leave behind. If Walsh refused to carry the pack down for her, she could at least gather the essentials. They'd made it this far. A brief detour wouldn't hurt anything.

Lisa wondered how he'd take the news. She'd thought about it all night. In fact, the prospect swam in and out of her dreams until she knew for certain it was the right thing to do. Sitting up, she combed fingers through her hair, drawing it from her eyes. As her right hand fell, the fresh dressing around her injured wrist reminded her how Walsh, a.k.a., Florence Nightingale extraordinaire, had produced it and wrapped it for her. Recalling his nearness, his insistence that she should see a doctor the minute they hit the town, gave her a warm, snug feeling. He used the word "they." Did that mean he would join her? Would he meet her father?

Giggling at the weirdness of showing up in the ER with a stranger, Lisa unzipped the sleeping bag from her body and checked out her ankle. Puffy toes protruded from the end of her dirty bandage and she frowned. As she unwound the tape, her foot throbbed in relief. She had a mind to leave it off for a while and enjoy the release, but there was no time. She wanted to get up, get out, and get busy.

Quickly re-wrapping her ankle, Lisa pulled on her boots and scooted out, careful not to bump her injured hand or foot.

"Good morning, Sunshine," Walsh greeted with a smile.

Light washed the haze from her eyes and took him in. Seated on the fireside log, he wore a brown, long-sleeved T-shirt and khaki-green cargo pants. His boots were laced high and tight up his ankle, like soldiers she'd seen on television. With no hair to speak of, his morning appearance was no different than his afternoon. Over a small open flame he cooked a pot of something that was steaming. Inhaling, she couldn't pick up any scent but campfire. Was he boiling water for coffee? Making soup?

Sliding out completely on her rear side, Lisa replied happily, "Good morning."

"Drink coffee?"

She wrinkled her nose. "No." She never touched the stuff. Lemon water was her start to the day.

Walsh tapped the log beside him. "Have a seat."

Limping over, she took the position offered and sat, but not too close. Things looked and felt a whole lot different in the morning. Allowing him to get close last night would not feel the same in the magnifying light of day. Her stomach growled loudly, reverberating up through her ribs.

Walsh grinned. "My breakfast menu consists of beef teriyaki or meatloaf. Have a preference?"

Not that she'd ever touch either one, but she wondered how he planned on whipping up one of those? Did he have a magic wand she didn't see?

"MRE meals," he said, as though reading her mind. "I've a pack full of them."

"I'm vegan."

"What's that?"

"I don't eat meat or anything derived from animals."

"Nothing?"

"Nothing."

Walsh grunted. "Well, I have a Chicken á la King meal. Pick the chicken out and there's a ton of vegetables left to be had."

Horrified by the prospect of consuming chicken-drenched vegetables, Lisa suppressed her displeasure and replied, "Thank you, but no. I'm fine. I can make it until lunch time." She'd be down in three hours tops—once she retrieved her backpack, that is.

Walsh frowned. "You can't go without eating. You'll need your energy to get down. It's a two-hour hike with two working legs." He dropped his gaze to hers and said, "Speaking of which, how's the ankle?"

"Good." Lisa reached down and skimmed her good hand over the gauzed area. "I re-taped it this morning and it's ready to go."

"And your wrist?"

"Tender but good."

Walsh nodded. "If you want, we can head down now. I don't need this." He reached for his pot of water and dumped it out on the ground.

"Er—actually..." She placed a hand to his forearm. "I have a favor to ask."

"What kind of favor?"

Staring into expectant green eyes, she gave way to the intensity of his gaze and blurted, "I want to get my backpack."

"What?"

"I want to get my backpack and take it down with me. All my collection data is in it, my camera—"

Walsh held up a hand. "Where is your pack?"

"At the site where I fell. I stashed it beneath a rock for safekeeping."

"We'll send someone up for it later."

"But it would be so much better to get it now."

"For who?"

Lisa paused. For her. But to voice as much would seem rude.

"I can't carry you and your pack down to town. It's one or the other."

"You don't have to carry me. I can make it down on my own. It'll just be slow-going, is all."

"You can't walk on that foot."

"I can, and—if I hadn't run into you last night—I'd be hiking down under my own power, and I'd make it just fine."

"I'm not letting you hike down alone."

Normally she would tell him exactly what he could do with his machismo, but at the moment, she needed his machismo mentality and strength to get her backpack and get it down the mountain. "Please, Walsh." She leaned into him ever so slightly. "That data is crucial to my research. We're getting ready to do a major tadpole release and it would be really helpful to know where the fungus has proliferated and where it hasn't." Ever so slightly, she squeezed her hand on his arm, her palm warmed by the contact with his cotton shirt. "My vials have that info."

Staring at her, she sensed something soften. Just behind his eyes—she could feel it. He was debating. "Listen, you don't have to carry the whole pack," she said quickly. "I'll grab my tubes and notes—my camera—and we'll go. Maybe I can call down and have Dale meet us halfway." After all, it was his fault she was in this predicament. If he hadn't ditched her the night before, she wouldn't have been alone, creating the perfect target for some lunatic.

"And if we run into trouble?"

Lisa gaped at him. "No one is going to bother us—not with you in tow."

A small smile entered his eyes. "I appreciate the vote of confidence, but...."

Vote of confidence? It was absurd to think anyone would mess with this man. She didn't care who they were dealing with—one look at Walsh would make any would-be assailant think twice.

When he dropped his gaze to her hand, she realized she was clutching hold of his arm and yanked it back. "So you'll do it?"

"I'll do it. Let's just hope I don't regret it."

On impulse, Lisa squeezed his hand. "You won't, Walsh. Promise."

Walsh held Lisa at the tree line, scanning the open area between sections of forest. Ambivalence coursed through him as visions of her fall inundated his mind. Going to her backpack was a bad idea. It was a waste of time and energy, a side trip he already regretted, except that Lisa seemed so excited. He didn't have the heart to tell her he'd changed his mind. Hovering by his side, he could feel her impatience, her readiness to go. The fact that she fit perfectly against his body as he hung his arm around her shoulders didn't help.

It was distracting.

"I don't see anything," she said and started forward.

He pulled her back. "Not yet."

Peering up at him, her hazel eyes leapt at him from beneath her pink bandana. "Why not?"

Because it didn't feel right. Something was off. Glancing in both directions, Walsh saw nothing within the caverns of forest across the way. Nothing up on the ridge. There was clearly no one in the open stretch of meadow between here and the base. There was no reason not to cross.

Other than his gut. He looked down at her booted sprained ankle. "Use the stick I gave you for weight support."

"Will do." Dutifully, she manned the wooden pole by her side, planting it forward.

Lisa was so carefree, as though she didn't understand the stakes. She wasn't stupid. Quite the contrary. She was intelligent and well-educated. She should know there was an element of serious danger in what they were doing, both to her health and safety. But from the minute she'd suggested the idea, she'd been a pit bull with a toy in its mouth. Getting the backpack would be easier than arguing with her.

Walsh gave her a nudge and the two crossed the grassy field, dodging occasional patches of boulders as he half-carried her, half-walked her over. With morning well underway, the sun peeked over the forest to his right, bathing the land in creamy tones of light. In the distance he could see floppy strands of grass poking up around a remote pond. Boulders appeared washed in white-gray as the sun reflected from their surface, and bright blue flowers stood out in clumps against the green. Colors were muted, a gradual awakening of what they would exhibit midday.

Once they reclaimed her backpack, they'd head past the pond and down. It would take them a half-hour longer than the route she'd originally planned to take, but with large sections of sloped terrain, it would be better for her foot.

Reaching the wall of trees, Walsh immediately searched for company—of any kind—deeper in the forest and behind them, the ledge above. He didn't want to run into a mountain cat or black bear any more than he wanted to run into their killer.

"Which way did you come out, do you remember?"

"Yes." She pointed. "The only way I could. I had to follow the curve of the ridge, about fifty yards that way."

Walsh gave a double-take. "Fifty yards?"

"Maybe less," she replied. Her enthusiasm dipped. "I'm not sure."

Now he really regretted the decision to go after her pack. Walking this much would take a toll on her foot—a prospect she didn't seem to mind, but one he cringed over inflicting. Messing around with a serious sprain was not smart. But staring into her face, he knew there was no way she'd turn around. Not when they'd already committed this far.

Clasping her upper arm, he grumbled between his teeth, "Let's go."

After several minutes of dodging rocks and ducking branches, Walsh was ready to hoist her onto his back, if he thought she'd let him. Hiking through the trees and around rocks and logs was doing nothing good for her foot. Conversation was minimal as he minded the terrain. The smell of densely packed pine trees hung in the air, intensified by the cool morning temperature. Lisa idly commented on the landscape, the beauty of nature, leaving him to maintain a vigilant watch for unexpected company as he waited for her to identify the location where she hid her pack.

After an hour of walking, she tugged at his shirt, exclaiming, "This is where I fell!"

Walsh looked around. Looked the same as the rest of the trees through which they'd traveled. More importantly, he saw no backpack. "Are you sure?"

"Yes." Pointing, she explained, "That's the boulder where I hid my backpack. I can see the blue from here."

Lisa hurried over and Walsh followed, one eye continuously scanning the trees, the other trailing her. Tossing her walking stick, she hobbled to the rock and pulled at her backpack.

"Hey, wait a minute." Walsh strode over. "Let me get that." She continued to tug and reaching over her, Walsh grabbed hold and hauled the pack out.

Struggling beneath him, she said breathlessly, "I got it."

Together, they dragged it clear and he stepped aside as she immediately dug into the top flap. He watched as she rummaged through the contents, pulling out a miscellany of objects. Glancing around the immediate vicinity, he asked, "Everything look okay?"

"So far, so good," she said, examining the tubes in her hand. Reaching in, she withdrew another bagged set. Turning, she beamed. "They made it without breaking."

"Glad to hear it. How about your camera?"

"I don't know." Rooting past clothing, she lifted the bulky camera free. Turning it back and forth in her hands, she pulled the lens cap off, switched it on and peered through the viewfinder. Aiming at him, she quickly adjusted the lens and pressed with an audible click. Pulling the camera from her face, she looked at the image and grinned. "Works like a charm!"

Taken aback, Walsh computed the fact that she'd just taken his picture, unsure how he felt about it. He didn't like strangers taking his photo, though he wasn't sure he counted Lisa as a stranger. Not completely. Not anymore.

Looping the camera around her neck, she stuffed one plastic bag of tubes in each jacket pocket, then reached in for her notepad. She patted her coat pockets, her shorts, then glanced at him. Her gaze darted about his person before settling on his canvas shoulder bag. "Can you carry this?"

"I guess." Walsh took the pad of paper from her and joked, "Sure you trust me with secrets this valuable?"

"Of course."

The tender quality to her reply caught him like a punch in the chest. He cleared his voice and replied, "Nothing I'd know the first thing about anyway." Flipping open his bag, he slipped the pad inside. Lisa continued to hunt through her backpack. Clearing out the mix of emotion pitching through his stomach, he asked, "Now what are you looking for? You don't have any live toads in there, do you?" he added with a playful smile.

She smacked him with a glare. "No. I just want to be sure everything is here."

Because she thought someone had gone through her things?

Doubtful, he thought, but remained mute. No need to antagonize. She was happy to have her data, and Walsh was going to leave it at that, though watching the camera hanging from her neck bang into her pack gave him pause. "Ya know...that camera of yours might prove more trouble than its worth."

Lisa jerked up to face him, the camera swinging with a thud against her chest. "What do you mean?"

"I mean, your test samples are the priority, right? Maybe we can leave the camera and come back for it later."

She hesitated and he swore she was about to object until she said, "You're right." Un-looping the bulky professional-grade camera from around her neck, she nodded. "I can leave this until later. Nobody is going to bother my stuff. Not if we shove it back under the rock and out of sight."

Walsh was surprised but pleased. After she lodged the camera deep between her clothing, she closed the top and he stowed the pack back in its hideaway.

"Okay." Straightening, he checked his watch and looked to her.

Her hair was pulled back and secured beneath her pink bandana, her eyes bright and eager, her lightly-tanned skin flushed. Although she didn't wear a drop of makeup, her complexion appeared made to perfection, her lashes thick and full, her brows defined, and her lips...well, her lips were pink and full and...perfect. She looked as though nothing unpleasant had happened and she was ready to conquer a fourteener.

Energized was the term he'd used to describe Lisa. *Energized and determined.* Two qualities she was going to need to get down. His pulse quickened. *And beautiful.* Lisa was definitely an attractive young woman. Tamping back a rush of desire, Walsh asked, "Ready?"

"Ready."

He smiled. Picking up the walking stick he'd crafted specially for her, he handed it to her. "Let's get to it."

Walsh led the way back through the trees, making a direct line east. There was no need to head back the way they'd come. At first Lisa had questioned his direction, but once he explained, she was fully on board.

Whatever you say, Walsh. Whatever you say.

If only she'd said that when he told her to go down the first time, none of this would have happened. But that was a woman for you. They didn't listen. They did what they wanted to do, when they wanted to do it, even if it landed them in trouble. At least every woman he'd ever known behaved that way. Women didn't understand logic. They didn't understand the way a man thought, the concerns he dealt with on a daily basis. Women flitted through life while men cleared their path. He swept a sideways glance at Lisa. He might not know this one very well, but the fact that she didn't listen to her own father was a clue. A giant clue. Wade had called this morning for a progress report. Seems Lisa's father had requested the call because he was worried. *Worried that she might stray off course with him?*

Stopping, Walsh held a branch for Lisa's ease of passage. Seems the man knew his daughter pretty well. According to Wade, instructions were to head straight down. *Okay, Walsh? Her father wants her coming straight down. Three hours.* Walsh countered, make it four and he'd deliver his charge. Wade agreed.

Once again, when they reached open range, Walsh paused, scanning the perimeter for visitors. Beside him, Lisa inhaled deeply, rolling her shoulders, stretching out her neck and arms. Gazing toward the distant mountain range, she sighed. "I never get tired of that view."

Scoping out the landscape, satisfied they were alone, Walsh released the tension in his chest and indulged in the alpine terrain with her. The sun was bright, accentuating colors and details. The bulk of heat was still yet to come, but the downpour of light was heavy, lighting the meadow grass a brilliant lime-green against a backdrop of darker evergreen. Embedded rocks and boulders were flinty-gray, wedged into the ground at random. Various wildflowers were scattered throughout, dual peaks stood rugged in the sky as though carved against a vivid blue canvas. Gouged from the tremendous pressure of tectonic shifts, these mountains had been literally ripped from the ground and thrust upward. Horizontal striations gave visual evidence to years of erosion, not to mention the marks of glacier movement.

Dwelling on the sheer force that created these mountains filled Walsh with a sense of awe. Unlike the dusty, dry desert mountains half a world away, these mountains were beautiful. Magnificent. The Rocky Mountains called to the wild in a man. They beckoned his thirst for adventure, dared thrill-seekers to scale their heights. The other mountains held war and strife, a wasteland of suffering and brutality. Death.

"Ever climb a fourteener, Walsh?"

Shaking the dreary memories from his mind, he glanced at Lisa. The innocence and openness in her eyes pulled at him. "No. The idea never made it to my bucket list."

"You should. It's one of the best feelings in the world."

"I take it you've done it?"

She nodded. "My dad and I climbed Pikes Peak a couple of years ago, and it was amazing. The views from the top were incredible. It felt as if I could see the whole world from one spot."

"Probably close," he remarked, not in the least surprised that she'd made it to the top. From what he'd seen, Lisa was certainly competent when it came to mountain terrain.

Removing her jacket, Lisa carefully tied it around her waist. Now that they were in the sun, Walsh was feeling the temperature rise himself, and wished he'd worn a short-sleeved T-shirt, but there would be no detours for a wardrobe change. They were going straight down, as he promised. "My shortcut begins on the other side of your pond." He pointed in the direction she'd traveled yesterday. "About a half mile more and we can cut through the trees—"

"Near the river." She nodded. "I know the way. It brings you down on the east side of town."

"So you know that the travel gradient is less steep that way."

"Yes, but it adds almost an hour to the trip. I usually take the other way because it's a more direct approach. My car is parked west of town."

"Under the circumstances, I think your foot would prefer the gentler terrain, don't you?"

She grinned. "If you insist. But as soon as we get down, I need to get these tubes to the lab."

Did the girl have the slightest concern for the well-being of her foot at all? How about a stop at the Emergency Room for an x-ray? According to Wade, that was her father's planned destination for his daughter, only no one told her. Walsh shook his head. Lisa was like dealing with a kid whose only concern was getting down to her playground the quickest way possible. Only *her* playground was a science lab. With a hand to her arm, he nudged her forward.

Let's go, Einstein.

Chapter Twelve

Hal Richardson set his chamomile tea aside and stared at the dark black hands of the cuckoo clock tacked to the wall by the mantle. Ten o'clock. Wade said his friend estimated Lisa's arrival down to be noon. Noon or one o'clock—because her ankle had been injured in a fall. Stress pushed in his stomach. Wade hadn't given much detail, claimed he didn't have much, but said she'd been injured in a fall and was on her way down this morning.

Thank God she was able to make it down of her own accord.

Hal didn't like the idea of her being up on that mountain alone, especially when there was a madman on the loose. She should have come down the night before with Dale. It would have been the sensible thing to do. Return to the mountain with a group from school and gather the data she needed then. But of course Lisa's toads got in the way of sensible thinking. When she was on the hunt, all else was blocked from her mind. He'd seen it firsthand when he accompanied her on one of her trips. Make that fact-finding mission. She mapped out where they were going to go, what they were going to do, and precisely how they were going to do it. Then, like the scientist she was, they had to document it all. Hal remembered being amused by his daughter's robotic nature, but he kept up with her, assisting the catch, swab, and recording of data. She barely spoke during the process, like he wasn't even there, but he didn't complain. Tracking the toads was her business, her deal. He was simply along for the ride.

Hal liked that his daughter was passionate about her work. It was important to love what you did for a living. But those toads of hers were causing a problem. She'd fallen and injured her ankle, and Hal had a sneaky suspicion that Wade knew more than he was telling. But that was Wade. He was a police officer first, friend second. He seemed confident Lisa would make it down, now that she was being escorted by this friend of his, McIntyre Walsh. Hal didn't know the man, but he trusted Wade's judgment. If Wade said the man was solid, the man was solid. If he could help his daughter get down safely, Hal was behind him.

Resting a hand on the nylon brace on his knee, Hal glanced out the plate glass windows of his living room. Floor to ceiling, he could see the entire south face of the mountain from the comfort of his leather recliner. Gazing out over the sweep of aspen and evergreen, he pressed his lips closed. Lisa was up there somewhere. If it wasn't for his recent knee surgery, he'd be up there too, escorting his daughter down to safety. Instead, he had to wait for others to do the job for him. It was a fact that didn't sit well with him.

Almost sixty years old, Hal remained a part of the summer search and rescue team. Wintertime kept him busy in the operating room. Between the Weekend Warriors up from the city and the slew of yearly tourists here for the snow skiing, his days were spent repairing broken bones and twisted knees. December through March was great for his medical practice, but in the summer, the need for his services slacked off, allowing him time for other pursuits.

Like rescuing ill-prepared hikers, he thought soberly, hating to link Lisa to that category. His daughter was no neophyte when it came to traversing the mountain. She had not only mastered the skills required for climbing—sheer rock faces included—but she had all the survivor skills down pat. Hal never worried when Lisa was on the mountain, though he stipulated she not go up alone. Prepared or not, there was always the possibility for an unexpected hazard.

A tremor zipped through Hal. Like a murderer on the hunt for young women.

His Bernese picked up his head, stared at him, then rose from his spot near the kitchen and plodded over. Without command, the dog rubbed up against his master. Hal stroked the silky black hair at his ears and murmured, "Good boy, Rocco. I know she'll be home soon." Satiny fur filled Hal's palm, soothing his nerves. Hal's breathing calmed. His mind settled. "She'll be home before you know it, don't you worry."

Lisa and Walsh stopped for a break, choosing a flat, rounded stone to sit on. Easing down, she tried not to think about the pain in her ankle. Within the confines of her boot, it was swelling, big time. They'd been hiking for over an hour, making pretty good time, and she didn't want to tell Walsh for fear he'd make her stop completely. Now that she had her test tubes in hand, all she could think about was getting them down to the lab and Professor Stevens.

"How's the ankle?" Walsh asked.

"Fine," she lied. "But a short break wouldn't hurt."

Pulling a bottle of water from his bag, he handed it to her. "Thirsty?"

"Yes," she said, more hungrily than she expected.

The rise in his brow suggested he heard the greed in her voice. "You okay?"

"Yes." Uncapping the bottle, she chugged, relishing the warm water as it flowed down her throat. Dry and scratchy didn't begin to describe how her vocal chords felt. Ripped and torn and tight as a funnel were more apt descriptions.

Lisa drank until the bands in her neck began to release, wiping the spillage from the corner of her mouth. Walsh stood over her, staring. "Do you have more?"

"Do you need more?"

"Don't you need water?"

"I'm good." He tapped the tan-green bag slung over his shoulder. "I have another bottle if you need it. No lemon," He winked, followed by a brief smile. "But the H2O will do you good."

Lulled by his tease, she smiled back at him. "I'll wait."

"You sure?"

"Yes." She felt guilty that he was giving his provisions to her and using none for himself. It wasn't right. She was thirsty, but she wasn't going to die without water. Besides, the river wasn't far from here. She could always take a drink then.

Unexpectedly, Walsh sat down beside her and reached for her calf. "Do you mind?" he asked, proceeding to set it on his thigh. "I'd rather see your ankle elevated as much as possible."

A flurry of nerves skittered through her midsection. "Sure, no problem," she replied, her gaze glued to his hands.

Gingerly, he removed her boot and inspected her foot. The touch of his fingers over the bandage at her ankle sent pulses through her flesh. He touched the underside of her toes and a shiver raced through her.

"You need to get off this ankle."

"I will. As soon as I get down."

Walsh moved his gaze between her face and her foot. "You're aggravating the injury."

Tamping down a flare of irritation, she said, "The walking stick is taking most of the weight."

His green eyes flashed. "Hardly. You can do serious damage if you're not careful. You should know that."

"I understand the ramifications. My father is an orthopedic surgeon. He'll take care of it once I make it down." Walsh grunted in displeasure. "What?" She had to get down the mountain in order to receive proper care for the injury, didn't she? "You have a better idea?"

"Heli-vac."

"What?"

"My friend Roan pilots the helicopter used for search and rescue. We could call him to evacuate you by air."

"I am *not* leaving this mountain by helicopter. That's ludicrous." Walsh held her gaze with his own brand of resistance. "It's silly, Walsh. Those are valuable resources. We don't need to waste them on me."

"Rescuing injured hikers is exactly the type of operation they run." Cupping his hand around her heel, he drew a light finger over the ugly bruises farther up her leg. "I think you fit the bill."

Lisa couldn't think about bills and operations. The delicate skim of his fingers on her bare skin fired electricity clear up her leg. Earlier she had removed her socks to accommodate her bandaged foot and now he was touching her, cradling her foot in the palm of his hands. It felt intimate, personal. "No," she blurted. "I don't need them to fly a helicopter up here to get me. I'm fine. A few more minutes and we can go." The warmth of his hand was beginning to melt into her skin. "Really."

"If you say so."

"I do."

Walsh let go of her foot and breathed in deeply. As she watched him, it seemed like his thoughts and emotion made a distinct retreat from view. It almost felt as though he considered himself responsible in some way, as though it was his duty and obligation to get her down in one piece—one healthy piece—and he was failing. But it wasn't his job. He was simply an aid, an assist to her goal of getting down and getting the help she needed. Her father would be waiting. He would see to her injuries and take care of them.

Lisa placed a hand to his arm. "Listen, you've been great." The statement drew his attention to her. "I want you to know that I appreciate everything you've done, continue to do, but I'll be in—"

Green eyes turned hot and fluid as though bracing for what she was about to say next. Lisa suddenly realized it was with good reason he stared at her so. He must have sensed her next words. *But I'll be in good hands once I'm down.*

As though she weren't in good hands at the moment. In very good hands.

Lisa felt a warm flush at her neck and cheeks and finished quietly, "I couldn't have done it without you."

The assertion felt weak. They both knew the sentiment had changed. They both knew what she had meant to say. The shift in mood was palpable. Lisa was busy planning the rest of her day—the part that didn't include him—while he was here making it happen.

Avoiding the heat of his gaze, Lisa glanced away. It was true. Once she made it down, her father would take over her care, and she'd get back to the lab and her life would go on. Without him.

It was then the full brunt of realization hit her. She didn't know this man. She hadn't known him before and wouldn't know him after. Once he saw her safely to the bottom, Walsh would return to his high-country home and she to the elegant appointments of her father's residence. It didn't seem fair. Feeling Walsh's gaze on her, Lisa looked at him, torn by the unspoken emotion swimming in those green eyes of his. Unfortunately, fair didn't have anything to do with it. It was Walsh's choice to live here, not hers. He chose to seal himself away from the world, away from people and everyday life. Feeling the newly formed lump in her throat, Lisa was antsy to go. Although her foot still rested atop his thigh, he no longer touched it, but instead, sat patiently waiting for her to recover. Quiet.

Well, recover she had, from both his touch and the reprieve from walking. She could not get wrapped up in some mountain recluse, not when she had a job to do. It wasn't wise. It wasn't smart. And Lisa prided herself on making intelligent choices. "I'm ready to go," she announced.

"We have time, if you need it."

"Nope," she replied, and pulled her leg from him. "I'm good. It's time."

Walsh stood by as she replaced her boot, carefully sliding it over her swollen foot. Mindful of the pain and tenderness, Lisa made a mental note to put more weight on her stick and less on her foot. Walsh was right about aggravating the injury. The less damage done now, the better her prospects in the future.

There was only one fairly steep descent between here and easier terrain, a single-file path that went above the river, eventually depositing them to a heavily-wooded section below. From there they could stop and grab some cool river water and then weave their way down, maintaining a fairly even keel over large areas covered by grass.

Scooting off the rock, Lisa stood. Walsh handed her the crooked but functional walking stick, and she exhaled a heavy breath, releasing a stream of tension she hadn't realized she'd been clenching in her chest. *Relax*, she told herself. *The trip will be over in no time and you'll be back in the lab where you belong.* Together, she and Walsh set off.

Scrubby weeds dotted their path interspersed with stepping stones and jutting rocks. The uneven ground was hard on her pace, but Lisa managed as well as she could. Her legs were in great physical condition, allowing her to handle the rugged terrain with the aid of her stick. Grateful it was her right hand injured and left foot, it made the rhythm easy to maintain—left hand and left foot worked the stick-and-limp while her right hand was free to rest. Walsh was right to take this route. She couldn't climb and hold a walking stick, a stick that was making all the difference as she "stepped-poked-swung" her way down the mountain.

"Oh!" Lisa cried out as she bumped into the back of Walsh. Like a solid wall, he stood entrenched in her path. "What happened? Why did—"

His hand flew up nearly smacking her in the face, gesturing silence.

Alarm bells went off in her head. Had he seen something?

Lifting to her tip-toes—her good ones—she peered over his shoulder in search of the problem. Was it a bear?

Shock mingled with confusion as Walsh drew a pistol from his rear waistband, a weapon she had no idea he'd been carrying. He wasn't going to shoot an animal, was he? He couldn't! She wouldn't stand for it!

Before Lisa could object, Walsh turned and willed her to be quiet. Staring into his hard, cold green eyes sent a chill down her spine. Something bad was happening.

Clutching his back, she hugged her body close to him as he inched forward. Like a shadow, she trailed him along the narrow path, one eye on the way ahead, one eye on the black barrel of his gun. Lisa wasn't a gun person. She didn't like them, didn't like the violence they wreaked. She was totally against them. To think she might see Walsh shoot something or someone completely unraveled her. She wanted no part in a shooting, but she wasn't a fool, either.

She wasn't going anywhere Walsh wasn't.

Seconds passed like the ticks of a time bomb, tracking their every step. Walsh's muscles felt like steel plates beneath her fingers, his movements precise and measured. Lisa's breathing shallowed, her chest tight with fear. Peeking from behind him, she couldn't see past the scraggly trees ahead, their branches rust-brown in death, but something had to have caused this precaution. But what?

A clearing opened and Walsh stopped. He looked up, down, swept his gaze over the ridge to their right. She followed the line of his gaze and saw nothing. Had he been mistaken? Had he seen anything at all? "What is it?" she whispered, unable to remain silent a moment longer.

"We have company."

She could barely hear him. Did he say company? What kind of company?

Walsh continued his advance, his gun leading the way. Out in the open, Lisa felt vulnerable, exposed, but oddly safe behind this wall of man. The first sounds of river roar permeated her skull. Yes. The river was below them. She couldn't see it from here, but she could hear it now and knew that if she peered over the edge of earth, she'd be treated to a gorgeous view of the mountain stream cutting between red mountain rock below. This section was flaming red due to the mineral hematite in the rocks, an iron oxide similar to rust.

Walsh remained ramrod straight. She was glad Walsh worked from an abundance of caution but she didn't understand. "Whatever you saw is gone," she told him.

Releasing her grip on him, she breathed deep and full.

"Lisa."

"What?" she asked, startled by the deadpan tone of Walsh's voice.

That's when she saw him. Following the line of Walsh's arm and gun, she saw the man from yesterday. Standing on a ledge above them, partially concealed behind a tree, he was staring. At them.

Panic lodged in her throat. Walsh's gun was raised. Was he going to shoot him?

Walsh didn't say a word. He simply stood his ground.

A pack of nerves swarmed her breast. Was he waiting for the other guy to shoot first? Then it dawned on her. The other man didn't have a gun. Walsh said he used a knife to kill that girl. "Walsh," she hissed. "You can't shoot him. He's unarmed."

Ignoring her, his gun remained leveled at the man above.

Lisa seized hold of his shirt. "Walsh, don't! Don't shoot!"

The man above had nothing in his hands, nothing pointed at them—didn't Walsh see that? The man was above them. They could pass below. He wouldn't attack them. Clearly he saw Walsh had a gun, understood he was willing to use it.

When Walsh began to move—backwards—Lisa stumbled. *They were leaving*?

Lisa struggled to glean what was happening as Walsh slowly pushed her back, toward the cliff. Eyeing the edge, she cried, "Walsh!" If he didn't stop, they'd go over the edge. Clutching hold of him, she pressed against him to stop. "Walsh, hold up!"

He stilled and Lisa breathed easier. Gun trained on the stranger, Walsh slid his free arm around her waist and pulled her close. "There's a bear," he whispered.

"A what?" Darting her gaze about, it quickly locked onto the ambling mass of black fur heading toward them. The breath escaped her. There was a bear! *Ohmigod*—could it get any worse?

"We need to get out of here."

The feather quiet of his voice understated the obvious as he stared into her eyes. Lisa latched onto him and uttered, "Where are we going to go?"

"Do you trust me?"

"Trust you?"

"Do you trust me," he repeated a hair more forcefully, his gaze darting back and forth across hers.

"Yes, but..." Lisa stammered over words and thoughts, her mind a jumble of confusion. She whipped a glance over his shoulder, acutely aware the bear had noticed them, acutely aware the stranger was still watching them. Perilously close was a disappearing edge, a sixty-plus fall to rocks and rushing water below. "Yes, yes," she cried, panic scraping at her heart. She trusted him. But what were they going to do?

Dropping his gaze to her body, her wrist, her ankle, and then the river, he returned to her face. Green eyes quietly but firmly drew her in as he secured his hand gently around her elbow. "You sure?"

Everything clicked. Lisa understood. She knew exactly what he meant. Sucking in deep breaths, she replied more calmly, "Yes, yes." She nodded vigorously. "I can do this."

A slip of pleasure moved into his gaze. "Let's do it. One, two, three—"

Walsh turned, yanked her body, and thrust them both over the edge of the cliff.

Chapter Thirteen

Walsh aimed for the deepest section of river as he thrust them over the edge. Lisa's screams were silenced upon impact. Ice-cold water swallowed them whole. Plunging deep, Walsh lost his grip on Lisa's arm. He reached wildly for her, but the powerful current swirled her away. With a hard scissor kick, Walsh erupted through the surface. "Lisa!"

Yards ahead of him, he thought he saw her brown head pop up then go under. "Lisa!" he yelled. The frigid cold shocked his skin, permeated his clothing, his flesh. Rivulets of water streamed down his face. Riding a swell of water, he launched into a series of strokes.

Where was she?

Scouring the water's surface, he saw nothing. Water swept him toward a cluster of large rocks, and he kicked hard to avoid a direct hit. Treading water as the current carried him downstream, Walsh didn't see Lisa. Icy water stiffened his muscles, slowed his reaction. He whipped his glance back, forward. Had he missed her? Had she surfaced? Was she behind him?

They had to get out of the water. It was too cold to spend more than a few minutes in its icy grip. Hypothermia would set in quickly. Buoyed and sucked in by the churn of current, Walsh fought to keep his head above water. For a moment, he could have sworn he saw her, but now she was nowhere to be seen. "Lisa!"

Damn it, he should have stayed up top! Shot the man— the bear, if need be—and ensured Lisa's safety. Instead, he'd come up with the brilliant plan to jump to their escape. Because he thought she could handle it.

A narrowing river channel came at him fast and furious, boulders pressing in from both sides. Walsh recalled there was a sharp drop-off ahead before the river gradually wound to more shallow depths. *Had she gone over?* His knee thwacked against a submerged rock. Biting back the pain, he made an instant decision. *Get out. Get on the shore, increase visibility.*

Searching for the nearest "out," Walsh pulled arms and legs in and rode the current down. Thrusting his hips upward, he minimized the impact of rocks hitting his backside. As the river widened, he twisted his body and pummeled hands and legs in a hard swim for shore. Head above water as he powered forward, Walsh combed the edge for the safest exit spot.

The riverbank was layered with rocks and sticks, crowded with trees offering no decent spot to depart, forcing him to settle for the quickest way out. Heading for a wedge of opening between two massive rocks, he grabbed a protruding mass of branches and hand-over-hand, hauled himself out. Water rushed over his feet as he dragged himself up and onto one of the rocks. Chest heaving, he swiped the water from his eyes and scanned the river for signs of Lisa.

Nothing.

Clothes coated his body with icy wet. The sun beat hot on his head. Walsh couldn't understand it. They jumped in together. She should have been right beside him. Standing, he cupped a hand to his brow and searched downstream. No bobbing head, no shriek for help. The river flowed at a pretty formidable rate through here, water levels high due to a monstrous year of snow. It was possible she could already be much farther down.

Shaking a chill from his body, Walsh ripped open the flap of his bag, dove a hand inside and hit Lisa's soggy notepad. He cringed. Her notes were soaked. Ruined. Brushing the disappointment aside, he located his binoculars and brought them to his eyes. Military grade, they survived the elements where paper would not. Sweeping his gaze over the water from shore-to-shore in triangular form, he began with the farthest point downstream, retracing the river to his current position and back. Nothing came into focus. There was no sign of her. Pressure built in his chest as he swept his gaze upstream.

Nothing. *Not a damn thing.*

She could have caught her foot. With numerous underwater entrapments, she could have been sucked under and gotten stuck beneath a rock. With a sprained ankle, she would have been powerless to resist the force of water. Images of Lisa drowning in the angry depths clawed at him. Walsh swung his binoculars downstream. No. Lisa was light. She would have popped up quicker than him, traveled easily over the rock-bottom river. She knew this terrain. She had experience. The river level remained deep for another mile or so before dumping into a mine field of rocks and boulders. There was a chance Lisa could get out beforehand.

If she had the strength. Walsh shoved the binoculars back into his bag, ripped the shirt from his body and tied it around his waist. He needed to get moving. If she survived, Lisa would need his help.

A reality thought he didn't need at the moment, he ejected it from his mind. Lisa was okay and he would find her. It was possible she never made it downstream. Maybe she sought a way out early. Leaping from rock-to-rock, Walsh climbed back up and scanned the walled cliff of red stone where they jumped, scouring the depths below. Sticking to his established triangle method of surveillance, he sought any sign of her. Pre-established patterns kept the brain from getting caught up on things it thought it wanted to focus on, leaving gaps in surveillance. Patterns equated to objectivity. Thoroughness.

But there was nothing.

Anger surged. Walsh would not lose her. He refused to lose her. Traversing the rocks until boots hit the ground, he took off running. "Lisa!"

Phone in hand, Hal paced his kitchen, doubt roiling his gut. "I don't like it, Wade. She's late. She should have been here by now. Your guy said noon, the latest one o'clock. It's one o'clock."

"I hear you, Hal. I tried to call him but he doesn't answer."

Both men understood cell service could be spotty. "Can you run a search on her number?" Hal asked. "Locate her using the cell towers?"

"I've got a guy working it right now."

"Good." Hal rustled the hair on Rocco's head. The dog hadn't left his side for the last hour. Rocco was his constant companion and could read Hal to the bone. The animal was smart. He knew his master was worried and he remained close, for comfort's sake. "Let me know as soon as you hear anything."

"Will do." Wade paused and Hal detected concern in the veteran's voice as he added, "She's gonna be okay, Hal. Hold on to that thought."

"I will."

Hal replaced the slim phone in its cradle and slumped onto a stool. Leaning on his elbows on the black granite counter, he focused on the iridescent flecks of blue scattered throughout the stone. Catching the light, they reminded him of the quartz he and Lisa used to find in abundance while hiking the mountain. When she was younger, she liked to collect them, amassing quite a collection of glittery rocks on her bookshelf.

As she grew older, her interests turned toward saving and preserving the wildlife. Entire summers were spent on the mountain where Hal barely heard from her.

"She's gonna be okay, Rocco," he murmured to his dog. "She's tough. She knows how to handle adverse circumstances. She's gonna be okay."

Rocco nudged his nose against Hal's thigh as though reassuring him it was true.

Dropping his head back, Hal closed his eyes. He stroked the fine hair of Rocco's head and cheeks and tried to convince himself of the same. Thoughts of Leanne gurgled to the surface.

Lisa's mother had been the cause of his daughter's first adverse circumstance in life. She passed away of ovarian cancer when Lisa was only twelve, and it had been the hardest year of their lives. Leanne had been his rock, his soul mate. High school sweethearts, there had been no other woman for him but Leanne. When she revealed her diagnosis, Hal remembered feeling as if she'd cut the heart from his chest. Throughout the ordeal, his wife had kept her spirits bright, but Hal could see the pain in her eyes. The treatment to save her life was slowly killing her, bit-by-bit, until one day she decided she was finished. Leanne said her goodbyes, held Lisa in her arms, and went to sleep. It was the last vision Hal had of her—mother and daughter, nestled in loving embrace.

He and Lisa cremated her, scattering her ashes over the mountain as Leanne requested. She wanted to be at one with nature. *His granola*, he used to call her. She'd always been happiest outdoors, drinking in the world, savoring the landscape. Like Lisa. Hal opened his eyes. They were two of a kind.

Allowing his gaze to drift through the living room windows, the mountain range, Hal marveled at the day. Not a cloud in the sky, clumps of evergreen covered the ridges interspersed with sections of aspen. Even when at home, Lisa preferred to sit out on the deck. Said she felt cramped indoors, as if one could be cramped in a five-thousand-square-foot home with floor to ceiling windows. Half the house consisted of windows, yet his daughter wanted to sit outside where she could breathe in the fresh air. Claimed if she could make a perfume out of pine trees, she would. Hal teased her that if successful, she'd end up smelling like a bottle of cleaning fluid. Lisa shrugged it off. She was an independent one. Always had been.

Brushing thoughts of the past aside, Hal focused on the present. Lisa was fine. She was a survivor. Headstrong and willful, he was banking on that streak of independence to see her home.

Rocco whimpered into Hal's hand, a cold nose prodding him to continue stroking his fur. Obliging, Hal found comfort in the gesture. Dog was man's best friend. It was certainly true in his case.

Walsh reached the shallows of the river and his heart sank. There was no sign of Lisa. Not on the shore, not in the water. Not in the surrounding trees. It was as if she'd disappeared into thin air. Panic hammered at him, but he refused to give in. Calm was the name of the game. He had to stay calm. She wasn't here, she wasn't here—those were the facts on the ground.

He glanced back upstream. He'd have to retrace his steps, recheck every inch of the river until he found some clue to her whereabouts. If she hadn't made it out, he would find her. If she'd somehow managed to escape, he would find her. His gaze was drawn to the border of trees, the boulders. The drum of river flow filled him. He would leave no stone unturned until he found Lisa, scooped her into his arms and held her close.

Turning on his heel, Walsh jogged upriver. He'd call Wade, but there was no reception. His cell phone had made it through the icy plunge only to come up empty on reception. Walsh glanced up into the sky. Not a cloud in sight, it was perfect flying weather. He'd contact Wade when he made it back to his camp. He would call him and get a search and rescue team up the mountain, stat. He'd get Roan in the air. Walsh would direct the search, and if they encountered the killer, he wouldn't hesitate.

He would do what he should have done the first time.

Returning to the spot where they jumped in, Walsh climbed over the rocks and peered into the center depths. The loud rush of water coursed through him, powerful currents churning the river around him. Dangerous vortexes formed behind boulders, vortexes that could suck a body under. He felt the rise of cool water mist on his face and bare chest. Glancing up, he searched reflexively for sight of the killer. High atop the wall of red-rock, Walsh scanned the area. Seeing no one overhead, he returned focus to the water, bracing himself for what he might find. If Lisa hadn't made it, he would have to accept the fact. Walsh ground his jaw. But he would also bring her home. Marines didn't leave anyone behind.

Leaning forward, he set hands to the grainy stone surface and examined every inch of water, searching for the pale yellow shirt. Several large logs had been trapped by the current amassing soggy weeds and sticks, but no Lisa. Continuing his search, he shoved the reality from the forefront of his mind. A female body would prove no match for this current.

Especially one the size of Lisa.

Unwilling to give up, Walsh moved boulder-to-boulder, scanning the water from every feasible vantage point. He worked methodically, carefully. He didn't take anything for granted. Following a line of boulders leading downstream, his heart leapt into his throat. There!

It was Lisa's royal blue jacket. Springing over the rocks until he gained better perspective, Walsh realized at once it was her jacket—and only her jacket. Relief flooded through him. It had become hooked on a rock, its sleeves swaying randomly with the current.

Exhaling heavily, Walsh's gut pitched. Her test tubes were in that jacket. Her notes were soaked, her samples destroyed. Everything important she had gathered from her backpack was lost. Lisa would be devastated. But she wasn't in it, a fact he considered positive. No drowned body left room for possibility. *Hope.*

Chapter Fourteen

Lisa hurried through the forest, heart thundering, branches smacking her face, her arms, as she made her escape. Walsh's idea had been smart. He'd been right to jump. She didn't hesitate. She'd held vertical, clenched her backside and landed feet first. After impact, she surfaced, tucked arms in, held her legs straight ahead and rode the current downstream as she'd been taught. Butt up, feet forward, Lisa let the river carry her safely over the hazards. She'd hit a few rocks on the way, but for the most part, she sailed through without issue until a shallow section of river stopped her cold.

Cold. Her entire body felt frozen stiff. Her ankle felt better—because it had lost feeling and was numb. It was only adrenaline that saw her out of that river and into the cover of forest, but the chill was catching up with her. She knew the risks. She had to get warm. Hypothermia was a killer.

Her body shook, her lips quivered, and the shade of trees overheard did nothing to help her cause. But clearing the scene of danger had been her first priority. Yes, Walsh's plan had been a good one, but something went wrong. Horribly wrong. After she hit bottom, she crawled out over a riverbed of pebbly softball-sized rocks and watched for him. Crouched within the cover of trees, she waited. He should have come cruising down the river right behind her, but he didn't.

Shivering, soaked to the bone, she'd waited. Walsh would come, she'd told herself. He had to come. But after five minutes, she abandoned the effort. If he was okay, he'd find her. He'd dump out in the same location and he'd track her down. He'd know she would high-tail it out through the shelter of forest—the only place she could have gone—and he would do the same. Lisa purposefully kept her track as straight as possible. No turns, no detours, she would make it as easy as possible for him to find her.

Pulse pounding, she tripped over a nip of stump. Dropping forward, she caught herself on her knees and flinched as her wrist gave way. She gasped. Streaks of pain shot up her arm.

Struggling to recover her breath, Lisa rolled to a sitting position, breathing in and out, deep and full. Calm down, she told herself.

Relax. Conserve energy. Think.

Glancing from dirt and rocks to trees and trunks, she inhaled deeply, controlling her exhale against the pound of pulse. Her legs were cramping. Her knees and back were bruised, her ankle throbbed. Her wrist fell limp, the bandage locking in a brutal cold. Although she hurt, she wouldn't feel the worst of it until later. Much later, when she stopped—stopped completely.

At the moment, she was fueled by fear.

Looking behind her, Lisa searched for signs of Walsh. Tree limbs hung suspended and quiet, trunks stood solid and mute. Browns and greens filled her vision. Silence filled her brain. Like an apparition, she imagined Walsh running toward her, joy coursing through his green-eyed gaze. He'd run to her, wrap his arms around her, and together they would escape to safety.

The image evaporated. Her heart fell. There was no Walsh. There was only Lisa.

She hugged arms to her body, her cold, wet clothing sucking mercilessly to her skin. A hard shiver began to take hold, her body visibly shaking beneath its grip. Warm. She had to get warm. *Sun.* She needed to get out into the sunshine, get dry. Easing up from the ground, Lisa took off in a stagger. Reality was taking its toll. Unable to hurry, she felt weak. Faint.

Lisa knew from experience that adrenaline withdrawal was like dropping a junkie onto hard pavement from a second-floor window. It stopped you dead in your tracks. It was abrupt. The strength and stamina from moments before gone, drained free in seconds. But Lisa couldn't stop. She might not be able to limp-run like she had no injuries, but she couldn't stop. Not yet.

On impulse, she pulled the phone from her pocket. Lisa frowned at the cracked screen. It had been an unlikely prospect to expect her phone to work, but she was disappointed just the same. She remembered the rock most likely responsible for the damage. She'd hit hard as she passed. So much for an all-weather protection case. Certainly didn't prove to be Lisa Richardson protection-proof. At least her watch survived.

Slipping the phone back into her pocket, she tensed as a strong shudder rattled her shoulders, her teeth. From where she crawled out, the river would follow a gradual slope down and past town, leaving her best route a direct shot in the opposite direction. Gauging her whereabouts, she estimated time. If she could travel straight down, she could make it in ninety minutes. The growing tenderness in her ankle reminded her that "straight down" wasn't an option. Checking the ground for a stick that could assist her walking, she spotted nothing suitable. Without Walsh, without a walking stick, she'd have to hobble her way down. She'd be lucky to make it in four hours.

Whatever. She'd make it when she made it, but before she went anywhere, she had to break this chill. Expelling a sigh, Lisa focused on the positive and headed down. It was one o'clock—the time they had estimated she'd be home. Her best hope at this point would be to make it down before dark.

Walsh arrived at his camp, his heart and lungs painfully constricted. After he grabbed her jacket, he'd run as much of the way as he could, scaling sheer rock face in some sections to cut time. Active duty in the military kept a man in supreme shape. Living on a mountain with nothing to do but pass the time fishing and thinking did not. At the moment, his heart was pounding so hard he feared he might have a heart attack, but he couldn't stop.

Lisa remained in serious danger.

Tossing her fleece into his tent, Walsh stripped the wet clothes from his body and tossed them in behind it. He changed his boots, changed his clothes, grabbed the necessities—water, food, ammunition—and packed them in a small backpack. His gun survived the icy plunge, but his bullets might not have. He had to reload. He had to contact Wade and let him know what was going on. Snagging his phone, he dialed but the call dropped. No signal. He began typing: *EMERGENCY. Trouble on way down. Lost contact with Lisa. Potential injury/hypothermia. Send team for evac. Last known coordinates are as follows.*

Walsh input the location as near as he could guesstimate and sent the text. Without actually mapping the location using his phone, he had no way of pinpointing the cliff above the river where they'd jumped. But pressed between a bear and a killer, there hadn't been time. Visions of an angry black bear mauling the killer brought Walsh pleasure. Hopefully nature took care of things for him on that count. As far as Lisa went, he would need help. Slipping the phone into his front pocket, he hoped the message went through.

Wade would take action. Once he received the message, he'd figure it out, cover all the bases. Roan Phillips was a helicopter pilot and the best in the business. Walsh had flown with him on a search and rescue earlier in the summer and walked away impressed. The guy had no military experience, yet he flew like a fighter pilot, the bird an extension of his mind. Walsh knew Roan would fly over the whole damned range to search for Lisa, zipping in and out of canyons until nightfall, if that's what it took. He was a professional. He'd get the job done.

In the meantime, Walsh had to run his own search and rescue. Lisa was in no condition to walk. If she made it down that river, she'd be cold and wet with nothing to change into. Glancing around as the thought struck, Walsh grabbed a sleeping bag and stuffed it into his pack. Slinging the over-stuffed nylon sack onto his back he took one last look around. Food, water, weapon, communication, warmth—he was set. It was time to find Lisa.

Lisa had never been so happy to see the sun in her life. Emerging from the forest of aspen, a sea of papery white barks speckled with black knots and canopy of fluttering leaves, she squinted against the bright sunlight. Before her lay an expansive meadow littered with yellow and blue blossoms. Across the plush sweep of grass, pine trees stood in the distance in all sizes and shapes, fixed in clusters that looked like families—parents, kids, tiny sprouts. She lingered, the urge to take a picture struck deep, an acute reminder she didn't have her camera.

Shaking the negative thought from her mind, Lisa inhaled the panorama and focused on the beauty. Warmth. Breathing in, she centered on the scent of nature, the warm sun baking her skin, the visual of land that filled her with peace, like a warm cup of tea. Edging clear of the trees, she dubbed the area clear. In every direction, there was no one around but her.

As sunshine soaked into her skin, Lisa ached for it to penetrate her every cell. She needed this, had yearned for it. Another shiver raced through her. It would take more than a few minutes drenching herself in sunlight to do the job. It would take work. Snapping her thoughts to attention, Lisa knew she had to act. She had to get out of these wet clothes sticking to her skin and get them dry, her body dry. She glanced about, finding no rocks close by, no boulders to use as drying platforms, which meant she'd have to dry her clothes on the grass. A prospect that didn't please her. It would add time to the equation—time she didn't have to spare. But what choice did she have?

Slipping the T-shirt from her body, followed by her shorts, socks and shoes, she spread them out over the grass. Despite the flood of sunshine, Lisa felt cold. Clenching against an involuntary shudder, she exhaled heavily. Vigorously, she rubbed her hands up and down her arms, one more forcefully than the other to create as much friction as possible. Within seconds, her skin warmed. She debated removing her bra and panties. They were wet, sticking to her skin, but with the growing heat from the sun, they shouldn't prove more than a discomfort. She wasn't prepared to get naked. Although unoccupied for the time being, this area was popular with hikers.

Naked. Lisa gritted her teeth against a hard shiver. She'd heard of hikers being found naked, dead from hypothermia because the brain became disoriented, delirious, and the hikers began to believe they were hot and shed their clothes. She glanced down at her body, the wet pink bra and polka-dot panties of the same color. At least her search and recovery team would find a woman in cute underwear.

Easing to the ground, Lisa sat. Continuing to rub her arms, she couldn't get warm. The heat didn't move beyond her upper arms. Her gaze moved to her feet. The bandage at her ankle was sopping wet, same with the one on her wrist. She needed to get the bandages off and dry them. Unlike her underwear, they wouldn't dry affixed to her body. Carefully unwrapping each, she laid them across the grass, smoothing the wrinkles and bends in material. Once dry, she would re-wrap. She compressed arms to her body, but it didn't help.

Fire. She needed a fire to get rid of the chill.

Leaning forward, Lisa reached for her shorts, tapping around a snapped pocket. *Yes!* Her magnesium stick and knife were still inside. In a few minutes she could light a fire and warm herself more thoroughly.

Surveying her immediate vicinity, Lisa analyzed where she could do so with minimal impact. She wasn't going to build a fire in the shade of trees, though she would have liked to. There was too much undergrowth that might accidentally burst into flame. Yet sitting out in the open sun without sunscreen was not smart. Her skin would burn crisper than a piece of white toast.

Then she remembered. She could use the aspen trees for sunscreen! Like a blast from her mind vault, she recalled several facts concerning aspens. The powdery white substance on their bark could be used as a sunscreen. Not a very powerful one, maybe SPF 5 or so, but it was better than nothing. Better yet, aspen bark could be used as aspirin. Her thoughts went directly to her ankle. She could break off a branch, scrape the outer bark, then chew flecks of inner bark as an analgesic. Heartened by her recall, Lisa glanced up at the line of trees, their leaves trembling in the light breeze. They looked like glittering stones dangling from the trees. Beautiful. Functional.

Rising, Lisa hurried to the nearest tree, rubbed her hands over the knotty bark, and wiped the powder over her face and arms, her chest and shoulders, including a swath over her thighs. She wasn't as concerned with her legs as she was her face, neck, and shoulders. Those were the sensitive spots. Next, she tip-toed across the forest floor, her bare feet pricked by rocks and the sharp edges of branches as she gathered the necessary kindling. Carrying handfuls of it, she formed a small bundle of tinder and set it on the ground, as close to the edge of trees as possible, but not within, and commenced to fire-building.

Since she was in the midst of virgin territory, she'd have to keep it small. Burning the grass would kill the microorganisms in the soil. If she had a shovel, she could build a mound fire by scooping out the mineral dirt from beneath the fertile top soil, and use it for her fire, sparing the ecosystem.

Reluctance pulled at her as she took in the pristine blades of green. Unfortunately, a fire was a "need" and not a "want" at this point in her travels.

Survival of the fittest, she rued. That, too, was a reality of nature.

Taking her knife blade to the magnesium stick, Lisa set flame to her kindling at once. Tossing a few twigs and small branches she'd found on the ground beneath the trees, she fanned the flames until she'd achieved a decent fire. Holding her palms near the blaze, she rubbed them together, then her arms and legs, transferring the warmth as widely as possible. Scooting close, she grimaced as smoke drifted into her face, seeped into her wet underwear. Unpleasant, but warmth was priority one, stinky or not. An audible growl rumbled through her stomach. Next on the agenda would be food. With the immediate edge of cold softened, the first item after warm-up would be to scout for food.

Walsh arrived at the river, climbing down to ground zero of their jump. He'd seen no sign of man or animal on his way, though he was locked and loaded and prepared for a confrontation with both. Gazing down into the fast-flowing green-hued water, Walsh couldn't see a thing. The midday sun cast a sheet of light over its surface, impeding his view of the depths below. The sound of the current filled his ears, white water swirling within his vision. Walsh couldn't see two feet under, let alone to the bottom—where Lisa could have been trapped.

Discharging the thought, he lifted his gaze and scanned the perimeter. *She isn't down there. She's alive.* Walsh moved his line of sight downstream. Lisa had to have floated ahead of him. The section of water they landed in was too deep for her to have gotten a foot stuck. That happened when people—usually rafters—tried to stand in the shallows of swift current. The weight of their bodies wedged foot and ankle between rocks and the current swept them sideways. During his jump, Walsh had hit nothing underwater. Lisa was lighter than him and would have popped up first. She had to have been ahead of him. If she had tried to stand and become stuck—which he doubted—it would have happened farther downstream.

Turning, Walsh leapt over rocks and hopped down to the gravelly bank. Traversing the uneven shore, he thought about Wade's brief text reply to his message: *Working on it now.*

Brief and to the point. It was Walsh's preferred mode of communication, but in this instance, he would like to have heard more. *Have you sent a team? Can you put them in contact with me?*

Glancing at his black wristwatch, Walsh grunted. It wasn't his job to push. Almost three o'clock—he still had plenty of time to find her and get her down, or call for transport with exact coordinates. Pressure pushed into his gut. "Find her" were the key words.

Chapter Fifteen

On the first ring, Hal grabbed the phone from an end table in his living room. "Have you found her?"

"Not yet. We've triangulated her position to a spot on the mountain. I've got a crew going up to search for her now."

"Oh thank God," Hal sputtered, his pulse beating erratically. "What happened?"

"They ran into some sort of trouble on the way down."

"Trouble?" His pulse tripped. "What kind of trouble?"

"My buddy didn't say, only that they ran into trouble and wanted a team sent up the mountain."

The blood drained from Hal's brain. The need for a team couldn't be good. Why would they need a team? Wasn't this friend of Wade's capable of getting her down? "You talked to him? You know this for a fact?"

"Text, not phone call."

"How long before they reach her?" Hal asked. "Any idea?"

"According to the coordinates, about two hours. That puts them at her last known location around four."

Hal understood the restraint in Wade's voice. Since they were en route to the bottom, their last known location might be useless, but at least it was a start. It was a big mountain, the expanse of terrain daunting for any search team. The more they could narrow her location down, the better. "Keep me posted."

"Will do."

"Thanks."

Hal hung up the phone, disturbed by a growing misgiving. Wade was keeping something from him. Other than stating the obvious—it would take time to locate Lisa, time to bring her down—Hal sensed there was something more to the details of her situation. Eyeing the kitchen phone as though it were about to leap up at him, Hal understood the stakes. Lost hikers without GPS locating devices could be hard to find, especially if they were moving.

Walking to the plate glass windows, he looked up, inundated by memories of past hikes. He and Lisa had crisscrossed that mountain many times, both winter and summer. Lisa was a skilled hiker. When going up for research, she took the same route down as a matter of routine. Environmentalism. Precaution. Not that he worried she couldn't handle unchartered territory, she could. The girl could climb anything put in front of her, but the acres of land and trees, cliffs and streams, equated to a lot of ground to cover. Without accurate information, locating Lisa could be difficult. Add her injuries and Hal understood the stakes had ticked up a notch.

With five hours of sunlight remaining, Wade's team would have to work fast—smart—all of which they did on a regular basis. Colorado's search and rescue teams were the best of the best. They knew the terrain, knew the odds. They'd rake that mountain over until they found her.

Them, he corrected. She wasn't alone. His daughter had company.

For that Hal was grateful.

Ending the call, Wade turned to Roan Phillips. Chomping at the bit to take the helicopter up, they both understood there was a protocol to follow. Wade might be top cop in the department, but he still had to follow the rules. Walsh's emergency text changed the facts on the ground, but Wade needed more specifics before he sent Roan up for evacuation. His search and rescue team would secure them.

"When are you going to tell him?" Roan asked, noting the omission regarding Walsh's text during his phone call with Hal Richardson.

"When we find his daughter alive and well," Wade replied.

"And if you don't?"

It was the obvious question, and one Wade didn't want to answer. Brushing past Roan, he said, "We will."

McIntyre Walsh was his first line of defense. If he could put one man on that mountain tasked with the job of finding Lisa and getting her down, it would be Walsh.

EMERGENCY. Trouble on way down. Lost contact with Lisa. Potential injury/hypothermia. Send team for evac. Last known coordinates are as follows.

The text message was ingrained in Wade's psyche. Lost contact with her? What the hell did that mean? How had they become separated in the first place? Wade had replied, asking for more details, but none had come. Walsh must be out of range. He wouldn't leave Wade hanging like that, not knowing his relationship to the girl's father.

Wade swiped a glance around the confines of his office, one of the fancier spaces he'd occupied as a police officer. He not only had the latest in technology to do his job, but expensive wood furniture, regional artwork, and two of the politest secretaries he'd ever worked with. Only the best for the police department of a ritzy ski resort. Wade massaged his brow. None of which would change conditions on the ground. Something had gone wrong. Terribly wrong.

Had they come into contact with their mountain killer? An animal? Another fall?

Wade shook the clutter of supposition from his mind. He couldn't dwell on what-ifs. He had a team en route, a group of four men and one woman, all exceptional in their ability to get the job done. Their skills included firearms, emergency medicine, cave and water rescue. Whatever Lisa and Walsh needed, these folks could provide. Wade hoped Walsh would find Lisa first. He was on location. He'd know best.

"Have we heard anything from the team?" Roan asked.

Breaking from his thoughts, Wade turned. Roan was a dream come true for the department. Not only did he possess exceptional piloting skill, he was an all-around good guy, with classic brunette good-looks and a smile that beamed all-

American popular. Men and women alike wanted Roan assigned to their case, though for very different reasons. Wade wanted him on board because he was good. Damn good. "Not yet. I don't expect to until they reach destination."

Roan nodded.

Wade shared his impatience. Once the team called, there would only be a few hours of flying light left, limiting Roan's services, should they be required. His aircraft boasted ample cargo space and a suspension system that delivered an incredibly smooth ride, almost like it'd been designed specifically to transport rescue victims from mountain to emergency room. Staring into the eyes of his number one pilot, Wade raked a hand through his hair. He hoped to hell they didn't need that particular feature.

Lisa collected the coals from her fire and scattered them about the base of the aspen trees, dispersing them as thoroughly as possible. She'd cleaned up as well as she could, pained by the fact she couldn't erase the black spot in the grass. The scorched circle of earth in the midst of lush green would be a lasting scar. But her fire had done its job. She had sufficiently rid the chill from her body and was ready to move on. Dressed and warm, she allowed her hair to fall loose around her shoulders. Her bandana was long gone in the river, probably halfway to town by now. A grumble of hunger persisted. No water, no food, she was beginning to feel the effects. If only she'd thought to take a few gulps of water before leaving the river. Unfortunately, her thoughts had been in emergency-mode.

Well-acquainted with what to eat in the wilderness, and what not eat, Lisa set off to conquer her next challenge. Berries would be her best bet. Serviceberries, thimbleberries, raspberries, anything she could get her hands on would suffice. Bears survived not only on berries but a variety of things, including cattails. If she could find them, cattails were a doubly good option for her because they served more than one function. Twist the tips and discover a light, fluffy interior perfect for kindling, or a source of warmth she could use to pack her clothing. The shaft could be used to make an arrow, though she was hardly a hunter. The base of the cattail was nature's spaghetti, and a great source of carbohydrates—the energy supply she'd need to keep going.

But Lisa hadn't seen the first cattail and surprisingly, the section of aspen and evergreen she'd come through had been unusually berry-free. She'd seen a slew of mushrooms, but wasn't about to touch the first one. Some were poisonous and she knew to steer clear, though she wasn't much for the fungus in general. Fungus. Who ate fungus? She'd have to be ten-days starved before she even considered eating one of those things!

Lisa shuddered at the thought. Berries. Berries were her friend.

With a brand new walking stick, she traveled the tree line, peering between pine branches and tree trunks in search of berry bushes, continually popping a watchful glance over her shoulder for followers. She remained vigilant for company—animal or beast—particularly the murderous kind. She didn't have an exact plan for what she'd do should she run into the killer, only that it was better she see him first.

Maintaining a steady pace, Lisa made good time until she came to a cliff. It wasn't a very steep drop off, maybe twenty feet or so, with a line of trees poking up here and there. Normally she'd travel ledge-to-ledge, stone-to-stone to get down, but at the moment, it was more than she could handle. To her right, the ground sloped upward. To her left, the earth sloped down. She chose the path of least resistance. Down was the name of this game.

Using everything and anything to aid her passage, Lisa plotted her course step-by-step. With no established trail, she was forced to pick and choose her way forward with caution. When she finally reached level terrain, her ankle raged, the pain hot and angry.

Expelling a sigh, she looked ahead and saw what appeared to be a gully forged through the aspen forest. The open channel of land was laden with massive stones, allowing only tufts of grass to grow between. Thankfully the boulders had no height to speak of and instead were rather flat, like they had been squished into the earth and polished over. Good news, she mused sullenly. She'd leave little to no human footprint.

Footprint. Dropping her gaze to her feet, she almost didn't want to look at her ankle. It was killing her. She was no doctor, but it was clear the hike was doing more harm. Her dad would be furious. How many times had she heard him lament about ill-prepared hikers and the havoc they wreaked on their bodies? Havoc *he* had to fix. Taking a deep breath, she trudged forward. Oh, well. If she had caused any serious damage, he'd be the man to fix it.

Spotting a fallen aspen tree several yards ahead, its center most likely split by lightning, Lisa saw a "seat" and headed straight for it. Time to take a break, elevate her foot, and rest for a while. Conveniently slanted at a thigh-height horizontal angle, she easily hitched her rear up and onto the smooth round trunk. Placing a hand on the knotty bark, she blew a heavy sigh. It felt good to sit on her nature bench.

Taking time to breathe, Lisa gazed around, derived strength from her environment. Strength she needed. She couldn't ignore the possibility of being stuck up here for another night. Last night she had lucked out. When Walsh showed up, her entire survival projection had shifted. He gave her warmth, water, and food. Well, tried to give her food, except beef jerky was not on her menu. Recalling how he apologized for no lemons made her smile. It was sweet of him to think of her preferences. And this morning when she asked him to retrieve her data from her backpack, he did. It wasn't his first choice, but he did. Her smile grew, and tears filled her eyes. It had been a kind gesture on his part, one that had been wasted. Their leap into the river might have saved their lives, but it destroyed her data.

Choking back her disappointment, Lisa knew the notepad in his bag would have been soaked, her jacket lost, her vials with it. The effort to get them had been all for nothing. Fortunately, Walsh insisted she leave her camera behind. At least she still had a chance to recover her photos.

Photos. Walsh's image popped into her brain. She'd taken a photo of him to prove her camera worked. He'd been totally off guard, the image capturing his face in soft lines, the deep brown of skin dark within the shadows of trees, his eyes a burst of spring. Retrieving the camera was the last thing he'd wanted to do, but he did. Because she asked him to. A lump rose to her throat.

If she wasn't careful, she could fall in love with a man who so unselfishly put aside his own concerns in favor of hers. Who moved like a mountain cat, stealthily, deadly. A man who lived alone in the mountains, fierce and independent. The description suddenly amused her. Explain *that* one to dad. Brushing tears from her eyes, she said, "I've met a man who lives in the wilderness and I've fallen in love."

Where are you going to live, high altitude?

Yes. Good point. How would that work, actually?

Softening her focus to the depths of forest, the quiet space between trees and brush, Lisa pushed the silly musings from her mind. Breathe, she told herself. In, out. In, out. Focus on recovery, not inane thoughts of a man you just met. It was effort wasted.

Ten more minutes and she'd get on her way. She'd continue this path and take it home. Home, where her research and her father and her friends awaited. Honing in on a lumpy brown pile near a tree, she sharpened her focus.

Was that what she thought it was?

Instantly she rose and shuffled over. Squatting down on her good leg, she examined the pile more closely. Large and clumpy, it looked like dog poop, like one of the many surprises her father's dog, Rocco, left behind in the yard. But this was no dog's doing. This came from a bear.

Automatically, she swung her head and searched around her. Heartbeats thumped between her ears, her throat. The *last* thing she needed was to run into a bear. No mace, no way to run, she'd be easy pickings. Narrowing in between the span of tree trunks, she consoled herself with the fact there was no bear staring her down like a five-star main course. Breathing easier, Lisa returned focus to the poop. It was semi-fresh, deposited within the last several hours.

Pleasure surged. And it was filled with berries. Berries!

Flipping her face from side-to-side, she delighted in the fact. It meant berries were likely nearby! In a split-second of decision, Lisa sought her stick and continued in the direction she'd begun. She was getting close to food. She could feel it.

Walsh reached the end of the river, the shallows where Lisa would have landed, had she made it through the rapids. It was the most likely place for her to exit, provided she rode the rapids without issue. Running the surrounding geography through his mind, he filtered potential escape routes. There was a wall of mountain to one side, stacks of boulders to the other, river and forest ahead. Walsh's gaze was drawn to the cave-like opening in the trees. There was only one way she could have gone. If she made it this far, she would have had to have gone through there.

Adjusting the hang of his backpack, he secured the gun at his waist and took off running, stopping sudden. The phone in his pocket vibrated. Pulling it free, he saw a message from Wade.

Team arrived at last known location according to Lisa's cell phone. Approx. half mile west of your place. No Lisa. Heading for your coordinates now.

Walsh furrowed his brow. Had they pinged her phone? Walsh typed furiously. *Her cell phone probably dead. In process of tracking her now.*

Wade replied, *Any more sighting of our attacker?*

He was referring to Walsh's subsequent text. If Wade was sending a team up, they needed to know this guy was active and in the vicinity. *None. Advise team to be on alert. Use description I gave you.*

Roger.

Walsh replaced his phone and took off running.

Lisa cried out in relief at the cluster of raspberry bushes near the base of an aspen tree. "Berries—I've found you!" Overcome with joy, she'd never been so happy to spot the red fruit in her life. Stabbing the walking stick along the ground, she hurried to them. Darting her gaze about the bush, she greedily plucked and stuffed them into her mouth. A sour tang exploded on her tongue. Groaning aloud, she reached for another handful. They were delicious! A bit on the tart side, but delicious. Absolutely delectable!

Keeping a wary eye out for hungry bears that might be angry with her for stealing their cache, she stuffed as many as she could into her mouth, chewing as fast as she could. The lack of water made them grainy as she swallowed, but she didn't care. She had food. Food!

Within minutes, Lisa stepped away from the bush. Best to let the first round settle before consuming another. Finding food had been a good thing, however it sharpened her need for water. In terms of survival, food was secondary to water. The human body could go a week without food. More, even, yet in the same time period, it would begin shutting down without water. But where? She glanced about. Where was her nearest source?

Lisa moved her gaze up the mountain, then down, around the trees, along the boulder-ridden grassy path. She'd been on an easterly course until she deviated in search of these berries. Glancing left and right, she tried to remember which way the river flowed in relation to her position. Was she east of it like she thought? Had she veered west without realizing it? With her cell phone dead, her compass app was no use.

Shaking her confusion, Lisa knew how to get the answer. Searching the ground for a stick, she found one, dug a space in the short grass and propped the stick up in a vertical position. Thankfully the sun was strong and clear and made a nice shadow. Lisa marked the end of the stick's shadow. Timing it with her watch, she waited fifteen minutes and marked the next shadow position. This gave her an east-west line. Glancing over her shoulder, she mentally retraced her steps. Closing in on six o'clock, she knew she had little chance of making it down before dark. At dark, maybe, but before...no way.

If she was correct in her assumption of where she was, she should run into a stream not too far downhill. She'd stop, drink, soak and elevate her ankle before continuing on her way. Memories of her last stop at a stream filled her with instant longing. Walsh had found her. He had carried her to his camp and taken care of her, sweeter care than she would have imagined possible from a man like him. Too bad he wasn't around at the moment. She could use his company.

Pulling her stick compass from the ground, she sighed, overcome by a wave of fatigue. Who was she kidding? She'd like more than his company. She'd like his smarts, his physique. A tiny thrill raced through her as she vividly recalled his body against hers while he carried her without effort, as though she were a doll. A toy. His muscles had been hard as any boulder-faced mountain she'd ever scaled, and probably equally cut. Ripped. Lisa suppressed a swell of desire. She'd bet Walsh's body was ripped to the core.

Chastising herself for indulging in images of his bare chest and arms, Lisa smiled. Walsh was good-looking in a wholly unique and intriguing way. When she called to mind his features—his high flat cheekbones, his dark skin and black hair, his stunning green eyes—Walsh struck her as part Native-American, part Middle Eastern. She remembered seeing a photograph once, a young girl on the cover of a magazine. If Lisa remembered correctly, the girl had been from Afghanistan, the photo depicting the devastation caused by war in her country. It was a shot taken before Lisa was born, but her photography instructor used it as a lesson on the power of capturing human emotion through the lens of a camera. The portrait definitely did the job, making one feel the pain through the haunted eyes of an innocent child.

Drawing her mind back to Walsh, Lisa was struck by the similarities in not only appearance, but situation. Over twenty years ago, the Middle East had been caught up in war and once again it raged today. Walsh would have seen children like her, innocents traumatized by the horrors of violence. She shuddered. What else he must have seen—horrible, life-changing things. She had merely viewed a photograph on a magazine, and it stuck with her. Lisa could only imagine what Walsh must live with. He was there. He had witnessed the suffering firsthand.

Tossing the stick into the trees, Lisa fought the sadness filling her heart. Walsh shouldn't have to live alone on a mountain because he'd been traumatized by war. He should be happy and carefree, enjoying life to the fullest. Imagining Walsh skipping through a meadow like some character from *The Sound of Music* made her laugh. There was nothing light and fancy-free about Walsh. The man was gristle and grit and steel to the core. Except for his heart. That was soft and sweet and nurturing. With a wistful sigh, Lisa picked her spirits off the ground and continued on her way. She wanted to see him again. Would she?

That was the question.

Continually panning the area for signs of Lisa, Walsh strode through the trees, pine giving way to aspen as he hiked by instinct. His gut never failed him. It had saved him and his unit more than once in the mountainous desert of Afghanistan, and it would save him and Lisa now. *Straight through.* If Lisa had come this way, she would have run straight through.

Run. The thought grated on him. She wouldn't have been able to run. She would have limped, at best. Hobbled, crawled. That jump and subsequent swim couldn't have helped her injuries. She'd have to be feeling the pain. But if he'd learned one thing about this woman, it was that pain wouldn't stop her. It didn't stop her from going after her backpack or from escaping a potential killer and a helluva cliff dive, and it wouldn't stop her now. She'd escape through a mountain forest and do whatever it took to make it to safety. Admiration welled. Lisa was a fighter. Not always focused on the right goal, he mused dryly, but a fighter nonetheless.

Emerging from the space of trees, Walsh paused. Overhead the sun was sinking, making way for night to move in. In another few hours it would be dark. Cold. Urgency pressed. There was no way she could spend another night on this mountain. She had no jacket, no means to start a fire... She'd freeze to death.

If she hadn't already. While he would like to shove the reality from his mind, Walsh couldn't. Lisa had to be cold. The icy water temp had taken its toll on him, and he'd been out in minutes. He couldn't imagine what it might have done to her. She'd have to be freezing. But with no dead body to say otherwise, he worked on the assumption that she was okay. Cold, but okay.

Kicking into action, Walsh stopped. An anomaly jumped out at him—a dark spot on the ground fifty feet away. Heart thumping, he strode over and dropped to a squat, reaching a finger to touch grass. He smelled his fingers, rubbed them together. Soot. Fire. Someone had built a fire here. Whipping his gaze about the ground, he searched for coals, remnants. There was nothing. Excitement surged. There weren't many hikers who would disperse a fire so thoroughly. But Lisa would.

Tingles rippled across his skin as he stared out over the vast meadow. Lisa had been here. With bold certainty, he knew he was on the right track. How far ahead she was, he didn't know, but Lisa had come this way. He was sure of it. Bolting upright, Walsh took off like a deer. She knew this land. She would know the quickest way down was due west then east.

Chapter Sixteen

Sitting behind his desk, Wade clenched the phone tightly in hand. Listening to one of his men report in, Wade did not like what he was hearing. Their mountain killer had struck again. "Where?"

"On the ridge near Larkspur Pass."

"Witnesses?"

"None. Boyfriend claims someone came in the tent overnight and stole the gun."

"The girl wasn't hurt?"

"The only good news."

Something inside Wade closed. Good news wasn't the term he'd use. Escalation was a bad sign. Their suspect might have spared a life this time, but the fact that he'd stolen a gun could only mean one thing. Walsh no longer stood the advantage in weaponry. If they didn't find him and Lisa soon, Wade didn't want to consider the consequences. He'd yet to tell Hal about their run-in with the suspected killer. The first encounter could have been a stranger, a person completely unconnected to the murders. But the second was no coincidence, a fact Wade could no longer ignore. "Thanks. Let me know if you get any more information."

"Will do."

Roan held his gaze but said nothing. Both men understood the stakes. The search and rescue team had come up empty. They searched the river, but there was no sign of Walsh or Lisa. They were splitting up, the search boundaries broadening.

Wade stood. "Take the helicopter. Do a fly-over of the river and every inch of the mountain downhill from there."

"Got it."

"I want every speck of land covered, you hear me?"

"Roger."

Roan turned to go and Wade grabbed his shoulder. "Take Canyon Laredo with you."

"Already called him."

Canyon Laredo was a part-time search and rescue paramedic who used to work for the department but now spent his time between rodeos and seriously-ill children on a charity dude ranch ten miles out of town. He and Roan grew up together and worked like hand-in-glove when it came to air operations. Canyon was Roan's eyes and ears when his were fixed on his instruments. Which they usually weren't, Wade mused. Roan flew a helicopter like most people rode bicycles. But Canyon would provide the necessary cover, should anyone decide to take a few pot shots at a police aircraft.

Pacing his kitchen, Hal Richardson peered into Adele Simms' black-brown eyes. His companion and owner of Adele's, a top-rated gourmet restaurant in the resort village, she understood what he was going through. While six o'clock should find her prepping for dinner at the restaurant, instead she was standing in the middle of his kitchen, insisting he needed her more than the restaurant did.

It was a point he couldn't argue. Lisa hadn't shown up yet. She hadn't called, and Wade Davis could tell him little more.

"Can I make you some tea?" Adele asked, her dark eyes swimming with concern, eyes lined in deep burgundy. A similar shade of blush enhanced the milky-white skin of her prominent cheekbones. Her narrow nose, defined jaw line, and perfectly formed mouth made her features extremely photographic though she shunned any such attention. Adele was quiet, private, and completely focused on him and his needs.

Hal shook his head. He couldn't eat, couldn't drink. He could only pace.

"Is there anyone we can call?" Placing slender fingers on his hand, she asked, "Have you talked to anyone on the team?"

"Wade will call when he knows something."

Suddenly, the sight of a helicopter in the distance caught his eye. Hal hurried to the window, Rocco close at his heel, metal dog tags clanging at his neck. Sweeping in from the west, the heli-bird made a wide curve up and over the town. It was headed up the south face.

Hal's blood ran cold. It was searching for Lisa.

The telephone rang and he ran to answer it, wincing at the stab of pain in his knee. Grabbing the phone, he clipped, "Hello?"

"Hal, Wade."

"What's going on?" he demanded, pulse pounding. "I saw a helicopter fly up the mountain." He flashed a gaze to Adele. "Have you heard something? Did they find Lisa? Is she injured?"

"Not yet. I did send Roan up to help with the operation, though."

Hal felt Adele's hands at his shoulder. "So you don't know anything more."

"Not exactly."

"What?" Disturbed by the hesitance he heard, Hal insisted, "Talk to me, Wade. What's going on?"

"It seems our killer has upped his game. We think it's possible he stole a gun from a couple of hikers overnight."

"Possible? You don't know for sure?"

"We don't have a positive ID, but it occurred in the same area that Walsh placed him earlier today."

"Walsh placed him somewhere today?" Hal gaped at Adele. "On their way down?" Wade remained silent, allowing the answer to sink in on its own. Hal felt weak, faint. This was his daughter they were talking about, not some nameless hiker on vacation. This was Lisa. "They saw him. They saw him and you think the killer is armed," Hal added flatly.

"Yes."

Hal latched onto Adele, her pensive gaze fixed on his. The overhead lights reflected huge white dots in her pupils, added shine to her glossy short-cropped black hair. She held no smile for him, no words of encouragement. She understood the gravity of the situation and wasn't about to sugarcoat it.

"Right now," Wade continued, "we have our best team on it. We're going to bring Lisa home safely and get this madman off the mountain."

"What can I do?" Hal asked.

"Nothing. We've got it covered."

It was a kick in the gut. Hal was part of the team, he was part of search and rescue, yet he could do nothing. Nothing. The phone slipped at his ear as he replied dully, "Let me know if anything changes."

"You know I will."

Hal hung up the phone and fought a rising tide of helplessness. Sliding an arm around Adele, he hugged her to him, pressed his chin to the top of her head. Small, petite, this woman was narrow in physique but powerful in support. She understood the emotions flowing through him. Lisa was all he had. Lisa was his to protect. He hadn't been able to save her mother, but he had to save her. There was no way he could stand the loss of them both.

Through the years he'd been a hawk about her diet, made sure she ate healthy, took good physical care of herself. Hal warned her of the dangers of high country, made sure she was trained, and skilled, and could survive the elements. He even went so far as to hire a personal trainer who taught her techniques in self-defense. Hal had done everything he could to ensure Lisa would be safe. Casting a reluctant gaze to the living room windows and beyond, Hal felt his power slipping away. The helicopter was a mere bug-sized dot in the distance. His daughter was somewhere below, alone, in danger, and there wasn't a damn thing he could do about it.

Lisa wanted to cry. She wanted to scream. She'd found the stream, but the veil of night was drawing closed, pushing out the last embers of twilight. She'd made good progress. She was halfway down, give or take, but she couldn't continue. While she understood this was going to be the case, surrendering to the finality of it was another matter. A part of her had clung to the possibility she might beat the night.

She could no longer.

She needed to be realistic. There was no way she could outrun Mother Nature. Night would fall hard and fast and with it the hammer of cold. It had been another cloudless day, leaving no atmospheric blanket of insulation to retain heat through the evening. If she didn't plan ahead and build a fire now, she'd be fighting another bout of biting cold. A mild tremor skirted through her as visceral memories of her earlier chill gripped her. Lisa understood the value of fire. It could mean the difference between life and death.

Surveying the forest floor, using the last remnants of daylight, she deemed the best place for fire would be in a level space of earth twenty feet from the stream. There was a large expanse of rock entrenched between the roots of several pine trees. There was a dead tree nearby—far enough away she didn't worry about catching it on fire, close enough to make a great source of kindling. She could use the tree next to it for shelter. With no jacket or sleeping bag, warmth and shelter would be the top priorities for the evening.

Analyzing the layout, Lisa deemed the low-level spread of branches and wide girth of the pine tree's trunk would provide the framework she needed for a rudimentary shelter. Gathering a miscellany of branches, Lisa worked to assemble a "mattress" that would act as a buffer zone between her and the stone-cold ground. Next, she needed to construct a few "walls" around the tree trunk, the rooftop provided courtesy of the existing tree branches. As she patted the limbs into place, sharp needles poked her skin and she cringed. Her sunburned skin was beginning to tighten and "pinch." Aspen sunscreen had its limitations. Working through the discomfort, she shaped her shelter. She wouldn't need much space, only enough to curl up and stay warm. It would be an uncomfortable night, but she'd make it. Once she built her fire, she could heat up some stones and strategically place them around her sleeping body to increase warmth retention. Anything to help ward off another bout with hypothermia.

Blowing a wisp of hair from her face, Lisa decided her refuge was sufficient. Time to build a fire. Rising, she turned and cried out—"Ouch!"—and fell to her knees. Her unfastened boot had twisted loose, wrenching her bad ankle in the process. Streaks of pain shot through her leg, the sensation throbbing and jabbing at the same time. Darn it, this was the last thing she needed! It felt like shards of glass cutting through her. Clutching her leg, she whimpered, gritting her teeth through the pain.

Easing to her side, she sat, wiping a chunk of sticky substance from the heel of her palm. "*Ugh,*" she groaned. She'd landed on a freshly broken branch covered in tree sap. Frustration welled. Why hadn't she been more careful?

Wiping the gunk from her hand onto the side of her shorts, Lisa refused to be knocked out by her injuries. Not when she was almost home. Water. Fire. Those were her concerns, not pain.

She had to ignore it. She had to drill her focus into the task ahead, not the pain in her ankle, though how she was going to walk was the question. Reaching down for her foot, she fully removed the boot. *Suck it up, Lisa. Suck it up and get moving before it's too late.*

Pushing up from the ground, she pulled in her leg and used her trusty stick to shuffle her way to the stream's edge. She lowered to all fours and scooped up water, slurping greedily. Icy water streamed down her throat, soothed the scratch-board of her vocal chords. Rivulets spilled down her chin, freezing the sensitive skin of her face. Suddenly gripped by thirst, Lisa drank until the bones in her hand felt frozen stiff, barely able to curve into a cup to collect the water. Lisa sat back against a rock, and realized the air temperature had dropped a few more degrees.

Fire. It was time to build a fire. Collecting the necessary material, she dusted off the rock surface and formed the basis for her fire. With a scrape from her knife, she sparked the magnesium stick until she achieved flame. In several minutes, her fire had doubled in size. Rubbing her hands vigorously together, she held them close, warming the edge off her chill. The heat of fire never felt so good. An unexpected shudder rocked her shoulders. It felt good, but she needed more. She needed it bigger, bolder, despite the risk to her whereabouts.

Glimpsing movement from the corner of her eye, she froze. Zeroing in on the spot, she held her breath. Her heart thumped. Again, it moved. Relief swept through her as a young elk popped its head up. The breath rushed from her lungs. *It was only an animal!*

Tension broke like a tidal wave, sending heartbeats drumming into her ribs. It was an elk out for a bite to eat. Lisa smiled, inhaled deeply to calm the unexpected battering in her chest. *Relax. There's nothing to worry about.* Her stomach growled. Actually, there was. She was hungry. Around her, sunlight suddenly lowered, as if dimmed by a switch. Breathing in and out, Lisa focused on what she could control. Fire. Warmth. Shelter. She was safe here. No one knew where she was. Tossing a large stick onto her fire, she reached for another. No one followed her. She was good. Alone, but good.

Fire was her focus. This was her mission at the moment.

No doubt help was on its way. Her father would have insisted they send a team up the mountain to look for her. All she had to do was hang on. This fire might even help them locate her. If they found her, perfect. If not, she'd hook up with help on the way down. The lower she hiked, the higher the chance of running into someone.

Running into someone. Lisa closed her eyes, warding off images of a cold-blooded killer. *Hikers.* She'd run into hikers. The killer didn't know where she was. Walsh didn't know where she was. She had to focus on the positive. Conditions weren't ideal, but she had enough to give her solace. She added sticks to her fire. Time to look for those rocks to heat her shelter next.

Walsh was halfway down the mountain when the first slivers of night crept over the mountain. Slants of shadows cut across treetops, walls of darkness formed over half of the grassy hillside. There was still no sign of Lisa, and with the light fading fast, his chances of finding her faded with it. It would be dark soon, and she was without light, without phone.

She was vulnerable.

Walsh expelled the thoughts. Lisa was strong. Capable. If anyone could survive the ordeal she'd suffered, she could. It was a concept that gave him comfort. She was a woman who gave him comfort. She wasn't self-centered or helpless. She wasn't whiny or weak. She was independent, like him. She was strong and determined and self-reliant, like him. With each passing hour, Walsh was beginning to realize how very much like him Lisa was. However, without the proper tools, she was as vulnerable as he would be in the chill of night. The human body could only endure so much. It was up to the power of the mind at that point. That's how people survived, because they believed they would. Willed it to be.

Hovering in place, he wasn't sure which way to go. Down was the sensible choice. Straight down. But this section of terrain was level in both directions, and both directions would eventually get her to where she was going. Lisa could have gone either way.

Pausing, Walsh tried to put himself in her position. She had no food. No water. The fire she'd built earlier was a sign that she'd been cold but recovered. The sun had been overhead all day. At this point, she'd be dry and warm. But hungry. Thirsty. The main river was west of here, but it had branches that ran through this area. If it were him, he'd want water. Water before food. Would Lisa agree?

At this point, there was no room for error. From what he'd seen, Lisa was no fool. She'd head for water, same as him. The phone in his pocket buzzed. Walsh pulled it free and read the message. *Status?*

No contact with anyone yet.

Dots moved across his screen indicating Wade was typing his reply. *Suspect might have stolen a gun. Consider him armed and dangerous. Helo in the air.*

Walsh read the words, allowing a fresh wave of concern to wash through him. The man had secured a weapon? Roan was flying overhead?

Wade was right to send him up. Daylight was waning fast, underscoring the need to find Lisa soon. Roan might be able to spot something from the air Walsh couldn't see from the ground. Typing, he replied, *Will advise when new status achieved.*

Roger.

Unsettled by the turn of events, Walsh tuned his mental radar to high alert. The gun pressing into the skin of his lower back would be of no consequence if the killer found Lisa first. Half-walking, half-jogging, Walsh escalated his trek down, scanning the landscape with a meticulous eye, continuously posing his question. *What doesn't fit?*

Nearby, an elk crooned into the cooling dusk. Squirrels squeaked and squealed like birds. A stream would intersect his path ahead. Inaudible from a distance, one would have to know its location in order to find it. Did Lisa know it? Had she come across it during one of her research trips?

He'd be there in minutes.

When he arrived, Walsh swept his glance up and down the length of the stream over rocks and trees, the low to mid-level shrubs, and expelled a sigh. Darkness seeped between trees, filled branches, rock crevices, puddled on the ground. Other than the muted babble of water at his feet, Walsh was alone. Impatience fired through his core. He was alone, *dammit!*

Dragging a hand over the soft buzz of his hair, he scanned the area. Trees, bushes, scraggly groundcover, boulders, rocks, river—but no Lisa. Where could she be? She couldn't have gone far. Had she taken a different route? Had he miscalculated? Had his gut steered him wrong? As he stood alone, desperation percolated through his midsection, up into his chest. He couldn't understand it. It was as if she'd disappeared.

Walsh experienced a flutter of pulse. It wasn't possible.

Suspect might have stolen a gun.

He'd heard no gunshot. Certain he'd tracked Lisa at least part of the way, he was close enough to have heard a gunshot. Closing his eyes, Walsh urged his brain to think, analyze. Dissect the situation. There was no way she could have gotten far after stopping to build a fire and traveling on a sprained ankle. Walking stick or not, Lisa was slow. Her pace was impeded. He had to be close.

Think. Focus. Sync sensory systems.

Steadying his thoughts, taking control of his breaths, Walsh released preconceived notions. *Allow the mind to expand. Breathe in, out.* Calm and centered, he opened to new possibility. Instinct took over. Gut. Standing rigid, rooted in the midst of evergreen, he gave himself up to the scents and sounds. Visions of Lisa formed in his mind. *Where would you go? Where are you?*

Tell me, Lisa. Talk to me.

Walsh dug into the quiet of his mind. Intuition was key. Breathing in, he picked up a new scent. Faint but familiar. Pine, wood, earth, and... Fine-tuning his senses, he sifted through the parts of the whole. Popping his eyes open, he focused on the scent. *Smoke.* Sniffing the air more pointedly, Walsh looked around. There was a fire. Excitement surged. Someone had built a fire.

Seeing nothing, he strode downstream. Lifting his nose, he inhaled deep and precise. Losing the scent, he jogged upstream. Yes—he could smell it. Running farther upstream, Walsh controlled his inhalations, specifically working to pick up on the distinct scent of burning wood. Nearly tripping over a dead log, he dodged an evergreen perched over the stream's edge. He scoured the forest for signs of flame. Walsh could smell it, but he couldn't see it. The obvious thing to do would be to call out her name, but on the off chance a killer was within hearing distance, he refrained.

Stepping on a branch, he cursed the loud crack. If he spooked her like he had last time, Lisa might hide, forcing him to reveal his position to anyone who might be looking on.

So be it. Pulling the gun from his pants, he held it ready. If there was anyone else around, he'd gladly take them on. It was more important to determine if the fire was hers.

Shoving heavy, pine needle-laden branches from his path, Walsh froze. In the heavy darkness, he saw the soft glow of flame.

Chapter Seventeen

Lisa's heart stopped. A branch had cracked in the distance. Was it another animal? Was someone there? She held her breath and waited for another sound. Nothing. Senses electrified, her pulse pounded freely, like it was running right through her skin!

What would she do if someone was coming? What if it was the wrong someone?

Fear zipped through her. Could be a hiker. She'd run into them on the trail many times. But the wrong hiker could end her life. Branches crunched repeatedly, sending her heart into her throat. *Ohmigod*—someone was running!

Whipping her glance around her fire, she sought the nearest weapon. A stone. Scrambling for it, she scraped her knee over sharp ground as she grabbed one of her heating stones to hurl at the intruder. *Ouch!*

Lisa bit back a cry. Too hot! Squeezing the tender tips of her burnt fingers, she searched for another. Tugging at a small boulder crushed between two larger stones, the gritty, grainy surface scratched her fingertips as she wedged it free. Winding back, she watched the darkness.

"Lisa!"

The hushed call of her name capped her motion. *Walsh*?

Clenching the rock with both hands, she held it against her body. Was that really Walsh? Excitement ballooned in her chest, but she feared to call back to him. What if it wasn't him?

But no one else knew her name. "Walsh!" she burst out. "Walsh, is that you?"

Out of the darkness, he appeared. Strong and rugged, his dark-colored shirt and pants blended into the night as the glow of fire cast shadows across his face. But not his eyes. They were vibrant green. Vivid. *Walsh.*

The two locked gazes before he came to her, pulling her up from the ground. Lisa dropped her rock and fell into his arms. Hugging her tightly, he murmured into her hair, "Thank God I found you."

Consumed by the sudden warmth of his embrace, the strength of his body, she uttered in disbelief, "How did you find me?"

Walsh said nothing, only held firm, infusing her body with relief. Ribbons of stress streamed from her limbs, wrung her body of any strength she had left. Surrendering to his hold, Lisa laughed through a sudden swell of tears. "I'm so glad you found me."

Squeezing, he released, but not too far as he held her close, moving his gaze back and forth over hers. "Are you okay?"

She nodded. "It's been a tough day, but I'm fine."

A smile pulled at his gaze, filled his eyes with a measured happiness. "You had a lot of people worried."

Including him? Tamping down a rise of nerves, she joked, "I had myself worried!"

Concern coiled around his gaze, tightening like a band around her heart. "You must be cold."

Tensing against an involuntary shudder, she replied, "A little." Short sleeves and shorts were no match for a cold Colorado night. One boot on, one socked foot, she looked pretty ragged. Briefly dropping her gaze to the soft dance of flames, she murmured, "I built a fire, a shelter. I'm good for the night."

She'd covered the basics but knew full well it would have been a struggle. She'd been considering staying awake all night by her fire. Noting the bulging backpack he wore, she hoped it included a blanket.

Walsh instantly slipped the pack from his back and un-latched the top, pulling out the orange satin-lined sleeping bag she'd slept in last night. "I brought this for you. I found your jacket and knew you'd be freezing."

He'd found her jacket? Was anything still in it? But a tide of gratitude drowned out everything but him. She didn't need her vials. She needed him. "Well, freezing might be a bit strong..."

Walsh unzipped it and wrapped it around her shoulders, pulling it to a close between them. "It's cold. It's going to get colder."

Abandoning her attempt at bravado, she sighed. Walsh had brought her his sleeping bag. He'd searched for her and brought her his bag to make sure she was warm. Nestling in the warmth engulfing her body, she met his gaze directly. Walsh was taking care of her. Such a simple gesture, yet she found it incredibly overwhelming, generous. Something deep inside her shifted. It was tender, loving. "Thank you," she said, her voice splitting in a whisper.

"You're welcome." Clicking into business mode, Walsh said, "You need to get off that foot." As he eased her back to the ground, he asked, "Where's your boot?"

"I took it off and left it by my shelter."

Crouching before her, concern swam in his gaze. "Have you had any water?"

"Yes. I drank from the stream."

"Good. But you have no food." Dipping back into his pack, he pulled out an MRE and a bag of beef jerky.

Her insides recoiled. He didn't seriously expect her to eat that, did he?

"You need to eat."

"I did."

He eyed her suspiciously. "What did you eat?"

"Berries. I found a bush-full on my way into this section of trees."

"Berries are not enough." He thrust the MRE toward her. "You need protein."

Reading the label, she noted his choice was beef ravioli. "I'm fine. I'll be fine until tomorrow."

Glaring at her, Walsh held the tan packet of food between them. "Don't be stupid."

"Stupid? Because I don't want to eat your ravioli?" His stare remained hardened, and she fought a primal reaction to strike back. Walsh knew she was a vegan. She didn't eat meat. Granted he was trying to be helpful, but in a pushy, demanding sort of way she didn't appreciate. But she did appreciate his presence. Reining in her annoyance, Lisa replied evenly, "I am not going to die of starvation. I appreciate your offer, but I'll be fine until tomorrow."

"And what happens if you don't make it home tomorrow?"

"What are you talking about? Of course I'll make it home—I'm halfway there!"

"Our killer has a gun."

The ground gave way beneath her, sucking her calm into a black hole. "What?"

Firelight flickered across his face as he informed her, "Wade told me the man stole a gun."

"How?"

"Don't know. Said he stole it somehow."

"Has he used it? Has he shot someone?"

"I didn't have time to ask questions. I was on the hunt for you."

Steamrolled by the fact that he'd risked himself on her behalf—continued to do so—made Lisa clam shut. She owed this man a debt of gratitude, not a game of twenty questions.

Holding the MRE between them, Walsh said, "It won't kill you to eat meat this one time. It's called surviving." When she didn't respond, he added, "I won't tell anyone."

Pulling the sleeping bag up around her neck and face, she burrowed into its warmth. *I won't tell anyone.* As if her vegan lifestyle was all for show. Pressing her lips into the satiny material, she shook her head. She'd be okay until morning.

Tossing the meal packet to the ground, Walsh pulled a phone from his pocket and began typing.

"Who are you texting?"

"Wade. I'm letting him know that I found you. They sent a team up for you. A helicopter, too."

"A helicopter?" Lisa balked. Was he sure? She hadn't heard the first sound.

Walsh nodded. "With it getting dark, they were worried."

The words struck hard. It was getting dark and she hadn't made it home. With no way to contact her dad, he would be beside himself. *Oh no...*

Images of a worried father clawed at her. Not only did he send up a search and rescue team, but a helicopter. He would have demanded they do everything possible to search for his daughter. After all, he volunteered a lot of time doing the very same for other families. It was only right they return the favor.

Watching as Walsh slipped the cell phone back into his pocket, she wondered about their next step. He would obviously stay the night with her. He'd insisted last night and she hadn't been in near as poor condition. Tonight was a different story. He knew she needed him.

Concealing a spurt of nerves, she turned, and focused on the fire. She did need him. Yet alone, secluded, it felt strange to have him near. Familiar and odd at the same time, like she knew him, like they were old friends, but she didn't know the first thing about him. Not really, other than her father's brief description. *He's a friend of Wade's. Ex-military, Special Forces.*

Lisa had no doubt she was in good hands. Strong hands. Capable hands. Suddenly drawn to Walsh's hands as he stoked the flames, throwing a few more sticks on top, she marveled at the soft quality of his skin. Brown and smooth, it appeared silken in the glow of fire. His fingers were long and well-shaped, his fingernails short and cleanly filed. They weren't the hands of a rugged outdoorsman, yet he was most certainly that. She moved her gaze up well-defined arms to his chest, to the light reflecting in his face. Shadows bounced from his brow to his nose, gathered beneath the solid line of his jaw. His attire had changed since morning. No longer dressed in long-sleeves, he wore a black T-shirt and olive cargo pants, his boots similar but different. He must have returned to his camp and changed into dry clothes after their plunge into the river.

Thoughts of her stomach flying into her chest, the shock of icy water when she hit, came rushing back. It all happened so fast. After sinking deep into the water, her reactions had been automatic. Amazingly hitting nothing in the murky depths, she had risen to the surface, kicked her legs up and in front of her and ridden the current downstream. It wasn't until she crawled out of the river that she realized she'd lost her jacket.

A jacket he had found.

It must have been unnerving to find her jacket and not her. Did he panic? Did he remain calm? Walsh said he'd been hunting for her. Images of a warrior on the hunt filled her mind as she envisioned him hiking the mountain, scouring the river, picking up her scent like a bloodhound. But how? How did he manage to find her on this huge space of mountain?

A squiggle of thrill raced through her. Because he was good. Because he was determined.

Because Walsh had made it his mission to find her.

Grabbing a headlamp from his pack, he rose. "I'm going to get more wood." Glancing around, he asked, "You said you built a shelter? Where?"

She nodded, pointing over her shoulder. "There, beneath that tree."

Acknowledging the direction indicated, he came to her, then set off for her shelter.

Through the darkness, she watched him. He was close, but the glow of her fire only reached so far, light petering into the night around them. She could see him bend over and check out her makeshift bedroom, could see the beams of light from his headlamp swing side-to-side as he assessed her handiwork. What would he think of it? Would he want to change it? Think it needed improvement?

Turning from him, Lisa braced herself for any disapproval he might deliver. She wasn't stupid for not eating meat. Her structure was rudimentary but sufficient. Settling her gaze on the ring of rocks around her fire, the idea to heat stones an added bit of cleverness on her part, Lisa knew she'd done the best that she could, given the circumstances.

Walsh returned, and after placing a tumble of scraggly branches on the ground by his side, crossed his legs and settled in.

Well? she wanted to ask. *Did I pass military muster*?

When it appeared Walsh was content with the silence, Lisa forced herself to accept the same. They didn't need to talk. Tomorrow she would be home and he would return to his mountaintop hideaway. He lived here, she lived in town. He'd been brave and courageous in taking care of her, but tomorrow it would end.

A prick of longing stabbed her heart, pushing tears behind her eyes. Grateful Walsh couldn't read her feelings, she filled her mind with the flames, the gentle sway of blue-orange rising to a golden yellow, and tried not to think. If she did, she'd realize how much she was coming to like Walsh. Maybe it was the romance of rescue or the thrill of escape, but she'd been thinking about him all day, hoping to see him, wishing him to do exactly as he had done. Come for her. Find her.

Save her from the villain who chased her.

Lisa felt his gaze. From the corner of her eye, she realized Walsh was staring at her. Curiosity pulled at her. "What?"

"Nothing."

Nothing? He was staring at her for nothing? Unable to match his heated gaze, the fire of thought churning behind those green eyes of his, Lisa turned back to the fire. Fine. If it was nothing, it was nothing. Didn't matter to her one way or the other. Shouldn't, anyway.

"Where did you learn how to take care of yourself?"

Confused, she glanced sideways and replied, "Um, my father?"

Hitching his chin toward her shelter, he asked, "He taught you the survivor skills you know?"

It dawned on her that Walsh wasn't speaking in general terms. He was referring to her camping skills. "Partially. He taught me a lot of them, but I learned a lot during high school and college. I was part of hiking clubs where we had experts come to our meetings and give presentations."

He grunted.

"What? Are they not up to your standards?"

Walsh nailed her with a sharp glance and held firm. "They're beyond my standards. They're beyond most people's standards."

Caught off guard by the blunt compliment, Lisa thrust her gaze back to the fire. So he had noticed. A scribble of excitement scurried through her breast and she had to suppress a chuckle. Good. She was glad he noticed.

"Most women would be dead by now."

Lisa swallowed but didn't respond, though she was heartened by the curt observation.

She'd always known she wasn't "most women," but to say it aloud would come across wrong. She took pride in her skills, her achievements. She strived to do her best in everything she did. It was her opinion that anything less would be a waste of time. Professor Stevens' words floated into her mind. *If you aren't in it to win it, get out of the race.* She couldn't agree with him more. Students came and went through the doors of his classroom claiming they wanted to be a part of the team, but many lacked the commitment necessary, and Professor Stevens booted them from his research.

Dale was one of those in jeopardy. While his intellect rivaled any student in the program, his will to hike and execute research projects lagged sorely behind. Where Dale disliked the outdoor aspect of their research, Lisa found pleasure in it. She would much rather spend her time in the fresh mountaintop air than in some lab painstakingly analyzing data. Both were necessary, but if she could choose only one, field operations were her preference.

When she realized Walsh was still staring at her, Lisa thought perhaps he had another question for her. But when she turned, what she saw staring back at her was anything but question. It was sharp and hungry, totally masculine and naked in its desire. She gulped. Was Walsh having thoughts about...?

She stopped herself from letting the idea unwind, trapping it in her chest in a tangle of emotion. She dropped her gaze, but her focus was lured to the round of his biceps, the ripped quality of his arms, the cord of blood vessel sliding over each. His arms pulsated with strength, shouted power and force. Sort of like his neck vein. He was tough, hardcore. Walsh was in superior physical shape, and surviving the rugged backcountry conditions came easy to him.

Tipping into a smile, he said, "You're something else, you know that?"

"Me?" she peeped, embarrassed by the chirp of her voice.

"Not only beautiful, but you're capable, smart. You skate circles around most women I've ever met."

Lisa couldn't get past the word beautiful. Beautiful? Had Walsh just called her beautiful?

But she didn't wear makeup or fuss with her hair. She wore plain T-shirts and shorts. Boots, not heels. No one had ever told her she was beautiful...not in physical terms.

"You must have a ton of guys after you."

No, actually, she didn't have any. Not really. The only man who had ever voiced his appreciation for her was Professor Stevens. Not that it was any guy's fault in particular for not noticing her. If truth be known, she wasn't exactly approachable. Relationships got in the way of her research, her time on the mountain. There might have been a few guys who'd made passes along the way, but once she hit her stride in college, that kind of attention seemed to dwindle.

"Are you dating someone?" he asked.

Struck by the personal nature of his question over the intimate ambiance of firelight, Lisa suppressed an abrupt rise of want. "I'm not, no."

"No?" He laughed and Lisa frowned. Walsh held his hands up as though warding off an imminent attack. "I don't mean anything bad, I'm just surprised. Have college guys lost their minds these days? If I were in college, I'd be all over you."

"Do you have a girlfriend?" she fired back, titillated by the turn in conversation to the very personal and suddenly intrigued to hear his answer.

"Me? A girlfriend?" He shook his head. "Not on your life."

"Why not?"

"Too much trouble, too much headache." Softening his edge, he added, "Besides, what kind of woman would want to spend her time up here with me?"

A smart woman. An outdoorsy woman. In that instant, unraveled by the fluidity in his gaze, Lisa realized a very bad thing. She liked Walsh. She liked him way more than she should.

An hour later, after dousing the flame, Walsh extended a hand to help Lisa from the ground. "Time for bed."

While she understood what he meant, the words still sent a flush of warmth through her chest, up her neck and cheeks. She'd enjoyed her time with him, their fireside chat. Mostly talk of what happened to her after their jump, how she made it this far. He confessed that he'd been worried about her, a confession she found quite pleasurable. It meant he cared. It meant she was coming to mean something to Walsh. And he, to her. They shared a bond—a bond of survival. It was an experience she'd never forget. More, these last forty-eight hours on the mountain had changed her. Gratified by her ability to survive, she found herself more captivated by him. Walsh was her equal when it came to handling the rugged terrain, the challenging situations. He was a man who enjoyed the outdoors, a man who appreciated the beauty of nature, a man who showed tenderness with someone in need. It felt like they were connected, like they were in this adventure together, against the odds, against the perils. It felt like they were a team.

Lisa gripped the hand Walsh offered. Though she popped up easily, her body protested. Picking up his backpack, he said, "Let me help you." Sliding an arm around her waist, he hugged her to him. "Want me to carry you?"

She looked at him. Was that supposed to be a joke?

Somewhat blinded by the deflected beam of his headlamp, she couldn't see into his eyes. Of course it wasn't a joke. It was an offer. An assist.

Not a romantic sweep off her feet. "Walking is fine."

Lisa didn't trust herself in his arms. She wouldn't want him to let go. She'd want him to carry her, hold her through the night. She'd been entertaining thoughts of him all evening, relishing his nearness, his warm, solid, masculine presence. Until her ordeal today, she had never realized the appeal of a man like Walsh. The arduous circumstances made her long for his touch.

Pulling the sleeping bag snugly around her body, Lisa allowed him to support the bulk of her weight as they walked to her shelter. The sooner she went to sleep, the sooner she'd wake up and get down the mountain. She'd get her injuries attended to, her life back to normal and her research back on track. After their discussion of boyfriend-girlfriend, Walsh didn't make another move toward the personal. They had participated in a factual exchange of events. A bond the two shared in hardship. He didn't make a pass at her, though if he had, she would have welcomed it.

When they made it to her shelter, they lowered together as one and she hesitated. How exactly was she going to do this? The sleeping bag was completely unzipped. She'd need to zip it closed, place it in position and slide inside. Glancing at Walsh, his light directed into the dark confines of her dwelling, she said, "I need to get the sleeping bag situated, I guess."

"About the sleeping bag..."

It suddenly occurred to her there was only one and it was wrapped around her body at the moment. The pack he carried was flat, empty. Empty of a sleeping bag, anyway. Walsh would be cold tonight in only short-sleeves and no jacket. "I'm sorry. Do I have the only sleeping bag?"

"You do."

"Oh." She glanced around, realizing in an instant where this was going. Visions of his body lying next to hers in the narrow confines of his sleeping bag rapidly became very real. Tangible. She and Walsh would be sleeping together this evening. Very closely together. Lisa gulped. "Well, um, we can share it."

Chapter Eighteen

Walsh wondered how she was going to take the news. He knew it wouldn't be comfortable for her sleeping with a stranger, but it was a helluva lot more comfortable than what he would have proposed, should the temperatures have been much colder. Survival ranked number one, and there was no greater source of warmth than two naked bodies pressed together. A fact he didn't have the heart to reveal, though he found the prospect appealing. Incredibly so. He tried to smile. "I didn't have time to grab two."

Lisa's mouth hung agape, as though she found it the lamest excuse on the planet. But truthfully, he hadn't anticipated another night on the mountain. In the back of his mind, maybe, but front and center had been his concern for her immediate warmth when he found her—a find he'd expected much sooner. As it stood, the two of them needed to stay warm, and there was only one sleeping bag.

"Well, er—I..." Lisa stammered like a fool. An incredibly cute fool, but it was clear she wasn't sure about the prospect of sleeping with him. She brushed hair from her face and asked in a tone that horribly missed its mark at nonchalance, "Sure, it's no problem. Do you think we'll both fit?"

"It will be tight, but we can make it. My bag is larger than most, and you, you're smaller than most." Innocent hazel eyes blinked and Walsh felt like a heel, almost like he should tough it out in the cold so she could maintain her sense of privacy.

"Almost" being the key word. "Don't worry. You're safe with me." The statement didn't seem to calm her as she tripped unwrapping the bag from her shoulders. Reaching to catch her, he asked, "Are you okay?"

"Um, hm."

Biting down on her lip, she was obviously biting back the pain of her ankle. Holding her narrow upper arm, Walsh helped her out of the sleeping bag and quickly folded it closed. Crawling inside her shelter, he stretched it out over the branches she'd carefully layered on the ground and had to admit, he was impressed. The woman knew how to build a shelter when the elements turned on her.

Sliding a hand over the corner of his bag, he turned his body within the tight space, careful not to knock down her walls and keep the direct beam of his lamp out of her eyes. Flipping the bulb to red, he gestured to her feet. "Let's get your boot off."

"Yes, of course," she replied and allowed him to help, offering no protest when he took it and set it alongside the other.

Zipping it partway closed, he said, "You slip inside first."

In the red hue of light, her hesitance was pronounced. Eerily so. She looked like a frightened victim in a bad horror flick, her pupils balls of red-toned white. All signs of ease had been wiped from her expression, replaced by a marked reluctance.

Walsh felt bad. Really bad. "I can sleep outside if you want me to."

"No, you don't have to."

Unsure whether to take the quick response as a sign she was okay with it or a sign of nerves, he reassured, "I won't die of frostbite."

"But you'll be cold." She glanced out the cave-like opening. "It's got to be thirty degrees!"

"I brought a long-sleeved T-shirt."

She cocked her head to the side and eyed him pointedly. "That won't be enough."

Walsh shrugged. He'd tried. "If you're sure..."

Lisa teetered on her response but ended with an, "I'm sure."

Discussion closed. Walsh held the bag open for her as she crept inside, wriggling until her feet were down to the end. Scooting as closely as possible to one side, she turned on her side and waited for him to slide in and spoon her. Walsh vacillated. Was that really a good idea? Cradling her within his arms could only lead to thoughts and feelings he shouldn't be having. "Now you move over, and let me slide in and you can hold onto my back. If you want to."

An awkward pause suggested she was visualizing the potential positions. Her reply confirmed it. "Okay. That sounds better. I mean *good*. Fine."

Walsh smiled, unable to suppress a swell of amusement. She was definitely an innocent. No boyfriend. He bet she spent all her time in the research lab with her toads and not in close quarters with the opposite sex.

Pulling the pistol from his waistband, he ignored the alarmed look in her eyes as he set it aside. He removed his boots, then worked his socked feet into the bag, sliding in behind them. He'd been in tighter spots than this and knew how to effectively manipulate his body, getting it where he needed it to be, when he needed it to be there. Let's hope he could wield the same control over his *entire* body.

Turning out his headlamp, Walsh set it next to his weapon and burrowed into place, marveling at the slender angles of her body as she adjusted to his presence. Lisa was slim. To feel her in the dark, he'd swear she was all bones, but he knew better. He'd seen her in action, knew there were muscles coating those bones. Bones. Bone. "Are you comfortable?" he asked, distracting himself from anything but her comfort.

"Yes."

Molded to his back, she felt like a skinny monkey. She didn't hold him, exactly, but without much room to maneuver, she was pressed smack-flat against him. "How's your ankle? Do you have enough room?"

Emitting a half-laugh, a low sound just behind his ear, she replied, "And if I don't?"

Good question. "Well, let me know if I'm squishing you," he said, already beginning to warm from the close contact within the insulated bag. "Maybe I can alter my position."

When Lisa didn't say anything, Walsh took it to mean she was fine. Fine. Visions of her face and body formed in his mind. Recalling the feel of her body when he'd hugged her earlier, the fragile quality of her hesitance at their sleeping arrangements... She was fine, all right. More than fine. He'd definitely like to be with a woman like her.

He hoped he hadn't gone too far. He had a few years on her, experience that meant the difference between handling a situation and allowing a situation to handle him. Lisa was young. Smart, tough, but she was young. Green.

"You know," she said, "it's said in survival situations that sleeping naked in a sleeping bag conducts more warmth between two bodies than wearing clothes."

It was a mere murmur, yet her words cut a hotwire through his core. Adrenaline flushed through him. *Was she proposing they sleep naked together?*

"I appreciate that you deferred to the second-best method."

Shot down. Smiling at the absurdity of where his thoughts had tried to go, he replied softly, "You're welcome." So much for the naïve factor, he mused. Should have known she was as well-versed in survival techniques as he.

Without warning, Lisa slid an arm over his body. She didn't move any other parts, only one arm, the other safely tucked between them. The feel of her bare skin against his arm was hot—hotter than any other part between them. Walsh waited to see if she'd press closer. If she'd go further. If he had his way, their positions would be reversed. He'd spoon her and scoop her close against his body, keep her warm and cozy all night long.

But that would lead to thoughts more sinister. Thoughts he couldn't control, though a part of him figured a one-night stand with a woman he was never going to see again wasn't criminal. Instead, it was the perfect combination.

Another part of him knew it was wrong-headed. Wade knew her, knew her father. It wouldn't be right. Releasing a sigh, Walsh thought, it was better this way. In the morning, she was leaving. They were leaving, heading down the mountain where he would deliver her safely to her father. And when he did, he would miss her. Spirited, willful, Lisa had been a breath of fresh air in his world. A ton of trouble and stress, but a breath of fresh air, renewing his faith in the human spirit.

Lisa definitely had spirit and then some. She was determined to do things her way, on her terms. Like chasing toads. Walsh thought about the single-minded focus she'd displayed when it came to the amphibians, how she disregarded her own safety for the pursuit of science, the cause for preservation. She seemed more interested in saving the toads than she was with saving herself. Walsh couldn't imagine having a daughter like Lisa. Worrying about her whereabouts would be a constant stress. It didn't matter that she was an adult. Walsh's older brother, Justin, had said it all. Handing the keys to his teenage daughter had been the worst day of his life. Said it was like watching an infant walk into a war zone. She had no clue what lay in wait for her.

Justin understood. He served, same as Walsh. He'd witnessed the worst of people, knew what they were capable of. A sudden onslaught of sights and sounds, blown off body parts, blood, dirt, gunfire assaulted him until he fought them off. War was ugly. Politicians were uglier. Corrupt. They were power brokers that served only themselves. Walsh wanted nothing to do with them or a society that turned a blind eye and allowed these people to retain their power. There was no honor anymore. No honor among thieves and whores, no honor among the ignorant masses that allowed them to prosper. It was a world to which he wouldn't return. Whether he spent his time on this mountain remained to be seen, but one thing he knew for certain, McIntyre Walsh would not rejoin as a normal member of society.

Quieting the notion, he realized it made the prospect of tomorrow all the sadder. He would miss looking out for Lisa. The last couple of days had been a refreshing change of pace, reminding him of what it was to be a Marine. Honor. Duty. Protect. All for a worthy cause. Lisa was definitely worthy. She wasn't silly or superficial, she wasn't shallow or stupid. She was smart, strong. When the going got tough, she got tougher. Exhaling heavily, he settled on the notion. Definitely worthy of a man's time and attention.

"Everything okay?"

His insides zipped taut. "Sure. Why do you ask?"

"You feel tense."

He was tense all right, in more ways than one. "Just trying to get used to this lumpy bed you made," he teased, drawing his mind from its gloom. "You know a lot about camping, but whoever taught you to construct a bed out of dead pine branches?"

"I used what I could," she replied, a hint of defense in her voice.

"Why didn't you use the green pine branches? Would have made for a more comfy slumber."

"I am not killing live branches from a tree."

Walsh chuckled. "You are such a granola." The arm she'd looped around his body tensed. Did she consider it an insult? Walsh figured she would be fine with the slang term. No big deal. It did describe her. "Did I say something wrong?" he asked.

"My dad used to call my mom that. Granola."

The drop in her tone warned this was sensitive territory. "Did she not like it?"

"I don't think she cared," Lisa murmured. "Not really."

Walsh didn't know if Lisa's mother was still in the picture, but he wasn't about to ask, not with the wistful longing whispering behind him. "It's not a negative term," he said. "It's just slang for nature girl."

"My mom was that, for sure."

"She still around?" he asked, despite himself.

"She passed away when I was twelve."

Walsh's heart splintered. "I'm sorry." Feeling her movement behind him, he asked, "You need me to move something?"

"No, you're fine. You're right. My mattress stinks."

"I was only teasing about that," he said, eyes wide open in the dark. It had been his way of mentally changing the subject. Was she doing the same?

Probably, he decided, asking, "Ever run into a bear before?"

"I've seen them, yes, but never up close and personal."

"I hope that bear we saw ate our friend today."

Lisa tapped his arm and said, "You don't mean that."

Indulging in the intimate gesture, the featherweight touch of her fingertips on his bare hand, he said, "I do, actually. The guy would deserve it, after the way he's been slaughtering women. At least it's natural," he added, glad she couldn't see the grin on his face. "Nature girl should appreciate nature at work, right?"

"Not exactly."

In the distance, a coyote howled.

"I've never run into one of those, either," she said, moving her hand slightly more snug against his.

"Me, neither," Walsh returned, mentally zeroing in on the bare skin connection. Reaching up with his bottom arm, he placed his free hand over hers. When she didn't object, Walsh breathed easier. Strange how in the dark he felt free to take the liberty of touching her this way. During daylight hours he wouldn't dream of it. It would be too forward, too intimate. But here, in the close contact of his sleeping bag, it was acceptable.

Desire surged through him. More than acceptable, it was pleasurable. Lisa's hand was warm and soft. He could feel the delicate bone structure of her fingers. Threading their fingers together would have been a natural move, but one he wasn't about to attempt. This was enough. Don't push it, he told himself. Enjoy the moment.

It was a moment that had been too long in coming. Too long since he'd snuggled up with a woman he cared about. But damn, there was nothing like it. Nothing else in this world that filled him with peace, calm, like the arms of a woman he loved. Loved.

His heart pinched. Tomorrow was going to be tough.

Chapter Nineteen

Walsh woke before dawn but stayed put until he felt Lisa begin to stir. Temperatures were still colder than her T-shirt and shorts would tolerate, would remain so in fact, well into the morning. He contemplated building a fire. He could have it ready and toasty warm by the time she got up, but he opted to stay put. There was time enough to huddle fireside. His time cuddled in the sleeping bag with her was limited. Extremely limited, and he wanted it to last.

Would prolong it for as long as he could.

As Lisa slowly came to life behind him, Walsh imagined the thoughts coursing through her mind. His hand covered hers, his thumb folded into her palm. With daylight upon them, would she feel embarrassed? Awkward?

With each increasing ray of light, he felt it. Their intimacy was slipping through his fingers. Soon they would be up, out, separate. In a matter of hours they would be down, their journey together at an end. Was it wrong to want to delay?

"Are you awake?" she whispered.

"I am." The moment of truth. The moment of reckoning. "How'd you sleep?"

"Like a rock, for most of the night."

"Good. A warm rock?"

"A warm rock," she repeated affectionately.

Glad for the smile he heard in her voice, Walsh asked, "How's the ankle?"

"That's what woke me."

Of course. All that hiking yesterday would have aggravated the injury, and they needed to get it elevated and tended to. Immediately, he began to unzip the bag. "We need to get you out of this bag and that foot up," he said, killing his indulgence on the spot. It was good while it lasted, but reality was back. Lisa had injuries that needed attention. She needed sustenance, too. Fuel for the trip down. Slipping free of the bag, he turned and paused. "Whoa. Someone got some sun."

Lisa frowned. "My sunscreen didn't work as well as I'd hoped."

Her cheeks were red, her nose burned. At some point it would make a nice tan, but at the moment, it looked like it hurt. "You had sunscreen? Talk about prepared..."

"Aspen tree bark powder. It was the best I could do."

Walsh picked up the gun lying by his headlamp and slid it into the back of his pants. "Who knew?"

As she pulled the sleeping bag from her body, Walsh could see the skin across her chest was lobster red and briefly wondered about the rest of her. She mentioned drying her clothes in the sun. Had she been completely naked? Inappropriate images bombarded him, images he quickly snuffed out. He helped her from the bag and she reached for her boots. He stopped her. "Let's take a look at that foot first."

She obliged, and Walsh took the opportunity to inspect her injury, running his hands over and around the swell of flesh. Although she needed medical attention, his intense scrutiny of her foot was partly for his own pleasure. He liked touching her, taking care of her. While Lisa was an extremely capable woman, a part of him enjoyed being her caretaker.

Made him feel needed. "You did some damage yesterday."

Reluctantly, she agreed. "Couldn't be helped."

Stretching out the bandage, he re-wrapped her foot, then helped her with her socks and boots. Assisting her as she crawled out, he lifted her to her feet, placed an arm around her waist and supported her as he walked her to the fire ring.

She groaned. "Ouch."

"Am I hurting you?"

"Everything hurts." Peering up at him, she returned a wry smile. "I think my bruises are catching up with me."

You couldn't tell to look at her. Other than a pronounced effort at movement, there were no horrific marks on her legs, only the red flush on her skin from too much sun and a sparse overlay of scratches. No serious marks on her arms. For a woman bruised and battered, Lisa looked pretty darn good. "Well, no one would know it to look at you," he said. "You wear bruises better than anyone I've ever seen." Lisa smiled at the compliment. Light, easy, they were developing a rapport and it felt good. Really good. "On the flip side, your hair's a rat's nest."

She scowled. "Thanks a lot."

He grinned. "I'm teasing. You couldn't look bad if you tried."

She nailed him with a wary gaze, clearly not sure if he was serious. But he was. Dead serious. Lisa looked good. Tousled hair, sleep in her eyes, skin a bit puffy from a solid night's rest... The woman looked damn good.

Leaving her in place, Walsh walked quickly back to their overnight shelter and picked up the sleeping bag and headlamp. The air was cold, and Lisa would be chilled in a matter of minutes. Unzipping the bag, he shook it free of any dirt and debris that might have filtered in and placed it around her shoulders. Tossing the light onto his pack, he watched her comb most of the tangles from her hair with her fingers. "I think you're ready for that photo shoot."

Lisa rolled her eyes. "I wouldn't go that far."

He would. He most definitely would. "Have a seat. I'm going to collect firewood."

"Do you think we need one?"

He stopped short. "You don't?"

"Shouldn't we head down?"

His spirits fell. "Sure. But you're going to be cold in only that T-shirt and shorts. Don't you want to wait and let the sun have a chance to come out and warm things up?"

Lisa smiled, her face opening into a thing of beauty. "Hiking warms my blood."

"That it does," he agreed, quelling a swell of disappointment. He wasn't ready for their campout to end, but as he gazed into intent hazel eyes, it was clear that she was ready to go. "First we need food and water." She nodded. About to give her a hard time about her non-meat ways, he decided against it. "Lucky for you I have a spare energy bar."

Her gaze lit up. "You do?"

"I do," he replied, taking satisfaction in the mix of surprise and gratitude he saw staring back at him. She wasn't the only one who'd come prepared for survival. He had a few skills of his own and no interest in forcing her to desert her principles. "Berry nut. I hope it's your favorite."

She grinned. "It's absolutely my favorite!"

Happy to have pleased her, Walsh grabbed his backpack and pulled out the bar. Tearing open one end of the shiny yellow packaging, he handed it to her. "Dig in."

Taking it from him, she asked, "What are you going to eat?"

"Beef ravioli, the meal of mountain men."

Lisa giggled. "Ravioli? Seriously?" Taking a bite from the energy bar, she chewed and winked. "Don't worry, your secret's safe with me."

Walsh pitched back a smirk. Apparently she didn't care for his comment last night about the vegan sneaking a bite of meat. "Very funny."

"Ravioli. Breakfast of champions."

Walsh grunted. She made it sound like sissy food. "I'll challenge you to a race, anytime, sweetheart. Anytime."

"Careful. I might take you up on it and show you up."

"You?"

She nodded. Taking another bite, she waggled her eyebrows. "Straight up the mountain."

Walsh laughed, thoroughly amused. The thought of Lisa outdoing him in a mountain climb was ridiculous. She was good, but he outweighed her in power and speed, tenfold. He trained for much more daunting challenges and had beat them, but he did like her spirit. She thought she could win, and that in itself was attractive. Very.

Ripping open his MRE, Walsh sucked the ravioli from inside the tan-brown packet, downing the contents within minutes. No formality, no manners, he ate like a man who needed to eat. This was about hunger fulfillment, not taste. Survival. Fancy pretense need not apply.

Lisa understood. She'd been known to ditch the etiquette herself on occasion. Once, she'd kneeled down on all fours and drunk water from a shallow pool collected on the surface of a boulder, like a dog. No bottle of spring water, no stream or lake for miles, she'd been completely high and dry—literally—and had to drink the standing water to stave off dehydration.

Speaking of water, she needed some, *bad*. Her throat felt like strips of bark, her sunburned skin stinging tight in the frigid mountain air. Her sunscreen had done its best to mitigate the damage, but it was no match for full-on, Colorado high country sunshine. She could use some aloe, but at the moment, a cool stream would go a long way toward easing the burn and quenching her thirst. "I need some water."

Crunching the empty packet in his fist, Walsh stuffed the paper into an outer pocket of his backpack. "Let's re-wrap your wrist first."

Without waiting for her reply, Walsh reached for her hand and sat, taking her down with him. Gingerly, he placed her injured wrist on his knee and carefully peeled off the bandage. Once again, she sat passively as he took control and deftly managed her injury, his wrapping pattern more precise and organized than hers. As he held her hand in his, their eyes met. "Thank you," she said abruptly, her thoughts split between his delicate hold and the muted heather-green of his eyes. "Thank you for everything you've done for me."

Walsh's mouth pulled at the corner, too reserved for a full-fledged smile, yet deep enough to reveal a dimple. "You're welcome. I'm glad I was around to help."

"Me, too." More than she imagined she would be. Walsh felt comfortable, secure. He felt like an ally, a friend. Her gaze lingered on his dark brows and high cheekbones, his browned skin... Walsh was attractive. He was strong and rugged, and good-looking. Different looking, interesting looking. Lisa's pulse quickened as he caught her staring.

"Ready?"

At the flush of warmth in her neck and cheeks, she swallowed. "Yes."

As he rose, she said, "We need to scatter the ashes." She handed him the sleeping bag, startled by the cool air. It was an instant chill to her warmed skin.

"Keep it."

"But I need to help you."

"Keep the bag," he said, gently pushing it back into her hands. "I'll take care of it faster alone."

Knowing he didn't mean it as an insult but unable to shake the blunt edge of his words, Lisa hung in place as Walsh went about the business of clearing the fire. Next, he dismantled her shelter and tossed the branches about the tree and nearby ground.

"Okay," he said. Reaching down for her walking stick, he swapped it for the sleeping bag and energy bar wrapper. Folding the bag lengthwise, he rolled it and crammed it into the main section of his backpack, tucking the wrapper in with it. "The way down from here is through those trees," he pointed, closing the pack and shifting it onto his back. "First stop, the stream."

"Perfect."

Allowing Walsh to assist, Lisa picked her way to the stream, careful not to misstep again and exacerbate her ankle. At the water's edge, she found a spot to sit, and cupping her good hand, filled her mouth with cold mountain water. Shocking, quenching. She placed a wet hand to her cheeks and nose, the water biting in a wonderfully refreshing sort of way.

"I bet that feels good," Walsh said, scooping a few sips of water for himself.

"Oh, it does," she moaned over the babble of water. "You have no idea. You probably never burn, do you?"

"Not usually."

Lucky for him. She doubted the military offered sun-screen to the soldiers battling in war zones. Camouflage face paint was about it, though it wasn't like he needed it. Walsh's skin was made for the sun, unlike hers. Combine her father's fair-haired complexion and her mother's pearly white skin, and she burned just thinking about the sun!

Splashing some water on her thighs, Lisa sucked in a gasp at the sharp chill. Gritting her teeth, she thought maybe the whole body spray wasn't such a good idea. The air was too cold and she underdressed.

Walsh took note of her reaction but said nothing. Drag-ging wet hands down his face, he wiped water over his fore-head, cheeks, and nose. It reminded her of a mountain bath, rinsing the dirt and grime off after a day's hike. Funny, but Walsh didn't smell. Not when she was close to him, not last night—his body scent was negligible. Well, she thought, looking down into the water, that's not entirely true. He had a scent, but a rugged one. A very male one.

After taking another few handfuls for drink, Lisa wanted to get moving. She needed to warm up and get her thoughts focused on topics other than Walsh and the smell of his skin. "I'm ready," she announced.

"Okay. Let's get to it," he said. Pulling the phone from his pocket, he began to type into the keypad.

Lisa chuckled. It was like he gave them a step-by-step account of their every move. She was glad for it, but it struck her as peculiar. It seemed so out of character for a man like Walsh.

He looked up. "Something funny?"

"You. You're like a scientist who inputs every detail while an experiment is underway."

"Is that a problem?"

"No." She gave a quick shake to her head. "It just seems weird coming from a guy like you."

He cocked his head. "And what exactly is a guy like me?"

"Oh, you know," she began, but paused, realizing she didn't know exactly. "You seem more the rugged individual who reports to no one but himself than conscientious note-taker."

"I'm a Marine. We report everything to our commanders."

Lisa looked at him. "But you're not a Marine anymore."

Walsh smiled. "Once a Marine, always a Marine. Besides, I'm responsible for getting you down safely. There are people waiting for you, and it's important to keep them abreast of our movements."

"You don't expect trouble, do you?"

"I always expect trouble and take precautions to avoid it."

What should have been a settling thought made her nervous. The killer wouldn't care about them. They were together now, headed down the mountain. Why chase them?

It seemed too much risk for someone who was committing crimes and didn't want to be caught. But Lisa had never concerned herself with how the criminal mind worked, and she didn't expect to start now. Her goal was survival, and Walsh would see to it that she did.

Taking her by the elbow, he escorted her as she gimped along with her walking stick. The hike shouldn't take too long from here, an hour or so under normal circumstances, three at the rate she was going. But that was fine with her. Lisa was enjoying her time with Walsh. Nature was awakening around them, a sprinkling of chirps and squeaks, animals darting about the trees and brush, dapples of light growing across the forest floor. Crisp and cool, the morning temperature remained too cold for comfort, but with Walsh close by, she felt warmed. Invigorated. He was so different from her in so many ways—big ways, small ways—yet they shared a love for the mountains.

Walsh had an appreciation for nature and it showed. He took care with the land, considered his impact. If he didn't love it, he wouldn't have chosen mountain living. There were

plenty of other places to hide—to decompress, she corrected—but Walsh chose Colorado high country, the heart of her
existence.

"So how long are you planning on staying up here?" she
asked.

"Haven't decided yet."

"Indefinitely?"

"For the time being," he replied, chucking a smile behind his reply.

"So I might run into you again sometime."

"You might."

Lisa wanted to ask if that would be okay with him, her
running into him again, enjoying a friendly visit. Thoughts
from last night peppered her mind, conjuring up pleasurable
feelings at the prospect of future visits. It had been nice to
share the sleeping bag with him. Cozy. Intimate. A flutter of
nerves swarmed her breast. Definitely nice. Nice enough
she'd like to get to know him more. Stealing a peek at him,
she wondered if he felt the same. She lingered on his profile,
the high ridge on his straight nose, his strong jaw line, the
determined set of his mouth. Did he want the same? He said
she was beautiful, asked if she had a boyfriend...

Could he see himself in that role? Could she?

A lump rose to her throat. Walsh was an attraction she
couldn't deny, a situation far from ideal, yet one she wanted
just the same.

Around them trees and leaves came alive with light. No
longer trekking through the chill of shadow, they were coming upon open land. Walsh walked ahead of her and looked
around, scanning the tree line, the grassy land between here
and the next patch of forest. He was searching for bad guys,
danger. She, on the other hand, was plain old enjoying the
view.

Joining him at the forest's edge, she soaked in the sight
of meadow and rocks, slanting sweeps of evergreen and aspen in the distance marking the way down. There were no
rocky mountain peaks to be seen from this vantage point, just

a reprieve in the mountainside, a gentle slope before the next steep drop that would eventually open the view to the town. "It's so beautiful, isn't it?"

"It is."

"I love it up here," she said breathlessly, losing herself in the terrain she adored. "I could stay here all day."

"Not today, you won't."

Lisa snapped her attention to him, protest hovering on her lips. Walsh returned a stern gaze. "No detours." His hand staunchly encircled her elbow. "We go straight down."

"What if I need to rest?" she challenged.

"Do you?"

No. But she bet if she claimed she did, he'd let her. Delight at the thought surged and she smiled. "No."

"Okay." Glancing in both directions, he said, "Let's go."

Suddenly she felt like a prisoner, Walsh marching her toward her captors. Across the swath of grass they traveled, slowing as the land gave way to a spill of boulders. One of earth's many gouges, it was a pretty tricky drop, at least for her condition. "Is there an easier way down?" she asked.

"Not nearby." Grunting, Walsh cursed under his breath. "I forgot about this section."

Craning her head, she thought, maybe it wasn't all that bad. The boulders were pretty big, a lot of them with flat, wide open surfaces. She could probably work her way from one to another with Walsh's help. Below, a collection of brown roofs were visible, a few of the higher-elevation homes in the valley. Around the bend to the west would be the village central where buildings became dense in proximity, but remained mostly brown and tan. Silver Creek was a western-themed resort town with a mildly European flair. As more international money flooded in, she expected that trend to increase. Her friend Kinsley's father was an investor in the resort and according to her, expansion was definitely on the horizon.

Walking to the edge, Walsh inspected the area below, perused their surroundings and ran through their options. Lisa could almost see his mind at work, running data like a computer, spitting out his best-case scenario for getting her down.

"I might be able to do it," she offered.

Pausing on her, his gaze darkened. "With only one good hand and one foot, you'll slip and fall."

"You might be surprised."

"I might—if I were inclined to let you try it, which I'm not."

Hmph. He might have a point, he might not. Lisa thought it was worth a try. She was about to insist when Walsh stepped away.

"Wait here," he instructed and headed toward the nearest line of trees. Lisa watched him jog in and waited while he did whatever investigation he was doing. She thought he knew this route. She thought *she* knew it, but when they came out of the trees, they were more east than she realized. Not that it was a big deal. It would still lead them down.

Trouble was, she couldn't travel just any terrain. She needed more slope than steep. Displeasure curled around her gut. It made her feel like a wimp. Granted, she was injured, but she didn't like special accommodations being made on her account. Leaning on her stick, she expelled a sigh. This stunk.

Minutes passed and still no Walsh. Taking a few steps in the direction he'd gone, Lisa grew concerned. There was no sign of him in the distant tree line. Nothing but black caverns tucked between branches of evergreen. How far was he going before he decided which way was best? Why didn't they just head through the trees and take it as it came? It couldn't be that bad.

Moving closer to the edge, Lisa peered down. It wasn't *that* far down. Maybe twenty feet to the first boulder, a cascade of smaller gray stones lay above it, as though strewn there from an avalanche or explosion. If she could navigate those without catching her ankle, she'd be fine. There were several cantilever-shaped rocks, some rounded, others pointed, most of which she could grab hold and use to steady her progress. She could probably do it.

It was certainly worth a try.

She studied the terrain farther down the mountain. The incline lessened considerably, dropping into a wide valley of grass and dirt punctured by a few rocks and bordered by young pine. Glancing back toward the trees where Walsh had disappeared, she willed him to return. Standing idle was not on her agenda.

A loud crack exploded the quiet. Pain ripped through her shoulder.

Spun by a powerful force, her knees buckled and she hit the ground. Lisa's mind went blank. All feeling went blank.

What the—?

She tried to make sense of what happened. She tried to get up, but her head swayed. Trying to move again, Lisa rolled off the cliff.

Chapter Twenty

At the sound of gunfire, Walsh froze. Every cell in his body echoed the crack of the bullet. *Lisa.*

Whirling, he took off running. Instantly transported back to the desert the day his best friend was shot, Walsh fought a rising panic. As he tore through trees, branches whipped his arms, lashed at his face—he ducked the worst of them. Urgency and dread tore through his skull.

A gunshot. Lisa was alone. Pumping his arms, he forced himself harder, faster, pummeling boots to the ground as he ran to her. Sprinting around a huge pine, he ran out into open field. There was no Lisa, only a man he'd seen before.

A man standing near where he'd left Lisa. A man he recognized, one he could kill with his bare hands. Pulling the gun from his waistline, Walsh fired, his first two rounds missing completely. Too far. The guy took off running in the opposite direction.

Walsh charged after him, firing another round at his back, but his aim was sporadic.

Evading a direct hit, the stranger took his own shot before escaping into the forest, the dark green of his shirt blending quickly into the trees.

"Damn it!"

Stopping short at the site he left Lisa, Walsh ground back his anger. He spotted her stick on the ground, but she was nowhere to be seen. Had she run? Instinct pushed his gaze over the edge of the short cliff and the earth gave way beneath him. *Lisa.*

Twenty feet below, her body lay splayed on the rocky terrain below. Blood oozed from beneath her T-shirt, crimson red against the pale yellow cotton. Her eyes stared up at him, vacant. Clammy fear punched him in the gut. Walsh jumped over and slid down the rocks to get to her.

"*Lisa*, talk to me. Are you okay?" Her dulled eyes trailed him, but she said nothing. "Don't move," he commanded, assessing her condition. She'd been shot in the shoulder. She'd fallen. Her back could be broken. She could have suffered a concussion. A thousand possibilities raced through his mind.

Walsh tore off his shirt, folded it lengthwise and carefully slid it under her wounded shoulder. Without closer inspection, he couldn't discern exit and entry status, what might have been affected internally. There was no time. Pulling ends up, he tied his shirt snug to create a crude tourniquet-like bandage. Folding the excess material over the top, he pressed the heel of his hand over the wound and applied pressure. Stop the bleeding was job number one.

Blood. There was a lot blood.

Snatching the phone from his pocket, he furiously typed. *EMERGENCY. Repeat EMERGENCY. Lisa down, gunshot wound. Suspect on run. Stat evac.* Walsh followed with his coordinates and sent the message. Setting the phone aside, he placed his free palm over her forehead, searching her eyes for response. "Can you hear me?"

She nodded. Almost imperceptible, but it was there. Checking her pulse, he found it spotty, erratic. Her sunburned skin had lost its tinge, her eyes, their luster.

No, dammit, no. You're not gonna die on me. A swarm of emotions took hold, mixing faces and places in Walsh's mind. A buddy from the unit had died in his arms. Gunshot to the chest, he never stood a chance of getting out alive. But Lisa did. They weren't hours from the nearest help. Her injury wasn't a gaping chest wound. It was shoulder—non life-threatening.

Except for the blood.

The sight of blood seeping into his shirt at her shoulder unsettled him. Dark and sticky, it dredged up painful memories. Single-handedly wrenching the pack from his back,

Walsh pulled out the sleeping bag and covered the length of her body with it. Next he lifted her ankles and slid the backpack beneath them. It wasn't perfect, but it was all he had.

"Hold on," he urged her, reapplying pressure to her wound. "You got this. Slow your breathing. Can you do that for me?" he asked, willing her to respond. "Can you calm your breathing?"

She simply stared.

Pressure squeezed his chest. Replacing his hand to her forehead, he said, "You're gonna be okay. You're gonna get through this." Walsh couldn't lose her—not now—not after they'd made it this far. They were less than an hour from reaching bottom. She had to stick with him. She couldn't give up. Not this close.

Close. Glancing over his shoulder on impulse, Walsh scanned the perimeter. Where had the guy come from? The entire way down today, Walsh hadn't seen a single person. No one. He'd looked, kept watch, but there had been no one to see. His phone vibrated on the rocks. Snatching it from the ground, he read. *Sending helo up. Report status.*

Maintaining one hand on her shoulder, Walsh thumb-typed his reply. *Gunshot wound. Bleeding. Shock. Possible back injury.* He hated to send the message. It would only escalate Wade's concern. But he had to get the message across. Things were bad. There was a killer on the loose. A killer Walsh should have downed with one shot, but firing while running didn't always mesh. His aim was rusty from lack of use.

"Walsh?"

"Shhhh…" he told her. "Don't try to talk. Save your energy. Breathe."

He wished he had something more substantive to place over her wound. His shirt was like putting a Band-Aid on a sucking chest wound. It was temporary. A stop-gap. He wanted to check the point of entry, evaluate her more thoroughly, but he wasn't about to release pressure. Not for something he couldn't fix.

At least the guy hadn't hit a vital organ. Unfortunately, Walsh couldn't rule out back or head injury, though he saw no blood coming from beneath her head. Eyeing the spot on her shoulder, he ground his jaw. Too much blood loss from any source was enough to kill a person.

Dammit—where was Roan?

Wade Davis keyed up his radio. Walsh's last message accelerated the situation. "Alpha One Hundred to Air One, you up yet?"

Static erupted on the line as Roan replied over the pulse of copter blades in the background, "En route, sir."

"Advise your medic we have a bullet wound, possible back injury."

"Roger."

"Report when you spot our victim."

"Copy. ETA, five minutes."

"Copy," Wade clipped, clenching the mic close to his mouth. Victim. He hated to refer to Hal's daughter as a victim. It felt like one of his own was down. *Gunshot wound. Bleeding. Shock. Possible back injury.*

Please, God, no. She was too young. This couldn't be happening to her. Speaking into his mic, Wade added, "Suspect on the loose, armed and dangerous."

"Roger."

Staring at the slew of paperwork on his desk, the myriad details and papers awaiting his signature, Wade put it all on hold. He had a crisis on his hands. A situation. There was a gunman loose on the mountain. Lisa had been shot. No telling how many more victims the guy might add to his list before they caught up with him.

One thing for certain, Wade was determined to make Lisa his last. Bringing the mic to his mouth, he pressed the button and called out, "Alpha One Hundred to Battalion Twenty."

"Battalion Twenty, go ahead."

"Have you started up the mountain yet?"

"Affirmative. Team is ten minutes in."

"ETA to victim's location?"

"Approximately thirty minutes."

"Copy. Helo is en route. Gunman is armed and considered dangerous."

"Roger."

Wade checked in with his other team next. "Alpha One Hundred to Battalion Five."

"Battalion Five, go ahead."

"Need you to deploy an ALS transport unit to the landing zone. They have located victim and will be transporting her to the LZ shortly."

"Copy."

Wade's cell phone rang. Checking the caller ID, he frowned. Hal Richardson. He answered the call knowing it wasn't fair to ignore him. "Wade Davis."

"Why is there a helicopter going up the mountain?"

The man was like a hawk perched on the limb of his residence, watching the scene unfold minute-by-minute. Wade hated to tell him, but Hal was a friend. He'd been on countless searches and knew the drill. No sense in sugarcoating it for him. "Lisa's taken a fall, Hal."

"What? How bad?"

"Don't know."

"You're sending an evac team for her?"

"Yes. We have her coordinates. There's a clearing nearby her location."

After a heavy pause, Hal asked, "What are you not telling me?"

"She's been shot, Hal."

"Shot?"

The gutted quality to Hal's voice cut deep. Wade didn't have a daughter but could imagine what his friend must be going through. If the same happened to any one of his sons, he'd be frantic. "Seems they ran into our killer on the way down." At least that was the assumption. With no positive ID, Wade was going with logic. He wasn't a man who believed in idle coincidence. "Guy took a shot from a distance and she fell."

"How bad? How bad is it, Wade? The truth. Give me the truth."

Heaving a sigh, he admitted, "I don't know." It was the truth. Walsh only suggested "possible back injury." There was nothing solid, no hard facts as to her condition. The more vague he could be with Hal, the better. Upsetting the man wouldn't help the situation. Not when he was powerless to do anything about it. "My guys are five minutes out. I'll call you as soon as I know something certain."

"Please," Hal said. "Please, as soon as you know."

"You're doing great," Walsh cooed, seconds ticking like a time bomb in his chest. "Help is on the way." Detecting a faint smile in her eyes, he moved his gaze to her lips, disturbed by their chalky quality. Maintaining gentle pressure on her wound, Walsh knew Lisa needed medical attention, and she needed it now. He was trained in emergency care. He knew what to look for, knew how to administer. But without supplies, there was nothing more he could do for her. Except to encourage her. "You're not going to let a silly little bullet stop you, are you? Heck, it's only a flesh wound." He hoped. Walsh hoped it hadn't hit an artery. The blood loss concerned him, but it could be attributed to her panic. Partially. He didn't want to think of her bleeding out. Gaze darting upward, he willed the helicopter to appear.

C'mon, Roan. This is an emergency. Get that angel up here.

A bullet ricocheted off the rocks behind him. Walsh ducked. Heart kicking wildly, he searched for the source. Hunching over Lisa's body, he estimated the shot must have come from the trees where the man had disappeared. At slightly higher elevation, the edge of forest followed the slope of mountain downward, giving the guy a direct shot.

Scrutinizing the evergreens, the shadows between, Walsh searched for signs of him.

"Walsh?"

Beneath him, fear gripped Lisa's eyes as she looked at his gun. He said nothing, splitting his attention between her and the threat. Waiting for a second shot, he whispered, "Shhh... Don't try to speak."

Walsh felt her begin to tremble, but couldn't afford to comfort her at the moment. He needed to stay alert, honed in on the trees around them. In the distance, he heard the rhythmic thump of blades. *Roan.* Visions of large green heli-birds flying overhead assaulted his focus as the sound grew close. Heart pounding anew, Walsh pushed the images away. That was another day, another place. Stay in the here and now.

Looking down at Lisa, one hand on her shoulder, the other tightly gripped around his weapon, he told her, "Helicopter's here. We're going to get you out of here."

Her gaze darted back and forth over his face, intermittently jumping to somewhere beyond him—somewhere in the trees where a gunman lay hidden, watching them, somewhere in the sky where help was on its way.

Walsh could feel the threat. A soldier knew when he was being watched. It was the air, in the senses. It was palpable. Visceral. An active shooter was on scene. Controlling the urge to scan the perimeter and locate his target, Walsh kept Lisa front and center in his sights. There would be time enough later to hunt the man down. Right now, his job was getting Lisa to safety. "We're almost there, okay? I need you to stay calm and let us do all the work."

Another gunshot rang out. At the sudden change in sound overhead, Walsh jerked his head to see the bird dip its nose abnormally before lifting up and flying away.

No! Every fiber in Walsh's body caught fire. Roan couldn't go! Raising his weapon, he searched the trees for sight of the gunman. He could take him out with one shot. One shot. All he needed was a visual.

But Walsh saw nothing. Nothing but his reinforcements leaving.

The helicopter turned and swooped back down, headed for the trees.

They must have seen the shooter, Walsh mused. They were trying to flush him out before landing. Sharpening his focus on the bird, Walsh saw a blond-haired man hanging halfway out of the open side door. Satisfaction unfurled deep inside him.

Canyon Laredo. Had to be. Not too many men sported red bandanas around their neck. The guy was a bull-riding cowboy and one of the few people Roan trusted to fly with him. Damn near sniper-caliber, too. Canyon could take a shot from the air and end it on the right spot, though Walsh knew it was unlikely to happen. Roan had thermal image capability on board. He'd locate the suspect and direct ground officers to him. Protocol. Procedure.

It was a process Walsh didn't have time for.

Wade's radio erupted in static. "Air One command."

"Command, go ahead. You found our victim?"

"Roger that, but we've got company. We're taking fire."

"Repeat?"

"We're taking fire. We have a gunman in the trees. One shot, near miss. Advise on landing."

Wade fumed inwardly. Their guy had the nerve to take a shot at a police helicopter? Anger streamed through his veins. It was a decision he'd regret. Wade would make sure of it. Closing his mind to the vengeance flowing through him, Wade informed, "Patient needs emergency transport. It's your call."

Through the static, Roan's voice peppered through the roar of blades pulsing in the background. "That's affirmative, Air One going in hot."

"Copy that," Wade replied. Knowing Walsh, he'd be armed and perfectly willing to assist in providing cover. "Will advise Battalion Twenty."

"Copy."

Wade contacted the other team and advised them what was going on. Still a ways out, he could only hope they came in fast and furious and stopped the guy cold—if Walsh didn't take care of it beforehand.

Walsh waved to Roan as they flew over, the helicopter sweeping low before landing in a clearing of grass and rocks thirty yards away. Broad sections of terrain were flat and level, making it possible for Roan to set his bird down wherever he wanted, but it was clear he was putting space between helo and gunman. Canyon hopped out before the skids hit the ground and took off running toward Walsh. Two other men followed behind with a stretcher, their shirts blown violently by the heavy push of air from the whir of blades.

"You're gonna be okay, Lisa. Helicopter has landed and help is on the way."

She tried to smile but couldn't quite manage. Her body continued to shake.

Over six foot in height and agile as a mountain cat, Canyon jogged down the rocks with ease and made it to them in seconds, trauma bag in hand. "What do we have?"

"Gunshot to the shoulder. Possible back injury." Walsh hadn't wanted to say anything to Lisa for fear he'd upset her, but there was no hiding it from Canyon. They needed to transport her as worst case, not best. Gazing down at her, Walsh's heart ached. The mention hadn't slipped by her. Panicky fear had been replaced with deep-seated concern.

Two uniformed men negotiated the gravelly decline with more effort, while Canyon busily removed bandages and tape from his bag. Roan would stay with the bird, taking it up if threatened by gunfire.

Surrounding her, each man took to his task, one taking over the bleeding wound from Walsh, the other checking Lisa's vitals. A long-haired brunette said in a tone more suitable for a day in the park, "You're going to okay, sweetheart. No worries here, okay?"

Walsh was glad to see Lisa had pasted her gaze to the paramedic. These men meant the difference between full recovery or not. Taking a backseat to the first aid, Walsh quietly took Lisa's hand into his and held firm. Gentle but firm. He wanted her to know he was still here, still with her. He'd like to fly down with her, but his presence would do nothing but get in the way.

Scanning the tree line in question, Walsh trained his weapon on any and every possible position the shooter could maintain. He planned to stay behind and finish what a stranger had started.

When the men had Lisa loaded and secured on the stretcher, they worked in clockwork unison to carry her up, straddling rocks as they climbed toward the helicopter. The constant pulse of blades in the background was reassuring to Walsh as he accompanied Lisa and the medics over. Roan would have her down in minutes and to the hospital from there.

Hurrying over level ground, they ducked as they neared the aircraft. Walsh released her hand as they loaded her in. The men took seats on either side of her. Sun glinted from Roan's gold-framed aviator shades, his hand already working his stick.

Walsh remained stationed outside.

Panic gripped her features as she registered the fact he was staying behind. "You're not coming?"

Roan revved the engines and Walsh couldn't hear the words over the powerful turbine, though he could see them on her lips. Shaking his head, he shouted over the increase of blades ripping wind against the bare skin of his chest and arms. "I'll see you in a few!"

Roan was wasting no time. As the bird lifted from the ground, Walsh blew her a kiss before he realized what he'd done. The gesture seemed to ease her fear, bringing a smile to her face. Relief swept through him. He was afraid the impromptu move might have been too much.

Ducking as he backed away, he felt a strange sense of peace swirling around the steel edge of his resolve. Something between them had changed. In the heat of crisis, the two had become something more than strangers on a mountain.

Hovering feet above the ground, Roan gave a fleeting wave and thumb up before powerful engines lifted the helo higher. Dipping the nose forward, the bird was off. Walsh watched them go, the sound reverberating in his chest.

He would join her after he settled the score.

No man would walk away from shooting Lisa. Not if Walsh had anything to say about it. Turning on his heel, he ran toward the trees. Their shooter was about to receive a visit from his worst nightmare.

Chapter Twenty-One

From the command post of his office, Wade dialed Hal's number. He would want to meet Lisa at the hospital.

Hal answered on the first ring. "How bad is it?"

"She's going to be fine," Wade said, relieved to be able to deliver good news. "She suffered a gunshot to the shoulder, but Walsh minimized the blood loss until my guys were able to take over."

"Walsh."

"He's a good man," Wade said, understanding the defeat in Hal's tone. Walsh was a man Hal didn't know yet, but one who had played a crucial role in saving his daughter's life. Hal was no stranger to trauma. Without Walsh, Lisa could have bled out on the mountain before help ever arrived.

"I need to meet this man," Hal said resignedly.

Wade chuckled. "Maybe on your next hiking trip. He doesn't make it to town very often."

"Is he some kind of recluse?"

"No." Wade shook his head. "Just a man who's lost his patience with civilians. He'll come around. I'm just not sure when." Truth be known, Wade had never expected him to stay up there this long, and had tried to lure him down on several occasions with an offer for a full-time position on the force, but Walsh wanted nothing to do with it. He didn't mind assisting Wade's team, but it would be on his terms, no one else's.

While Walsh never went into detail on his grievance with the military, Wade heard bits and pieces from the other guys. Walsh had a man down. He went back for him but was ordered to stand down. Retreat. Walsh wouldn't stand down or retreat if it meant leaving a man behind. It went against the very fiber of his nature. According to the stories Wade heard,

Walsh ignored the order and it cost him. Seems it was a price he'd been willing to pay. Walsh retrieved his man, returning the soldier to his family, who was forever grateful. Then, at his first opportunity, he left the service and returned home.

Home. Wade sighed. Living in the wild was no home. It was a hideout. Why Walsh didn't go to Colorado Springs and be near his brother, Justin, and his family, didn't make sense. The two got along. Justin was ex-military, could empathize with Walsh's situation. Why not start fresh in friendly territory?

A squawk from the radio broke Wade's reverie. "Gotta go, Hal. I'll see you at the hospital."

"Will do, and thanks, Wade, for everything."

"Wouldn't have done it any other way." Ending the call, he clipped into his mic, "Copy, Battalion Twenty. You're on scene. Be advised McIntyre Walsh is in theater. Repeat, one of our own is in theater. Take necessary precaution."

"Battalion Twenty, copy. I know Walsh by sight."

Exhaling heavily, the noose around Wade's chest loosened. Good. Last thing he needed was friendly fire to take out one of his best men. "Roger. Advise when suspect located."

"Roger."

Wade was concerned about Walsh. Normally he exhibited military precision when it came to his work. Objective, focused, he got the job done. But this was personal. He'd been directly involved with Lisa and wouldn't take kindly to coming under attack. Walsh would want to pursue the man and make certain he put an end to the killing spree.

Wade wanted the suspect brought in for questioning, not brought down with a bullet to his head—a feat Walsh could manage with his eyes closed. A shot Walsh might feel justified in taking. Reaching for his cell phone, Wade began to type a message. *Suspect wanted alive.*

Staring at the words, a wave of ambivalence washed through him. Walsh was no amateur. He understood the stakes. He understood he wasn't on the battlefield of war where killing the enemy came with the territory. Jabbing the backspace button until the screen was clear, Wade retyped. *Be advised, team on scene. Battalion Twenty nearing your location Update status when possible.* Pressing send, he re-secured the cell phone to his belt and began to pace. The message had been sent. Police Chief Wade Davis would deal with whatever consequences landed on his desk in the aftermath.

Walsh ran toward the section of trees where he'd seen the shooter run. If he was still in there, Walsh would find him. If he'd gone, Walsh would hunt him down. He would make him pay for what he did to Lisa, tried to do to him. The phone in his pocket vibrated. Checking the message, he grunted. *Be advised. Battalion Twenty nearing your location.* It was the last thing he needed. Not only did he have to be on alert for his suspect, he had to be wary of friendlies in the arena. *Update status when possible.*

Don't worry, Wade. You'll be the first to know.

Slowing to a jog as he reached the outskirts of pine, Walsh angled his back and hugged the wide berth of an ever-green, leading with his gun. Mission one remained: locate and neutralize suspect. Fine-tuning his senses, Walsh honed in on every sight, every sound. He scanned his immediate vicinity for threats before moving his gaze farther into the distance. Searching between trees and bushes, he looked for anything out of the ordinary. Any color, shape or movement that didn't seem right, didn't belong. Calming his breathing, his pulse, Walsh played his usual game as he sifted through the terrain. *What doesn't fit?*

Mentally stripping the landscape to trunks and branches, his eyes grazed every inch of brown, green, and gray in trian-gular fashion. The man's green shirt would allow him easy camouflage. Motion was the key. Keeping his footsteps light and his head down, Walsh crept forward, swiping his glance from side-to-side-ahead before advancing. His movements were soundless, the air still. Inhaling fully, he dialed back his thoughts and gave in to instinct.

Let his gut lead the way. Watch for movement. *Feel for it.*

Peering through pine and brush, he searched for the enemy. He picked his way over rocks jutting from the ground, examined a fallen tree several yards ahead. It was the perfect cover for a man looking to conceal himself. Gun ready, he searched the ground, the length of the tree, the area behind. Satisfied no one was there, Walsh advanced. Slowly, he edged behind a tree, scoped the area beyond. There was a small clearing lit up by a break in the canopy, a spotlight shining upon one section of forest. He paused, straining to hear, listening for any sounds that might give away a man on the run.

Walsh heard nothing but the sound of his own breath. Moving through the area, his forefinger curled around the trigger, Walsh continued a three-hundred and sixty degree scan of his surroundings.

From here the ridge opened and sloped gently downward. Thirty yards to his left, sunlight drenched the landscape, a mix of scraggly-branched trees and rust-colored boulders. As he paused at the tree line, heat gathered on his neck and shoulders, his body temperature raised by the flush of adrenaline. Gazing out over the grassy hill, another thick layer of trees below, Walsh saw no one.

Then again, he didn't expect to. His quarry would be in hiding.

His intuition hummed, drawing his gaze to a group of boulders.

Suddenly, at the sound of voices, Walsh turned. Hikers? Wade's SAR team?

Looking back through the trees, he concealed himself while he searched for the source. Better he saw them before they saw him. Down across the clearing, he spotted a figure darting behind the cluster of massive rocks. Walsh took off running. That was no idle hiker. That was his shooter!

Voices shouted but Walsh ignored them. Leaping over rocks like track hurdles, he kept his gaze on his target. Gun aimed like an extension of his arm, he prepared to fire.

An arm shot up from behind the boulder and fired. Walsh ducked, then fired off one of his own. Behind him, male voices yelled.

Jumping sideways, Walsh dodged a rock, then sailed over a small bush as he ran. Out in the open now, he had no cover. But a moving target would be hard to hit, even for a professional. Sprinting straight across the grass, he charged for the boulder, ready to fire upon sight.

Walsh slowed. Breathing labored, he circled the rock like a cat ready to pounce. Cupping left hand under right, he steadied his weapon, then whipped it quickly behind the boulder where he'd last seen the man.

Shocked to see no one, he proceeded with measured step, finger tense on the trigger. Sun hot on his bare chest, Walsh squinted. He analyzed the terrain, digested the threat. There was a group of boulders below this one, then a forty-foot dash to the cover of trees. Doubtful his target could have run the distance in the time it took Walsh to get here.

But he was taking no chances. Senses on heightened alert, Walsh inched forward, scanning the stone surfaces. There was no need to run. Not with plenty of places to hide right here. Easing over to another rock, Walsh knew he had to be close. He leapt down, sweeping his gaze over the tumble of stone. *Show yourself. Give me the satisfaction and show yourself now.*

Behind him, a man shouted his name. "Walsh!"

Walsh recognized the voice but didn't acknowledge him. This loser was his.

Jumping to the ground, he landed hard. Spots for concealment were dwindling. Walsh was closing in. Like tracking a hot scent, he could feel it. Sweat slicked his arm as he led with his gun. Wade's men would not deprive him the pleasure of taking this scumbag in with his own two hands. Lisa's shooter belonged to him.

Catching a brown head of hair dash from rocks ten feet ahead, Walsh fired.

The bullet ricocheted off the rock by the guy's head.

"Walsh!"

Don't get excited, pal. It was nothing more than a teaser shot. If he'd wanted to hit him, he could have. Better to bait the fool into unloading his weapon out of panic, leaving him wide open for take-down.

Crouching, Walsh snaked along the rocks, dodging behind one as he spied the black barrel of a gun sticking out from behind a stone. In a flash, it fired, then disappeared.

Ducking as the bullet kicked up dust near his head, Walsh grunted. *Lucky shot.* Angling around the rock, weapon raised cheek-level, he looked for sight of his target, stopping short when he saw him running for the trees. Walsh stood and fired. The man whirled and the two locked gazes. Twenty feet separated them.

Twenty short feet. Steel coated Walsh's heart as he held steady. One shot and the man would be dead. One, right between the eyes.

The guy held his ground, gun pointed at Walsh. Faintly registering the presence of Wade's men, Walsh held his target in his crosshairs. *Go ahead. Give me justification.*

Taking a shot, the bullet hit a rock several yards away. Backing away, the guy stumbled, tripped, and took off in a mad dash. Walsh fired, taking him out with a shot to the leg. Crying out in pain, the guy crumpled to the ground.

Sprinting toward him, Walsh closed the distance in seconds.

The man raised his gun to fire at close range. Walsh fired first, popping the gun from the man's hand as he yelped. *Stupid decision.*

Stuffing gun in his waistband, Walsh straddled him, shoving his head to the ground with an angry thrust. He would have buried a fist in the guy's face as well, but not with company, he wouldn't.

Writhing beneath him, the guy clawed a bloodied hand at Walsh, smearing blood over his arm. "Give it up," Walsh growled. "You're finished."

Fury ripped through the man's gaze. A leg kicked Walsh in the back.

"*Sonofa*—" Leaning forward, Walsh pinned the man's arms over his head with a savage thrust of his elbow into his chest. Squeezing his thighs, he locked the man's body beneath him. Staring into the eyes of a killer, Walsh wanted to snap his neck. He could do it with his bare hands and never look back. Rage flashed as images of Lisa's bleeding body shot into his mind. It would be easy. *Snap*.

Three men from search and rescue gathered around him. "Walsh."

Logging their nearness, he stuffed his emotion back and rose, yanking the man from the ground. Wrenching the guy's arms behind his back, Walsh held himself in tight check. "I'm taking him down."

Exchanging a glance between them, then back to Walsh, no one objected. They understood that he was one of them, trusted by their commander. Backing off, the youngest of the three bent over and secured the stolen gun.

Walsh thrust the guy forward and he gasped, slumping forward, a growing blood stain spreading over his pant leg. The senior team member eyed the injury caused by Walsh's gunshot. "We need to wrap that."

Walsh would have preferred to let the man suffer. He pictured dragging the man and his bloodied leg down the mountain, same as Lisa had to drag her injured body down, but relinquished the thought. These men were only going by the book, a protocol he wasn't going to break out of respect for them. "Go ahead, but I'm holding on to him in the meanwhile."

Dropping to a knee, the team member wasted no time in gathering supplies from his black nylon pack. Walsh shoved the suspect to the ground, loosening his hold only enough to allow the paramedic to treat the wound. Deftly, silently, the man went about the business of cleaning the wound and wrapping it with sterile bandage.

Walsh could see the calculations running through the suspect's mind, how he could use this to his advantage, how he could make his escape. Walsh almost wished he'd try it. All he needed was a reason.

The SAR team radioed Wade. *Suspect in hand. Bringing him down.* Wade confirmed, then asked about Walsh. The man confirmed his presence.

"Tell him Lisa is on the table."

The man looked to Walsh. *Lisa was on the table. She was in surgery.*

Nodding, gripped by a sudden impatience, Walsh controlled the urge to hoist the suspect up from the ground and drag his butt down the mountain this second.

Walsh wanted to be there for Lisa. He needed to know she was going to be okay.

There was no way he could accept the alternative.

Chapter Twenty-Two

Masked and dressed in sterile gown and gloves, Hal Richardson watched from the corner of the operating room as the surgeons worked on his daughter. Machines bleeped, staff moved in coordinated silence as they assisted the trauma physician and his P.A. The women were competent, the best of the best, but observing as a spectator, Hal felt helpless, unnerved by the sight of his daughter's flesh and blood as the doctors cut and stitched beneath a bright overhead light. Hal had operated a thousand times, knew the anatomy exposed at their fingertips. Working feverishly to repair the damage caused by the gunshot and control blood loss, Hal could only hope they saved the nerves, allowing Lisa to retain full motion of her shoulder.

Glancing toward the monitors, Hal cataloged the information: pulse, blood pressure, oxygen saturation level. The anesthesiologist was good. He'd worked with the man hundreds of times and trusted him. Moving his focus back to the patient—his daughter—Hal's heart ached.

She had to be okay. He needed her to come through with minimal complications; however, he knew the odds. He knew the dangers. The bullet had almost gone clear through save for a small tear to the axillary artery. Too much blood loss would cause complications for anyone. Lisa was healthy. Borderline anemic, low pressure, but healthy.

Hal tried to ignore the facts and figures running through his mind. He tried to turn off the physician in him and simply be her dad. He was here as support. He was here for himself as much as for her. He was here because he needed to be.

At the moment, there was no place else in the world he could be.

At the tap on his shoulder, Hal turned. A nurse whispered, "There's someone here who needs to see you."

"What?" Shock and confusion streamed through his veins. "Adele?"

The woman shook her head. "A man named Walsh."

Comprehension flooded as he registered the name. Flicking a glance to his daughter's body, the doctors gathered around her, Hal needed to speak to this man. It was because of him his daughter had a fighting chance.

Hurrying out behind the nurse, Hal followed her out of the sterile operating suite, pulling the mask away from his face as they passed the scheduling desk. An orderly passed, nodding as he pushed an equipment cart into a storage room. Slowing, Hal settled on the stranger in his midst.

In the hallway, a lone man stood rigid. Dark-skinned and physically built like one would expect from a Marine, the man had the most penetrating green eyes Hal had ever seen. They bore holes straight through him yet weren't threatening. Instead, they were oddly calm. Quiet. Wearing a starched green shirt reserved for medical staff and a dirty pair of cargo pants and all-terrain boots, Hal noted the bloodstains. Was it Lisa's blood? His own?

"Mr. Walsh?"

"Dr. Richardson," he acknowledged.

Hal went over to him and extended a hand. "Thank you." At a loss for anything more profound, the simple words came automatically. What did one say to the man responsible for saving his daughter's life? A complete stranger who went out of his way to ensure her safety when he didn't have to?

Hal repeated the only thing he knew to say. "Thank you for everything you've done."

Walsh accepted his gratitude with a brisk handshake. "How is she?" he asked, his gaze moving over Hal's shoulder, down the suite of operating rooms.

"In surgery. Her condition is stable. She's suffered a lot of blood loss, but she's hanging in there."

"She's a tough one."

"Tougher than she should be, sometimes."

A small smile tugged at the Marine's mouth, but the motion did not reach his eyes. They remained still, intense. "That grit saved her more than a couple of times."

Hal nodded, intrigued by the obvious emotion behind this man's words. What exactly happened on that mountain? Had Wade not told him the whole story? Had Lisa met with more hardship than he let on?

There were a million questions Hal wanted to ask, but none more important than one. "Will you stay? Will you stay until she's out of surgery?"

The man shifted his weight from heel to heel. Glancing to the nurses' desk, he hesitated.

Hal was stunned. What—he couldn't be leaving? Certainly he hadn't come all this way to turn around and leave. *He doesn't make it to town very often.* Wade's words echoed in Hal's mind. *Just a man who's lost his patience with civilians.* The comment drifted between them like a whisper of mountain breeze. Intangible, floating beyond grasp.

"Please, stay. Lisa will want to see you, I'm sure of it."

Walsh's expression absorbed the hit.

Bingo. This man had come to see the woman, not the patient.

Casting an uncomfortable glance at his attire, Walsh appeared on the verge of walking away—something Hal couldn't allow. "Sarah," he clipped to a nurse sitting behind the desk. "Can you get Mr. Walsh a cup of coffee?" Addressing the man directly, he asked, "Do you take it black?"

As Sarah rose, Walsh backed up a step and said, "I'll get it myself."

"Fine," Hal replied, thankful for the open window. "She shouldn't be in there much longer. Can I find you in the waiting room?"

"Call Wade," he said bluntly. "He knows how to get ahold of me."

And with that, the man smacked a metal plate on the wall and exited through automated doors opening ahead of him. Hal watched him go, fresh curiosity filling his mind. Who was he? How did he fit in with Lisa?

Hal wanted to follow him, probe him more fully for details of what happened up there. He needed to know every last one, but first he had to see his daughter through surgery. Pivoting, Hal thanked Sarah and returned to the operating room. Lisa might have made it to the safety of the hospital, but she wasn't out of danger yet.

While sitting in the waiting room, Walsh kept his focus on Wade. The Police Chief's face was friendly, but intense, the lines around his eyes adding years to his appearance, the starched shirt collar pinching the skin at his neck. Mid-fifties at most, Walsh thought Wade looked haggard and old. Stressed. But it came with the job. Walsh's duty was done. The Police Chief's was just beginning. Evidence, investigation, Wade and the lawyers still had to prove their case to a jury.

Walsh wanted no part in the process. It was as corrupt as everything else in this world, but he knew he couldn't evade it. Not entirely. He was a witness. His testimony would be crucial in putting the man behind bars and keeping him there.

Wade clapped a hand to Walsh's back, massaging the muscles at his neck. "I appreciate everything you did up there. I know her father appreciates it as much as I do."

For different reasons, Walsh knew. Wade had his suspect in custody and Hal had his daughter. Simple, straightforward, it made sense. Walsh considered his own reasons for doing what he did, and that's where sensibility eroded. At first, it had been easy. He witnessed a situation unfolding—a crime—and understood the perils. A stranger was following a lone woman as she hiked. Good guy, bad guy. Easy equation. When he warned her to head down and she refused, Walsh should have let it go. She was a grown adult. He'd warned her as any responsible adult would, and she chose not to heed his advice. Simple. Foolish, but simple. Why had he continued to shadow her movements?

Because she was attractive? He was a man, she was a woman—a very attractive young woman. That made sense, but was that it? Leaning forward, he dropped his arms to his legs, interlacing his fingers in a tight fist. Walsh tried to convince himself it was a matter of nature. Pure and simple.

But he couldn't.

Because it wasn't. It went beyond boy meets girl, finds girl attractive and follows her. Walsh couldn't let go of his identity. At his core, he was Marine. Always would be. Lisa had been in danger and it was his job to see her out of it. He enjoyed the game. He felt alive when hunting a target. But there was more to it. Lisa made him feel alive.

Competent, determined, she challenged his image of women. There had been women in the corps, but none like her, none with an air of naiveté. Marine women shared Lisa's strength and agility, her intelligence and will, but they lacked her purity, her softness. Her eager enthusiasm. That part was new to him. Watching her chase those toads had made him smile. It brought humor back into his life. Not in a mocking way but in a joyful way. Because she was thoroughly engrossed in what she was doing, committed to her cause above all else.

There weren't a lot of people he could say that about. Visions of her tumbling over the mountain ridge and subsequently finding her by the stream in the dark coursed through him like hot rods of desire. When he saw her there, the worst-case scenarios that had been rolling through his mind evaporated. It felt like a second chance. Where most women would have waited for someone to come and rescue them—most *people* would have waited, called for help and waited—Lisa picked herself up and got out of harm's way.

Admiration streamed through him. Lisa was a survivor. When he lost her in the river, any normal person would have feared the worst, but his gut told him otherwise. That's when he knew. That's when he knew without a shadow of a doubt that when he found her, he didn't want to let her go. He couldn't. There would never be another like her to come along in his lifetime.

"More coffee?" Wade asked him.

"No thanks."

"I like the green."

"What?" Walsh turned his head and looked at him. *What was he talking about?*

Amusement danced in Wade's dark eyes as they roamed over the stiff cotton shirt Walsh wore. "It compliments your eyes."

Walsh grunted. "Yeah. Right." He was in no mood for jokes. Battling a slew of soft emotion, of quicksand feelings he didn't want to be feeling, he popped up from his seat in an instant of decision. "I gotta go."

"Go?" Wade asked, rising with him.

"Yeah."

"But what about Lisa? Aren't you going to wait until she's out of surgery?"

Debating, Walsh remained planted in place. He wanted to. He wanted to make sure she was okay, talk to her, let her know he was glad she'd pulled through. But a bigger part of him wanted to hold her, comfort her, let her know how much he cared.

Staring into the seasoned gaze of Wade Davis, a man who could see right through him if given the chance, Walsh decided it was best to leave well enough alone until he sorted through his maze of emotion. He might say something he regretted.

Walsh was familiar with trauma patients. She'd made it this far. She'd be fine. "Lisa's in good hands. There's nothing I can do for her."

Hal Richardson appeared in the doorway of the waiting room, his gaze fixing on Walsh. "She's made it through surgery."

In the wake of those words, the tide broke, slashing the knot free from Walsh's heart. She made it through. He knew she would but reeled off a silent prayer of thanks just the same.

Wade placed a hand to Walsh's shoulder and squeezed. "That's good news, Hal."

"She's going to ICU. You can see her once they have her settled," he said to Walsh. "I've given word to the staff to allow you in."

Walsh remained in place, immobile. He didn't thank Lisa's father for the privilege. He didn't set off on his way to go see her. He stood, hands and legs bound stiff by shackles of emotion.

A queer look entered Dr. Richardson's gaze. Switching to Wade, the doctor's confusion faded, replaced by question. It was as if he already knew.

"I'm glad to hear she's pulled through," Walsh said. Lisa hadn't struggled so hard to up and fail in the end. It wasn't in her DNA. She was a fighter. She didn't give in.

Unlike him. "But I'm—"

"But you're going," Hal finished for him.

Surprised by the presumptive statement, Walsh paused. Centering on the man's hazel gaze, a piercing resemblance to Lisa's and delivering the same bite of intelligence, Walsh felt a stab of guilt, like he'd been caught red-handed. This was Lisa's father. He expected the man who saved his daughter to care enough to stay and see her when she awoke.

Walsh swallowed, bothered by the sharp wedge in his throat. This wasn't his gig. He didn't do sappy and emotional. He did his job. He made sure that Lisa received medical care, brought the man responsible to authorities, and would help with the prosecution. He wasn't ready for any more at the moment.

In the tight circle of men, Walsh could feel the man's scathing assessment. His daughter would expect a visit from the man she'd trusted to help get her safely down the mountain when she awoke. If for nothing more than to thank him.

Unfortunately, Walsh couldn't be that man. "I'm glad she's doing well, but this is not my place."

"Your place to what? Live and work like a normal human being, or have the simple decency to show a woman that you care?"

Walsh stiffened. "I think my actions speak for themselves."

"I think you're right." Without another word, the doctor left the room.

Beside him, Wade rubbed his chin and muttered, "I've never seen that side of Hal before."

"What side?"

He turned, his expression sober. "The kick-a-man-in-the-teeth side."

Chapter Twenty-Three

Walsh sat alone in front of his campfire, jabbing logs to stoke the flames higher, stronger. Heat. He wanted more heat, more intensity. He wanted to feel the burn against his skin. It had been forty-eight hours since he walked out of the hospital. Forty-eight long hours trapped as a prisoner in his own mind. Wade had texted. *Lisa awake and asking for you.*

Asking for him? Asking about him, or for him? She knew his story. She knew he lived on the mountain, preferred the solitude to the sanctimonious. Did she expect that to change?

He saved a life. He saved lots of lives. It's what he did. It's what lots of men did. He wasn't special. There was nothing special or extraordinary about what he did for her. He was a man who saw a crime in progress and handled it. He took care of business, same as any other would have done if met with the same conditions. Suddenly realizing the stick in his hand had caught flame, Walsh tossed it into the fire. *He was nothing special.*

Only one question remained. Would every other man sit on a friggin' mountaintop, torturing himself over the simple act of assisting a woman in need?

Walsh was disgusted with himself. He'd been acting like a fool, running through make-believe scenarios of him and Lisa getting together, sharing a life together. It was idiotic. He wasn't ready to move into an apartment, share his personal space, live a normal life, maybe get married, have kids. A dog. Walsh spit. Forget ready—he wasn't sure he even wanted it—any of it! Images of Lisa hiking through the trees, her pink bandana bobbing up and over the rocky landscape as she climbed, he right behind her, admiring her legs, her agility as they scaled another fourteener...

Crap. Who was he kidding?

He wanted nothing more than to spend time with Lisa—hike, fish, make love. He'd even help her chase toads, if she wanted. Save them from extinction, he corrected coolly, mildly amused as he recalled that indignant tone of hers when he'd first questioned her decision to stay on the mountain despite a murderer on the loose. Turning her nose up at him, she'd been so damned cute. Fierce, unhappy, but unavoidably appealing when she'd refused his words of warning. It had been the first night he stayed with her. The first night he realized he wasn't going anywhere until he saw her safely down the mountain. He was nothing special, but she was. Very.

I think my actions speak for themselves.

I think you're right.

Lisa's father had pegged him cold. He knew a runner when he saw one. The man read Walsh's reluctance with the precision of a fighter jet. Shot him down, too. *Don't want to stay and see my daughter?*

Go to hell.

Walsh would have had the same response, had he been her father.

We don't want a dog. We don't want your dirty laundry. We're getting a divorce. Sour memories curdled in Walsh's stomach. Even his brother Justin had refused to help. His wife didn't like dogs, didn't want the responsibility, so he refused his brother in need and Walsh lost his last friend—man's best friend.

Every time Walsh thought about returning to a normal life, he thought about the people with whom he'd be sharing space. People wanted easy. They didn't want to put themselves out, didn't want to sacrifice. People were self-centered and selfish. Why should he think Lisa would prove any different? They'd known each other for three days—*three days*—how could he be sure of anything in that length of time? He'd dated Tracy for three years before they married, and look how she treated him.

Walsh stoked the fire, a stream of sparks drifting upward into the night. He wasn't tired, couldn't sleep if he had to. He could only think. It reminded him of nights in the desert when it was his turn to sit watch for his unit. Wired for sound, he would pace the perimeter, continuously securing his unit's position while the men slept. Soldiers needed sleep to rejuvenate their bodies. They also needed support from back home, from their superiors in Washington, D.C.

Mesmerized by smoke and flame, thoughts of Lisa and visions of his future, Walsh knew he needed to make a decision. He was at a crossroads, that pivot point in time that determined one's future. Staring into the dark night, the pitch black silence, Walsh thought about his last life course change. Marines had missions. They had jobs to do, people to protect, land to defend, families waiting back home. It was a mission he'd abandoned, and for what?

Trees and rocks, rivers and streams. Food, air, water.

That's what he traded for a career in the military. The basics. He had the necessities. What more did he need?

Night closed in around him. Cold seeped into his bones.

Isolation turned against him.

It wasn't about need anymore. Meeting Lisa had opened the door to want. Hungry, persistent, it was a desire he couldn't shake. Walsh wanted Lisa. He wanted her in ways that rattled him. He wanted her every day, every way, twenty-four-seven. He'd wanted another woman this way. Pined for her from across the ocean, only to learn she hadn't been doing the same. She'd been unfaithful. Disloyal. She broke his trust in the deepest ways possible.

Lisa was different. He couldn't imagine her treating him that way. Couldn't imagine her walking away from a commitment, distance or not. She was made of fiber and grit. Remembering how she felt in his arms, the slender frame of her body against his, the delicate arch of her bare foot as he cradled it within his hands, Walsh surrendered to the feelings coursing through him. She was made of soft, sweet warm flesh.

Closing his eyes, he tried to ward off images of her body, but he couldn't. They bombarded him, permeated him. The ease of her smile, the spark in her eyes, her penchant for pink. Pressing his lids tightly closed, he brought knees to chest and wrapped his arms around his legs. Immersing himself in the smell of smoke, the chill of darkness, he pressed forehead to his knees. He tried not to want what he couldn't have. He tried not to muck up the water. Lisa was a young woman with a full life—in science, in college. She had friends, colleagues. She had goals, a mission. He lived on a mountain in a tent. What could he offer her?

For the first time since leaving his unit, Walsh felt the desire to be part of a team, part of a whole greater than himself. Like his brothers in the corps, people were stronger as a team, united in common goal. It gave life purpose, depth. Being part of the Marines had given his life meaning. Walsh's heart burst, pent-up desire dribbled free. These days his life had no meaning. He had no goal to achieve, nothing to fight for, no brotherhood, no family...

He was a unit of one.

Lisa slumped against the kitchen counter of her father's home. Her dad was making this harder than it needed to be. He was holding her too tightly, refusing any and all reason. He was afraid. She understood. But it wasn't rational. It was personal.

"It's an unnecessary risk," he said. Lines creased his forehead, carved either side of his mouth as he held her in his gaze. His very stern gaze. "You have no idea how lucky you are."

She did. She understood the anatomy, the arteries, the nerves, the millimeters that made the difference between life and death. But it was old news. The bullet had been shot from a handgun, from a distance. Caliber, speed, proximity. It was a simple matter of mechanics, mathematics. Her father's reaction was not. That was a matter of emotion. Fear.

Pushing off from the cold granite, she walked past him into the living room, her gaze inescapably drawn through the plate glass windows and up the mountain range, same as it had been every day since her return home from the hospital. She needed to get back there. She needed to hike, to work. She needed to stay relevant in the research she loved.

She needed to see Walsh. "Dad, I'm fine. I need to get back to work. Besides," she said, dragging a hand over her head and down the silky hair of her ponytail, "I'm tired of doing nothing."

Well, *nothing* was an understatement. She'd been consumed with physical rehab for the last three weeks, working to strengthen and maintain complete mobility in her right shoulder, keep the rest of her body flexible and strong. The bullet had grazed her scapula as it passed through. Working with a therapist at an outpatient clinic, she'd managed to fully maintain motion in the shoulder and she was ready to put it to use. Her dad understood this. But he didn't understand that the toad season was dwindling. The animals were readying for hibernation, and if she didn't go up now, she'd miss any chance at contributing to the research she began back in June.

This was her project, her baby. She was one of the lead researchers on the team and Professor Stevens was relying on her. He'd said as much when he came to visit her at the hospital. Mixed feelings swirled in her chest. She'd been happy to see him, but it felt awkward. Like he didn't belong in her personal space.

Feeling the sharp edge of her father's gaze, Lisa turned. "Dad, I've rested. I'm healed." She pulled down the cap-sleeve of her T-shirt to reveal the scar. Slim and pink, it was well on its way to becoming nothing more than a memory. "It's good, see? I'm good. Totally good."

"You're not good."

"I am."

Her father frowned. "You're not, but what do I know? I'm just an orthopedic surgeon trained in the anatomy of bones and joints and all things trauma."

Lisa didn't mean to laugh, but his face was so serious, so stern, she couldn't help herself.

Hal Richardson crossed his arms and glared at her. "Something amusing?"

"No." She shook her head and went to him. Sliding her arms around his waist, she hugged him firmly. "No. Nothing amusing at all. I appreciate your concern, I do, but I'm okay."

Nestling into the comfort and familiarity of his wiry frame, Lisa breathed in the scent of him. Her father was everything to her. He was her friend, her parent, her hiking companion, her intellectual challenge, but she needed him to give her space. She needed to go up the mountain, and she needed to go now, for more reasons than she could explain. "I love you, Dad, but I need to go up."

Slackening, he dropped his chin to her head with a ragged sigh. It was a sure sign she'd won. Ultimately, he would relinquish his objections and not stand in her way.

"It'll be okay, Dad. Dale is going up with me, and he promised not to ditch me this time. I'm not carrying a pack, only using my legs. My arm will be free and clear of anything hazardous."

Memories of her last trip up the mountain curled around her heart. Dale left because Walsh told him a murderer was on the loose—a warning she foolishly ignored. Tight, uncomfortable, the recollection picked at her like the snagged threads of a sweater. But if she hadn't ignored the warning, she wouldn't have gotten to know Walsh the way she did.

Stealing a peek out the window, longing wound through her. Layers of pine interspersed with aspen blanketed the mountain, concealing the wildlife and humans beneath. She had unsettled business on that mountain. More than her toads, she had unfinished business with Walsh. If it hadn't been for him, she could have died up there.

Walsh. She had expected to see him after her surgery. She'd expected to see him and share the relief over what had happened, apologizing to him for what she needlessly put him through. But he never showed. Her father said he'd been to the hospital but left the minute he heard she was out of surgery. Lisa had been crushed. She couldn't deny it. It hurt. She'd been looking forward to seeing Walsh more than anyone else, but he hadn't come.

It had been her father who sat with her, kept her company. Her friends. Her colleagues. Professor Stevens. Lisa closed her eyes, recalling the way he'd tried to hold her hand, comfort her in her time of distress. But she hadn't wanted Professor Stevens to hold her hand. She'd wanted it to be Walsh. Walsh and Walsh alone.

But he didn't come. His life was on the mountain, not sitting bedside with a woman he hardly knew. It was silly for her to think otherwise. Sillier for her to want more from him.

At least he'd been considerate enough to deliver her backpack to the police department. After her release from the hospital, she found it waiting at her father's home. The first thing she'd done when she spotted it was to grab her camera and check her pictures. The one of him. The one she'd taken when he escorted her back to her pack to collect her samples, the ones she subsequently lost in the river. The high quality resolution of the image had captured the color of his eyes with amazing clarity. It had been an unguarded moment. He hadn't expected her to turn the lens on him. But she had. And she was glad she had. The photograph was all she had of him.

Pathetic, that's what she was, Lisa thought, rolling her head away from the window. Downright pathetic. But that didn't prevent her from wanting closure. She and Walsh might not have a future together, but they had a past. A past to which she had to close the door on or she'd never be able to move forward.

"Will you promise to carry the PLB with you this time?" her father asked.

"Yes." The personal locator beacon was his failsafe way to ensure he would know how to find her at all times. Unlike spotty cell coverage, the device would transmit a message, allowing him to locate her exact position using satellite technology. "But I'm sure I'll be fine," she said, unable to fully convince herself of the same. Trouble was, her lack of conviction didn't stem from the physical concern. It was rooted in the emotional. "Really, I will."

Running a hand over her hair, her dad rubbed her back and held on tight. "I know you will be," he murmured. "I know you will."

Lisa's cell phone rang. Moving back, she answered, "Hey, Kinsley."

"Hey. Are we still on for lunch?"

Lisa checked her watch, checked her dad's expression, and slowly replied, "Yes. We're still on. One o'clock, right?"

"Yes. At The Oasis."

"Okay, see you there."

Ending the call, Lisa watched her father retreat to the kitchen, Rocco close at his heel. She had her own life, and her dad would let her live it, same as he always had. Watching Rocco stand obediently by her father's side, his body absently leaning in for the hand he knew would stroke the fur at his ears, Lisa found herself longing for things she'd never wanted before. She'd always prided herself on independence, freedom, yet lately she found herself yearning for companionship, warmth and comfort. Like her dad and his dog. Like couples strolling the college campus. It was weird.

Slipping the phone into her back pocket, she slung the leather backpack-style purse over her good shoulder and headed out for her lunch date. Life was wonderful but weird.

Kinsley Fairchild stood waiting outside the entrance to The Oasis. Their favorite hangout during the day, the restaurant was located stream-side with plenty of *al fresco* dining available and the freshest menu around, next to Adele's. But Adele's restaurant was open for dinner only. Expensive dinners, gourmet dinners, using only the finest locally-grown organic ingredients available. The Oasis was casual and hip and invited guests to linger.

As Lisa approached the brick and timber building, its entrance flanked by built-in rock planters laden with colorful flowers, sunlight deepening the gold tones in the wood exterior, she spotted Kinsley. She was tall and slender, her glossy black hair falling well past her breasts in the latest wavy style, a sharp contrast to her creamy white skin and pale blue fitted tank top. Dressed in navy short-shorts and strappy flats, a petite purse hanging hip-level from a gold chain, Kinsley drew male attention like a magnet.

Lisa waved, excited to see her. The two were different on the outside, but kindred spirits on the inside. Both sunscreen fanatics, animal activists, vegans, they bonded when Kinsley's parents bought a home in the valley, dividing their time between San Francisco and Colorado. Her father was a big-time developer, a key player in establishing the local ski resort, a role that caused a ton of friction between father and daughter. An animal-activist and popular blogger, Kinsley was dead set against the resort and its upcoming plans for major expansion. Lisa agreed. She didn't want to see the entire mountain taken over by ski runs.

"You're looking well," Kinsley said, leaning in for a kiss to each cheek. She opened the restaurant's door, allowing Lisa to enter ahead of her.

"I feel great," Lisa replied in passing, hit by wafts of baking banana bread. They passed white-clothed tables laden with plates of leafy green salads piled high with avocados, asparagus, and salmon, bowls of lime-green soup, gazpacho and carrot as they headed outside for a seat-yourself-table by the water. Lisa's stomach growled. "I had no idea how hungry I was!" she exclaimed as they walked outdoors.

"The Oasis will do that to you!" Kinsley pitched back.

"I could really go for some Tabouleh right now." Lowering into a seat beneath a wide umbrella, its yellow and white stripes awash with sunlight, Lisa eyed a shot glass filled with dense, bright green liquid on a nearby table and said, "Add some wheatgrass juice to my order. I need to build up my energy stores!"

"They have a brand new roasted red pepper hummus to die for. The best of the best."

Lisa nodded. "Bring it on!" she exclaimed, soaking in the atmosphere of stream-side dining. Beyond the stone paved patio and across a patch of short-cropped grass, the Silver Creek flowed through town, its banks swollen with fast-rushing water. Its bank was buffered with stacks of large, flat rocks, squared off and embedded in the slope of earth to create walls and steps. The proximity of water and tables was the main reason Lisa liked to eat at The Oasis. That, and the incredible food. She could sit here all day. Had, on many occasions, going over notes and research, for term papers and exam prep.

A male waiter appeared table-side, automatically filling their glasses with ice-cold water. "Care for lemon or cucumber with your water?"

"Lemon," Lisa replied.

"I'll try the cucumber." Kinsley smiled. "And will you bring a few extra slices? I'm in need of a detox."

"Sure thing."

Lisa shook her head. "Late night with Sebastian?"

"The man likes his wine, I'll give him that."

"As do you." Lisa enjoyed a private smile. The more expensive, the better.

Kinsley shrugged. "We all have our addictions."

And her friend wasn't concerned about the first one. "So, I'm headed up the mountain tomorrow," Lisa tossed out, eager to get Kinsley's opinion.

Reaching for her water, Kinsley asked, "So soon?" Relaxing back into her chair, she added, "Are you sure that's a good idea?"

"What?" Lisa extended her legs out into the sunshine, free from the shade of the umbrella. Too many days cramped indoors faded her natural tan, not to mention the depleting effect to her stores of vitamin D. "You sound like my father."

"He doesn't want you to go? Maybe you should listen to him. I mean, he is a doctor. He knows what's best."

"And so do I. I'm healed, I'm good, I'm ready to go."

"Is it Professor Stevens? Is he pushing you?"

"No, of course not," Lisa replied, irritated that Kinsley would assume he held such power over her. "It's me. I want to go. I miss it. You, of all people, should understand that."

Kinsley paused. "Is this about that guy up there?"

"What guy?" she asked, knowing full well "what guy" Kinsley was referring to.

"The one who took care of you when you had your accident."

"No. And my getting shot wasn't an accident. I was the victim of a crime."

"You know what I mean," Kinsley replied, cocking a quick brow as the realization set in. Sharp and quick, her dark brown eyes nailed Lisa. "It is, isn't it? You want to go back up there and see this guy, don't you?"

"I probably won't see him." Lisa cast a glance to the stream, channels of water rolling over one another as they rushed downstream. It reminded her of the stream where Walsh first found her. Not nearly as big, but the flow of water conjured up images of the encounter, how he scared the crap out of her but made up for it with his carrying her back to his camp.

Lisa tamped back a flutter of pulse. More than made up for it. "I'm going up to the ponds where Dale and I originally found the toads. Walsh doesn't hang out around ponds and frogs."

"Walsh," Kinsley said in a rush of breath. "*That's* his name. That's the guy you like."

Lisa fired what she hoped was a warning glare. "I never said I liked him."

"You didn't have to. It was written all over your face. He was all you could talk about in the hospital."

Lisa gaped at her friend. Had she run on that much about Walsh? Glancing at the ground, the uneven pattern of tawny brown stones, she couldn't recall. It must have been the drugs. She'd been sedated, taking some heavy-duty painkillers. *Oh, no...* She felt a tightening in her chest. Had it been obvious to everyone? Did everyone know how she felt?

"So I get that you want to see him again," Kinsley picked up, "but do you really think hiking up the mountain is necessary? Can't you just call the guy and ask him down for a drink?"

Lisa burst out laughing. "Walsh? Walsh doesn't come 'down for a drink.' He *lives* on the mountain. Or did you forget that part?"

"All the time?"

"All the time," Lisa repeated, swamped by an unexpected sadness. "He lives up there," she repeated, a wistful breath escaping her lips. "Full-time."

"Forever?"

Lisa didn't know how to answer that one.

"Wow," Kinsley murmured, taking another sip of her water. "You sure know how to pick 'em. First your unattainable professor and now some mountain recluse." She raised her glass in toast. "Way to go, Lisa."

Struck by the observation, Lisa mulled it over. Was she picking men she couldn't have? The hard ones? The difficult to attain? Was she subconsciously sabotaging her relationships before they had a chance to begin?

If she were going to be honest, Lisa would have to admit that she did have a thing for Professor Stevens, and he had it back for her. But with a strict "no dating students" policy, it was kind of hard to have a relationship. They spent tons of time together, but it never went anywhere outside the lab room. 'Course, Lisa didn't have time for "serious." She was too busy with her research.

Across the table, Kinsley smirked. "Love sucks, doesn't it?"

"Wouldn't know," Lisa mumbled in reply.

"First you can't get them out of your mind, next you can't get them off of your back." Kinsley shook her long dark waves and sniffed. "Well, you know what they say..."

Lisa waited for the remainder but Kinsley merely winked and said, "Doesn't matter anyway."

"What doesn't matter?"

"Unless you're moving onto the mountain, your feelings don't matter, right?"

Lisa looked at Kinsley, an odd realization forming in her mind. But they should matter. She shouldn't have to give up on someone because their situation was difficult, should she? They could work around it. They could make it happen. But as the arguments threaded through her mind, reality settled in. It was a fantasy. Her feelings were nothing more than silly and ridiculous. McIntyre Walsh lived on a mountain because he chose to live there. He had no plans to come down and live like a normal person, and she had no plans to move up there and live like a recluse.

None. Dropping her gaze to the white tablecloth, Lisa succumbed to defeat. There would be no Walsh and Lisa. It was wrong to fight the inevitable.

Chapter Twenty-Four

Depositing her breakfast bowl into the sink, Lisa pulled the stainless steel faucet head and rinsed the yogurt clean from the red ceramic dish, dropping it into the dishwasher. Grabbing her fanny pack from the counter, she slipped a small notepad and pen inside, followed by her cell phone. She wasn't taking a backpack on this trip, but that didn't mean she couldn't take the essentials, like her camera, her research notes. Dale would carry the bulk of toad swabbing supplies, leaving her with nothing to do but snap photos along the way.

"Where's your PLB?" her father asked, placing a hand to the polished stone counter, eyeing her expectantly.

Lisa yanked it from her fanny pack for him to see. "Right here."

"Good. What time is Dale coming to get you?"

"Any time now."

"And you promise to take it easy."

Lisa groaned under her breath. "Yes," she replied. Zipping the bag closed, she buckled it around her waist.

"I don't need to talk with Dale, do I?"

Giving an exaggerated roll of eyes for her father's benefit, she said, "No, Dad. I think you can trust me."

He smiled, his eyes glittering beneath the teardrop lighting overhead. "I know I can, but it makes me feel better to run through the list."

"Five times?"

"Twenty-five times, until I feel secure." Chuckling at his mother-hen mode, he said, "And you'll indulge me because you love your old man and don't want to cause him undue hardship."

She laughed. Dressed casually in jeans and faded blue T-shirt, her dad looked relaxed. Happy. "There's nothing old about you, Dad."

"Appreciate the vote of confidence."

The doorbell rang and Lisa went for it. "I'll be home before five, so don't call the teams on me until well after, okay?"

"I'll call them when I deem it necessary, young lady."

Shaking her head, she opened the door and the breath rushed from her lungs.

"Hello, Lisa."

She gaped. "Walsh..."

Looking past her, he said quietly, "I came to see you."

She trembled, the shock at seeing McIntyre Walsh on her doorstep riddling her body with doubt. What was he doing here? How did he find her? Why now?

"Lisa?" her father called out in mild concern.

"Walsh, I don't know what to say. What are you doing here?"

"I came to see you." His supple green gaze dropped to her shoulder. "How's the arm?"

Shakily, she rolled it up for his perusal. "Fine."

"I'm glad." A small smile crept onto his face. "Can we talk?" Again, his gaze darted over her shoulder. Was her father standing behind her? Was he still in the kitchen?

"Um, sure." Lisa called out over her shoulder, "I'm going outside for a sec." Before her dad had a chance to reply, she closed the door. *Walsh was here.*

Following him down the stone steps of her father's entryway, her thoughts bounced in a thousand different directions. Walsh was here—at her home. What did that mean? What did he want? She couldn't ignore the explosion of nerves in her belly or the pound of her heart. She could only hope it meant one thing.

Walking out into the morning sunshine, Walsh paused several feet from her. He seemed uncertain, hesitant, the sunlight reflecting his eyes in an unusual molten green. Fluid with emotion, yet they appeared crisp in the bright light. He looked good. Normal. Dressed in a pair of jeans and running shoes, the snug-fitting khaki T-shirt set off the brown of his skin, outlined the muscular build of the body she remembered from the last day she saw him. There weren't too many things she remembered from that day with clarity, but she did remember Walsh's rippled abs and muscular pecs as he stood outside the helicopter. Lisa gulped. Walsh. A man she'd fantasized about seeing over and over again ever since.

Turning to face her, Walsh held her in his gaze in what felt like a tender caress. "How have you been?"

The soft tone of his voice swept her from her feet. "Fine," she blurted. "Great."

Walsh nodded. "I'm glad to hear it. You had me worried there for a while."

Did she? If so, why didn't he stay and tell her? Why not let her know that he cared?

"I see you bought a new bandana."

Lisa touched her head. It wasn't new, only different. A lighter shade of pink.

"Did you get your backpack okay?"

"I did, thanks," she replied, confused as to where this was going. Had Walsh come to make small talk? Check up on his pack delivery?

A smile pulled at the corner of his mouth. "I know how you are about your toads."

Lisa stared at him. Thoughts and emotions collided in her chest, drained from her body as she dropped her hand to her side. She felt trapped in a morph of reality. What was going on?

Digging hands into his front pockets, Walsh tossed his gaze to the ground and then hit her head on with his words. "You're mad at me. You're mad that I didn't stick around."

"I'm not mad at you, Walsh." Surprised by the absurdity of the statement, Lisa replied, "I'm confused. I don't understand why you didn't stay and see me after surgery. My father said you were there, at the hospital. Why did you leave?"

Walsh glanced away, his focus drifting up the mountain across the valley, the mountain where their ordeal took place. His expression seemed so sad, so distant, Lisa feared what he might say next, though waited breathlessly for his every word.

Drawing his gaze back to her, he said, "I wasn't sure I could handle it. I wasn't sure I was ready."

"Ready for what? A visit? Since when is that a stretch for a guy like you?"

A smile eased onto his lips, sexier than it should be. Lisa's heart kicked as he mirrored back, "A guy like me. There you go again, acting as though you know me."

"Don't I?" she questioned, a sliver of fear pricking her heart.

His smile broadened. "You do. That's the problem."

"Problem?" The man was making no sense.

Walsh nodded. "I went up on that mountain because I'd lost faith in people. They lied, abandoned, let me down from the inside out. I didn't want anything to do with them." A brief chuckle erupted as he said, "You were right. A part of me didn't like people."

Lisa crossed her arms over her chest, more as a defense to what she heard than in judgment.

"Until you." The intensity of his gaze markedly heated as he said, "I never thought I'd meet anyone like you. You're like me in so many ways, yet different. When you were shot, I thought it was over. For the briefest of seconds, I thought my life was over before it had a chance to start again. And that's when I knew."

Goosebumps raced across her skin, up her neck, tingling in the fine hairs at her nape.

"I knew I couldn't live without you. I couldn't stand the thought of something happening to you, interrupting the only glimmer of joy I'd felt in a very long time."

"What are you saying, Walsh?" Embarrassed by the creaky quality of her voice, she uttered, "What does this mean?"

"It means I've signed a lease on an apartment outside of town. I bought a truck, talked to Wade about a job. I'd like to get a dog, but thought I better ask you how you feel about them first. Do you like dogs, Lisa?"

She burst forward, throwing her arms around his neck. "I love dogs! I absolutely love them!"

Encircling his arms around her body, Walsh hugged her to him. Hard. Desperate. Burying his face into her neck, he whispered fiercely, "I'm so glad. I'm so glad that you do."

Excitement and thrill gushed free, streamed through her arms and legs, sapping her of strength. Walsh was here. He'd moved off the mountain because of her, because he wanted to be with her. It was everything she imagined, hoped for. Lisa was certain it had to be difficult for him. Making such a drastic change couldn't come easy, but he'd done it.

Fireworks shot through her heart. For her.

Centering on the man in her arms, the solid embrace, the powerful connection, Lisa savored his cologne. Woodsy, with a hint of spice, it was rugged and smelled exactly like what she'd expect a man like Walsh to wear.

A man like Walsh.

"I love you, Lisa." Guttural, hungry, his voice was layered with need as he spoke close to her ear. "I want you to know that. I'll take it slow, but I have no intention of letting you go. Not after I worked so hard to find you."

Thrill zipped through her heart, and she squeezed him as hard as she could. "I love you, too!"

For a moment, the two were locked in a vise-like embrace that seemed to get stronger, harder, yet nowhere near close enough. Immersing her mind in him, savoring the feel of his body, his scent, Lisa realized he might be right about one thing. She didn't know him—not the facts and details of his life's history, maybe, but she did know his core. More than ever before in her life, Lisa had no doubt she knew this man's heart, the fiber of his being, the values that made him who he was. McIntyre Walsh was a good man, a decent man. He'd experienced some hard times, but they didn't blacken his heart. On the contrary, they deepened it. Walsh had proven himself to her on more than one occasion. He was a man to be trusted, a man with very deep feelings, a man she could lose herself in.

"Lisa."

Snapped from her reverie by the familiar voice, she jerked her head from Walsh. "Dale!"

Walsh released her and turned, surprised to see her hiking partner.

Dale moved a stunned gaze between her and Walsh. "What's going on? I thought we were hiking today."

Walsh eyed her pointedly. "Hiking?"

Mindful of the reproach staring back at her, she replied, "Yes. Dale and I had planned on hiking up the mountain today so I could check on the toads."

"It's too soon," Walsh said. Shooting a wary glance to her injured shoulder, he said, "You're not ready for that."

"I'm not carrying a backpack or anything." She tapped the bag at her waist. "Just this fanny pack."

"Your body needs rest, Lisa. You can't stress it with a hike up the mountain. I know you. You'll push yourself beyond the limit."

Now look who was talking about "who knowing whom." Walsh didn't know that she wouldn't be anything but careful. He only knew the hiker who'd been hiking at a hundred percent, not the one who'd been lectured by several physicians as to the danger of long-term damage to her body. Lisa wasn't risking that, not when she had a lifetime of living on the mountain ahead of her.

Living on the mountain. Walsh wasn't living on the mountain anymore. Unable to suppress a fresh squeal of emotion, she grinned. "I'll have you know that I'm not going to do anything that will jeopardize my shoulder. Trust me, easy and slow is my new motto."

Walsh cocked his head. "Since when?"

"Since five doctors and one boyfriend have scolded me as to the opposite."

An unabashed pleasure seized his face, one that clearly stemmed from her labeling him "boyfriend." It was the most boyish grin she'd ever seen, and strange to see on his very manly face.

"Glad to hear it," he replied, all concern erased from his features.

"Uh, are we still going hiking?" Dale asked.

Lisa had completely forgotten he was standing right next to her. Was she? Looking to Walsh, his presence all-consuming, she didn't want to do anything but spend time with him and explore the new aspect of their relationship. She couldn't imagine sharing the words "I love you" and then walking off—there was no way!

"Mind if I join you?" Walsh asked. "Promise I won't interfere."

Dale looked at him with an odd aversion, like Walsh presented some sort of threat to the process of toad sampling.

Quickly catching on, Walsh said, "Or not."

Not about to let Walsh go, Lisa encircled her hands around his arm and asked, "Do you mind, Dale?"

In that instant, all three seemed to realize Dale was the third wheel, the imbalance in the equation. "Uh, I guess not."

Not the most convincing of replies, Lisa prodded, "Are you sure?" While she wanted to be with Walsh more than anything at the moment, she had made a commitment to hike with Dale today.

"Actually, since the only reason you need me is to carry your backpack and keep you company," he said, "why don't you just let him take you?"

Lisa heard the silent, *You'd rather have him by your side, anyway.*

While she hated to take him up on his halfhearted offer, he did offer and she wanted so badly to accept. "If you're sure..."

"I'm sure." Running a hand through the lengths of his brown hair, he appeared visibly relieved. "I'll let Professor Stevens know."

Brushing the personal insinuation aside with ease, Lisa replied, "Good idea." Privately, she added, the sooner he knew she was taken, the better. It might mean less opportunity within the doctoral program, but so be it. In her heart of hearts, Lisa knew Professor Stevens had offered her the position of teaching assistant as his way of getting past the hurdle of his "no dating students" policy. They'd be colleagues, equals. It would allow them to take their attraction to the next level.

Unfortunately, the good professor didn't realize her attraction for him had disappeared since Walsh had entered her life. "Tell him I'll bring the samples in tomorrow."

Taking a step backward, Dale nodded. "Sure thing. I'll go get the backpack."

Wasting no time, he hurried back to his car, dragged the pack out of his backseat, and then dumped it on the ground before Walsh. Turning on his heel, he made a quick departure.

As Lisa watched him drive away, a wave of melancholy overcame her. Change was in the air. Dale had served a purpose, been a friend, but the look in his eyes had said it all. He'd been replaced. Professor Stevens had been replaced. No longer the front-and-center people in her life, that position now belonged to this man.

"You think he's upset?" Walsh asked.

"A little. But Dale's not the kinda guy to let it bother him for too long. Hiking isn't his first passion. Besides, he used to get distracted on the mountain way too easily."

Sliding an arm around her waist, Walsh said, "I can understand why." Nuzzling close, he whispered, "You're pretty distracting."

Clenching arms to her body as she staved off a sudden wave of gooseflesh, she giggled. "Dale was distracted by the toads, not me."

"Silly boy." Nipping her ear in what felt like the most normal of actions, Walsh added, "I'll consider it my lucky day."

Turning within his arm, she asked, "What?"

"You will let me go toad hunting with you, won't you?" He winked. "If I promise not to get distracted?"

Lisa laughed. Deep, penetrating, the sensation reaching every crevice of her body. "I can't imagine you getting distracted."

"Watch me."

Chapter Twenty-Five

Lying on top of soft mountain grass, resting comfortably on the bent hand of her good arm, Lisa pondered the distant mountain range, the future that lay ahead for them. Walsh was stretched out beside her, perched back on his elbows, his legs extended and crossed in front of him. The natural earth tones of his shirt blended with the scenery, making him appear right at home in the midst of nature. It also softened his looks, made them sultry and one hundred percent appealing. She was totally at odds with the environment in her bright pink T-shirt and blue shorts—unless she was a flower whereby she'd fit right in.

Taking a deep breath, Lisa felt totally relaxed. With the temperature hovering near a comfortable seventy-two, the afternoon had been absolute bliss. Amazing. The hike up had been filled with getting-to-know-you conversation followed by a curiosity on Walsh's part when it came to toad hunting. She would have sworn he'd been truly captivated by the process, enjoying it as much as she. True to his word, he didn't fall prey to distraction, but instead, was distracting in and of himself. His constant close proximity tangled her concentration, tripped up her normal discipline as she fell victim to his smile, his laugh, his comments and his confessions.

Lisa had hurt to hear the synopsis of his past. It was unconscionable what people were capable of, how different his past experience was from hers. Fortunately their discussion of dog breeds lightened the mood quite a bit. He wanted a chocolate Lab, she a Border Collie. When they revealed their choices, each looked at the other like they were aliens. A chocolate Lab? A Border Collie?

That's when she decided it must be true what they say about people and dogs; people choose pets based on their own image, or rather how they saw themselves. According to the theory, Walsh and a chocolate Lab were a perfect fit. Dark brown fur with pale green eyes, the breed was known for its lovable, loyal side yet were also incredibly hard workers. Trained in the sport of hunting, the Lab was a dog that fit Walsh like the T-shirt that caked his torso. Perfect. To the bone.

Lisa liked the Collie for its agility and intelligence, two traits she prided in herself. Collies were also friendly and loved the outdoors. Funny, but even her dad's dog, Rocco, seemed to fit the description. Strong and lovable, the Bernese was a natural watchdog and friend for life. Intelligent, too. Come to think of it, all three of the breeds were excellent choices.

How did one choose?

"Compromise," Walsh had said. "We compromise." Lisa had waited and laughed uproariously when he answered, "It's simple. We get two."

Warm feelings coursed through her as she recalled their conversation. Walsh was sweet, but stubborn. Same as her, she guessed, though no one had ever called her sweet. Which was fine. She'd take smart and snappy any day of the week.

Looking over at him, Lisa thought it was a great beginning.

"So, have you thought about what you're going to do? Do you think you'll accept the position offered by Chief Davis?"

"Probably. It's the only type of work I'm suited for."

"Well, you're obviously good at it. Do you not enjoy it?"

He shrugged. "It's a job."

Mulling over the deadpan delivery, she mused out loud, "But not your passion."

"Not particularly."

"What would be?"

Walsh glanced sideways and smirked, "Other than you?"

She smiled and lightly punched his side. "Other than me."

He grunted. "I don't know. I liked the Marines, working with a unit, ridding the world of bad guys."

"Do you want to go back?"

"I'll never go back."

Quick, blunt, there was no hesitation.

The renouncement gave her some measure of relief. It meant she wouldn't lose him to months of deployment. But Lisa would, if that's what he wanted to do. She'd let him go and love him from afar. "How about working with hikers? You could be a guide up the mountain."

Grimacing as though the mere thought were painful, he replied, "No, thanks. I think I'll leave that one to you."

"There must be *something* you'd love to do."

Curiosity settled in his gaze. Narrowing in on her, he asked, "What's the matter, worried I'll become some working stiff who hates my job and wants to quit?"

"No, not really." Lisa lowered her gaze and stamped out a flutter of angst in her breast. Hitting hard and fast, the feelings unnerved her. The fear. Insecurity. Lifting to face him directly, she confessed, "I'm worried you won't want to stay in Colorado."

A tidal wave of emotion swamped his gaze. Reaching over, Walsh placed a finger beneath her chin. "I'll always want to stay in Colorado, so long as you're here." Pausing, he said, "I can't promise you I'll be the man you want me to be, but I promise I won't leave you until you want me to."

Quivers of delight electrified her senses. "Walsh, I'll never want you to leave."

He raised his brow. "How can you be so sure?"

The point-blank question undercut her pleasure. How could she be?

Staring into eyes that held her, caressed her, made her feel safe and secure and protected—loved—how *couldn't* she be? There was no more complete man for her than him. From the physical to the mental, from his heart to his soul, Lisa felt a bond with Walsh like she never had before. They were meant for one another. She didn't know how it would work, the details, the everyday, but the thought of him leaving was more than she could bear. Lisa wanted him here, with her. She trusted him.

A squiggle of desire zipped through her. She loved him. "I can be sure of you." The proclamation settled in her core. "That's all I need."

Pleasure pushed the question from his gaze. "Good. Besides, I'm not going anywhere until I put that guy that shot you behind bars for life."

The mention gave Lisa a reality check. "You don't think he'll get off, do you?"

"Not a chance. Not with me in the picture, he won't. Besides, Wade says the evidence against him is solid. The search and rescue team found the guy's camp, including the knife he used to kill that girl. A few DNA tests will be all they need to put him away for life."

Lisa suspected Walsh would enjoy the prospect of enacting justice with his own two hands, but would never ask him about it. She didn't have to. It was etched in the hard green of his eyes each and every time he spoke of the man.

Shaking the brutal images from her mind, Lisa said, "I'm glad no one else will have to worry about him while up on the mountain."

"Me, too." Walsh ran a hand through the hair falling free from her bandana, caressing her cheek. He traced the line of her cheek, her jaw, opened the floodgates for a channel of emotion to flow between them. Walsh wouldn't let her go through an ordeal like that again. Like a guardian angel, a knight-in-shining-armor, he would protect her. "Have you thought about what you plan to do with the rest of your life?"

"Huh?"

"You've been grilling me—what about you? What happens after you finish your doctorate? Are you going to teach, conduct research?"

"I don't know." She gave a gentle shake to her head as she contemplated the question, turning it over in her mind. "I haven't really thought about it."

Walsh dropped his head back and laughed. "Why do I find that hard to believe?"

She blinked. Was it? Before him, she'd planned on staying active in the program at the university, but now...working side-by-side with Professor Stevens might prove difficult.

Awkward. She'd definitely continue her pursuit to save the boreal toad from extinction, but that could take many forms. What form she'd ultimately choose to stay involved remained to be seen. "I'm going to play it by ear," she said.

"You strike me as a planner, not a play-it-by-ear kinda gal."

"I do?"

"You do." Leaning over, Walsh assumed an intimate and not-for-public-consumption look in his eyes. "There's something I want you to plan," he said, lowering his lips to hers. Grazing them ever so lightly, he whispered, "Lots of this."

Rubbing slowly, painstakingly, he covered her mouth with his setting her insides on fire. Lisa couldn't hear, couldn't see, the sensation at her mouth shredding her belly. She'd fantasized about their first kiss so many times, but it had never been like this.

Walsh dipped his tongue into her mouth and she groaned. Warm desire flooded her loins, rumbled through the shreds in her stomach. It wiped her brain clear of everything but him. Sliding a hand behind her neck, he pulled her close, his movements turning eager, hungry—urgent. Mind spinning, Lisa didn't know how to react except to surrender. There wasn't anything else she could do if she'd wanted. She could only feel him. Could only breathe him, taste him, as he eased her back to the ground, deepening his kiss, his exploration of her mouth and lips, her cheek.

Lisa craned her head back, allowing him full reign of her neck and collarbone, trembling as she anticipated his next move. She didn't know what he planned or where this desire would take them, but she knew she wanted it. She wanted him, and nothing more than him. In this moment, she wanted to be here, with Walsh, in his arms, on the mountain, together at last.

# # #

The End

Lisa's Fave Granola

2 cups rolled oats
½ cup pumpkin seed, natural, not salted or roasted
¼ cup ground flax seed
½ cup maple syrup
¼ cup melted butter
1 tsp orange zest
½ tsp vanilla extract
1 tsp cinnamon
½ cup raisins

Preheat oven to 300°F. In a large bowl, combine rolled oats, pumpkin and flax seed. Mix well. For the granola "glue" mix together maple syrup, melted butter, orange zest and vanilla extract. Whisk well and pour over oat and seed mixture. Mix all ingredients until well blended. **Note**: this might be easier done with your hands. If you like the orange zest, go ahead and add some more. It's a nice compliment to the maple syrup.

Cover baking sheet with foil (nonstick types work best) and evenly spread granola mixture out over the pan. Bake for 20 minutes, turning granola mix once or twice during the baking process with a spatula. Add raisins and bake for 5 minutes longer.

Remove from oven and allow to cool on a metal rack. For options on this recipe, I'd toss in hazelnuts or almonds, maybe add a dash of nutmeg or fancy pumpkin spice flavoring?

About the Author:

Dianne Venetta lives in Central Florida with her husband, two children and part-time Yellow Lab Cody-boy! An avid gardener, she spends her spare time growing organic vegetables, surprised by what she finds there every day. Who knew there were so many amazing similarities between men and plants? Women, life and love and her discoveries along the way provide for never-ending fun on her garden blog: BloominThyme.com. When she's not knee-deep in dirt or writing, Dianne also contributes garden advice to various websites.

You can also find her on twitter @DianneVenetta and facebook.com/DianneVenetta. Plus, learn how you can become a member of her street team, Bloomin' Warriors, where you'll be eligible for special discounts, advance excerpts, author swag and unique gift items throughout the year. For full details, be sure to check out her website, DianneVenetta.com.

Other novels by Dianne Venetta:
Mystery/Romantic Adventure Fiction
Silver Creek Series:
NOT WITHOUT YOU #1
BECAUSE OF YOU #2
ALL ABOUT YOU #3
ONLY WITH YOU #4

Mystery/Romance Fiction
Ladd Springs Series:
LADD SPRINGS #1
LADD FORTUNE #2
HOTEL LADD #3
LADD HAVEN #4
LOSING LADD #5
LADD CHRISTMAS #6

Romantic Women's Fiction
The Gables Trilogy:
JENNIFER'S GARDEN
LUST ON THE ROCKS
WHISPER PRIVILEGES

Women's Fiction
CONDEMN ME NOT

www.ingramcontent.com/pod-product-compliance
Lightning Source LLC
Chambersburg PA
CBHW032209190626
46810CB00019B/2398